LARGE PRINT
EDITION

BLACKMAIL

AT THE

GALLIANO CLUB

CARMEN AMATO

ALSO AVAILABLE IN LARGE PRINT

GALLIANO CLUB SERIES
ROAD TO THE GALLIANO CLUB: Prequel
MURDER AT THE GALLIANO CLUB: Book 1
BLACKMAIL AT THE GALLIANO CLUB: Book 2
REVENGE AT THE GALLIANO CLUB: Book 3

DEDICATION

The Galliano Club series is dedicated to the memory
of

Celine McIndoe

First cousin. First playmate. First and best friend.
My maid of honor.

In our hearts forever.

COPYRIGHT

Published 2024 by Laurel & Croton

ISBN Large Print: 979-8-9891403-3-6

Key characters in the Galliano Club series

Luca Lombardo: Orphaned in Italy, Luca doesn't own the Galliano Club, but it's all he has after losing his wife and baby to the Spanish influenza shortly after arriving in America. *His secret:* He killed the man who murdered his parents. *He wants:* To truly be an American.

Karol Dombrowski: From Poland, Karol has one of the most dangerous jobs at the Lido Premium mill and lives in the same boarding house as Luca. *His secret:* Karol is ambitious but sees no opportunity to move ahead. *He wants:* A position of influence to improve the lives of fellow newcomers to America.

Owen Forbes Fisher: A graduate of Syracuse University, Owen is the accountant for the Lido Premium mill. *His secret:* He fears his wife will leave him for a richer and more socially connected man. *He wants:* To be an admired figure in Lido's high society.

Ruth Cross: A former Broadway chorus girl, Ruth

rents the apartment over the Galliano Club and runs the Tapping Toes School of Dance. *Her secret:* She was once convicted of public indecency and lewd behavior and spent time in jail. *She wants:* To be more than Luca Lombardo's friend.

Tess Kennedy: A graduate of Vassar College, Class of 1924, Tess works in the prestigious First National Bank of Lido. *Her secret:* She is a brilliant mathematician. *She wants:* To break the bonds of family and societal expectations for women and decide her own future.

Benny Rotolo: Previously a hitman for Chicago's North Side gang, Benny was chased out by Al Capone and came to Lido where his cousin lives. *His secret:* He's wanted for murder in Chicago. *He wants:* To build a bootlegging empire with the Galliano Club as his signature speakeasy.

Hanna Gorski: An artist's model and young widow, Hanna is on the hunt for the person who killed her sister and dumped the body in the Mohawk River near Lido. *Her secret:* She has ties to Al Capone's Chicago Outfit. *She wants:* Revenge for her sister's murder.

Eighteenth Amendment - Prohibition of Intoxicating Liquors, effective 16 January 1920

Section 1. After one year from the ratification of this article the manufacture, sale, or transportation of intoxicating liquors within, the importation thereof into, or the exportation thereof from the United States and all territory subject to the jurisdiction thereof for beverage purposes is hereby prohibited.

Section 2. The Congress and the several States shall have concurrent power to enforce this article by appropriate legislation.

Volstead Prohibition Enforcement Act, 28 October 1919

Sixty-sixth Congress of The United States of America;

To prohibit intoxicating beverages, and to regulate the manufacture, production, use, and sale of high-proof spirits for other than beverage purposes, and to insure an ample supply of alcohol and promote its use in scientific research and in the development of fuel, dye, and other lawful industries.

Be it enacted by the Senate and House of Representatives of the United States of America in Congress assembled, that the short title of this Act shall be the "National Prohibition Act."

. . . The words "beer, wine, or other intoxicating malt or vinous liquors" . . . shall be hereafter construed to mean any such beverages which contain one-half of 1 per centum or more of alcohol by volume . . .

"Nobody's on the legit." – Al Capone

CHAPTER 1

The Funeral

Saint Rocco's Catholic Church, guardian of the East Lido neighborhood, had never seen a funeral like this. Priests from three different churches were on the altar to concelebrate the service, assisted by twice as many acolytes. Those who'd been unable to get a seat filled the side aisles and blocked the confessionals. There were so many bouquets of lilies that the air was heavy with their cloying scent.

Jimmy Zambrano was finally being laid to rest.

He had been one of the leaders of the Italian community in East Lido. A devout Catholic, a family man, the long-serving foreman of the Lido Premium Copper and Brass rolling mill, and a murder victim whose body was found in the Mohawk River after weeks of fruitless searching.

Not only was all of East Lido packed into the church, but many who otherwise would never step foot in the Italian enclave were there as well. Nathan Packham, the owner of Lido Premium, sat with Henry Blick, who was the mill's all-powerful operations manager as well as Packham's nephew and heir. They were joined by Mayor John Peabody and Lido's chief of police, a stout man in a formidable blue uniform. More uniforms indicated the New York State Troopers who'd finally found Jimmy's body.

Only the Procopio family, including Nick Procopio's bootlegger cousin, Benny Rotolo, was missing from the funeral. Whispers had swirled through East Lido before the service, but no one expected any of them to show.

After all, it was Nick Procopio, the deputy foreman at Lido Premium, who'd strangled the man they were there to mourn.

Half expecting a thunderbolt to arc over the altar and strike him dead for his sins, Luca Lombardo rose to his feet as the casket went by, held high on the shoulders of the pallbearers. The solemn-faced priests followed, one swinging the smoking incense burner. Next came three acolytes, two with large candles and the one in the middle carrying a gold crucifix that was taller than the boy by more than an arm's length.

The organ wailed out Ave Maria from the choir loft above. The music muffled the clanking of the brass burner and the last few involuntary sobs.

As the casket passed each pew, the mourners filed out and processed up the center aisle after it. Jimmy's widow Carmella Zambrano and her children left the first pew, putting them directly behind the tall gold cross and guttering candles. Together with his wife Louise, Vito Spinelli, the owner of the Galliano Club and Luca's boss, accompanied the dead man's family.

Luca joined the procession behind Vito, along with Guido Serra, the Galliano Club's stout doorman. The center aisle was soon swollen with people shuffling through the cloud of incense. The organ music set a measured pace. Luca found himself mentally intoning the words to Ave Maria, the language of the church coming back to him as if it was yesterday instead of a decade ago that he was a teen in Calabria, reluctantly studying for the priesthood.

The double doors at the rear swung open, sending a welcome gust of fresh air into the church. The procession slowed to a stop. Luca caught a glimpse of his friend Karol Dombrowski supporting a corner of the casket. The pallbearers were crew chiefs at the Lido Premium mill. The dead man had hired them all. Karol, who roomed in the same boarding house as Luca, was the only Polish crew chief. His blonde head stood out amid the sea of dark-haired Italians.

Voices rose in a final prayer for Jimmy's soul. Once again, Luca remembered the words without effort.

. . . nunc et in hóra mórtis nóstrae. Amen.

He nearly choked on the final phrase. Now and at the hour of our death. The hour of Jimmy's death had been weeks ago. What might have been the hour of Luca's own death was all too recent.

Up ahead, Vito put his hand on Carmella Zambrano's shoulder. She leaned into him. Vito's wife Louise hugged Sonny, the oldest Zambrano child.

Luca felt the sting of loneliness.

At least tonight Vito was sober and clear-eyed, a fitting tribute to a close friend as well as his own role as the unofficial mayor of East Lido.

The pallbearers carried the casket through the double doors. The crowd streamed out and filled the wide steps of the church to watch it be loaded into a hearse for the ride to the church's cemetery. There would be no internment. It was early November and the ground in upstate New York was already frozen. Jimmy would rest in the Saint Rocco Cemetery mausoleum until spring.

Luca and Guido stayed with Vito and Louise Spinelli, forming a cluster by the Zambrano family as half a dozen flashbulbs went off. Reporters had not been allowed in the church, but that didn't mean that the funeral wasn't news.

The Lido Premium representatives and the mayor murmured their sympathies to Carmella Zambrano and left in their fancy automobiles as more flashbulbs popped and startled the crowd. An informal receiving line formed. Karol and the other pallbearers spoke to her next.

Vito's soup-strainer mustache trembled with emotion as he turned to Luca. "Jimmy can rest in peace now, no?"

"That's right," Luca said. The boss was looking for reassurance. "It's over."

"We'll drink a toast. With Carmella."

Luca nodded. A members-only outfit, normally the Galliano Club was closed on Sunday. Tonight all the rules were out the window. Even women were invited.

Karol made his way through the crowd. Luca handed over his friend's fedora, which had been left in the pew. "Come have a beer at the club," Luca said. "Drink a toast to Jimmy."

"You know I'll be at the Warsaw Club."

Not even Jimmy Zambrano's funeral could break down the wall between the Italian workers who belonged to the Galliano Club in East Lido, and the Polish workers who patronized the Warsaw Club on the south side of the city, near Holy Angels Church.

Before Luca could reply, a palpable ripple of unease went through the crowd. A space opened in the middle. Vito said something that Luca didn't catch. Carmella

Zambrano gasped.

Maria Teresa Procopio was on the sidewalk, chin held high. The widow of the man who'd killed Jimmy was a slight woman who nonetheless was known to be more than a match for her late husband.

A cinnamon sunset was stealing the light, but Luca could still see the woman's red eyes and lines of grief aging her face. Dusky hair was scraped into a bun and a long black dress showed below the hem of her knee-length coat. Thin hands clutched a beaded purse against her chest like a shield. Oddly enough, Luca was reminded of his dead wife Rafaella, who was still a teenager when she died.

"On behalf of my children and myself," Maria Teresa said to Carmella, loud enough for everyone on the church steps to hear. "I offer condolences for your loss. Your Jimmy, may his soul rest in peace, was a good man."

"Thank you." Carmella's voice was surprisingly strong.

"That's all I come to say."

"I understand."

Maria Teresa's gaze slid to Luca.

He touched the brim of his fedora in acknowledgment.

"Lucky Lombardo," Maria Teresa said with ice in

her voice.

The newspapers had gleefully dubbed him "Lucky" for his narrow escape from Nick Procopio's copper wire garrote, the same wire that killed Jimmy. Clubbed on the head by policeman Sean O'Malley's nightstick, Nick's dying words had been "In the river," the clue that led to the eventual discovery of Jimmy's body in the Mohawk River.

Lucky. Luca hated the nickname.

"Everybody's hero now." Maria Teresa spat hard.

The gobbet landed in front of Luca. He didn't move.

Luca had nothing to say to Maria Teresa Procopio, although there were burning questions he wished she could answer. Did she know her husband was in the bootleg beer business with Benny Rotolo? When did she know that Nick killed Jimmy? The same night? And most important of all, did she know that Nick didn't put Jimmy's body in the river but left it behind the Galliano Club for someone else to find?

Maria Teresa walked away. The crowd remained silent, stunned at her audacity. Two weeks ago she'd been another East Lido wife and mother. Now she was the widow of a murderer and scandalous enough to show her face at the victim's funeral.

Vito cleared his throat and took Carmella's elbow. His actions broke the spell and there was a general clatter down the stairs. An undulating line of wool coats was soon strung out along Hamilton Street as the crowd made its way to the Galliano Club. No weeping, just low murmurs and the scratch of shoe leather on sidewalks gritty with sand to prevent skidding on winter ice.

Luca heard "Procopio" murmured a few times. Nick's funeral was the next day but few would go.

"Hey, Lucky!" It was Bill Gifford, one of the reporters from the Lido Daily Clipper. "Lucky Lombardo! Waddaya think? Did Procopio kill the woman from the river, too?"

"How would I know?" Luca tried to push past. He'd been as surprised as anyone when divers pulled the half-naked dead woman from the Mohawk River after finding Jimmy's body.

"Did he confess like he confessed to Zambrano?"

"No," Luca said shortly and plowed ahead.

He unlocked the front door of the club at 601 Hamilton Street. The crowd streamed through the vestibule and into the saloon, shedding coats and hats and scarves. Wives and daughters marveled at the long mahogany bar, brass footrail, and man-sized bottle of golden Liquore Galliano mounted on the wall that gave the club its name. Luca whipped off his coat and started filling pitchers from the keg of beer hidden in the clever well under the bar.

Tossing aside his jacket, Sonny Zambrano came behind the bar, too. "I can do that."

A senior at Lido Free Academy, the kid washed dishes and swept the floor at the club after school. Sonny was like his late father, wiry frame, Roman nose, and a big appetite for work.

"Nobody expects you to work tonight," Luca said.

Sonny wiped his eyes with the cuff of his shirt. "Put me to work or I'll go crazy."

Luca handed him an empty pitcher. Sonny began filling it while Luca opened jugs of farm-pressed cider and bottles of tonic from the West End brewery in Utica.

The saloon was jammed. Carmella Zambrano was surrounded by the other ladies. Everyone soon had a glass in hand. Luca poured fizzy lemon-lime rickey for himself and Sonny.

"To Jimmy," Vito said, raising his voice to be heard above the drone of voices. He held his glass high. "Jimmy Zambrano. Friend. Father. Husband. Foreman. May Saint Peter keep him too busy to talk about our sins until we meet again. Salute!"

"Salute!" The word filled the saloon, rattling the pictures of the club's baseball team above the dark green paneling and the empty bottles on glass shelves that winged away from the Liquore Galliano. Clouds of tobacco smoke scudded across the pressed-tin ceiling.

Still behind the bar, Luca touched his glass to Sonny's. The speech had hit the right balance between sadness and humor.

And truth.

More toasts were made. The weight of sorrow was replaced with relief that the mystery of Jimmy's long disappearance was finally over. There was a sense of justice, too. A killer was dead. Life would go on. Jimmy's legacy meant that the Zambrano family would always have a place in the community.

Vito replaced Sonny behind the bar so the kid could empty ashtrays. For Luca, the next hour was like old times. Laughter and tobacco smoke swirled throughout the saloon as he and Vito poured beer and filled bowls with pickled onions, pretzels and candied lemon peel. They opened box after box of Torrone nougat candy.

Stories about Jimmy kept coming, everyone eager to share something funny or clever. The crew chiefs held the floor retelling Jimmy's mishap with a chemical mix that ate the leather fingers off his work gloves and famously marked his work boots with pink whorls. How he kept the mill going with double strength coffee during the grueling extra shifts to complete the Boston Maritime contract. Gio Tulipano topped them all, with an account of teaching Jimmy how to operate the crane that serviced the giant wire roller machines. The crane hook got stuck in the Number Four roller for an entire day as Jimmy sweated bullets and invented new ways to swear in both English and Italian.

After two hours, the crowd began to thin. Luca saw a contingent of wives, including Carmella Zambrano and Vito's wife Louise, head for the door.

"Are you all right?" Luca intercepted the group by the vestibule. "Can I do anything?"

"Thank you for taking care of Sonny," Carmella said with a nod toward her son across the room. Even in a sack-like black dress, she was a handsome woman who had displayed a spine of steel during the search for Jimmy.

Luca swallowed a rush of stomach-curdling guilt. "He's a good kid."

"You're keeping him that way. Tutoring him in Latin, too." Carmella touched Luca's cheek. "You're the club now, Luca, the way Vito used to be. He's all right tonight but everyone knows he's sick. If it wasn't for you, I don't know what would happen. This place is the center of everything in East Lido."

"It's everything to me, too," Luca managed to say, which was the truth.

Carmella made a show of looking over Luca's

shoulder at the crowded saloon. "Where's your girl? Sonny tells me her name is Tessa."

Luca gave a smile. Tess Kennedy was his Tessa.

"She's in Saratoga," he explained. "Her aunt's taking the cure. She'll be back soon."

"She'd better hurry if she wants to keep you." Carmella smiled back. "Sonny tells me you get plenty of letters. Lady letters he calls them. Ladies writing you letters because they saw your picture in the newspaper."

Luca shook his head. "I'm not interested in those ladies."

"Get married, Luca. You shouldn't be alone."

Guido opened the door for her. Carmella joined her friends outside. Luca watched the women pass by the big plate glass window with GALLIANO CLUB est. 1912 traced in curving gold letters across it.

It took all his self control not to run after Carmella and beg her forgiveness. Tell her that Nick Procopio's last words "In the river" weren't a confession after all. Tell her who was really responsible for putting Jimmy's body in the river.

Her good friends Vito Spinelli and Luca Lombardo.

Luca would never forget finding Jimmy's body in the alley behind the club. The mad scramble to hide it in Vito's Packard from the Antonelli brothers when they came to deliver bootleg beer. Rumors and the dawning belief that someone was trying to frame Vito for murder.

The first impulse was to take Jimmy's body to the church. When that proved impossible, Vito and Luca tried the mill and were stymied yet again.

Jimmy's secret fishing spot was the last resort. Luca said a prayer before they pushed the body over the riverbank. He'd never forget the splash.

Luca carried that sound inside himself, like a stone in his heart. It wasn't the oldest stone, nor the heaviest.

Those belonged to the night he killed a man named Humberto Orsini.

CHAPTER 2

Not bigger, stronger, or braver

If Ruth Cross was bigger and stronger and braver, she'd lunge across the table, shove that drumstick down Officer Sean O'Malley's throat and watch him choke. With a smile on her face.

But she wasn't bigger or stronger or braver.

Ruth huddled into her flannel dressing gown. Across the table from her, the strapping policeman devoured a plate of fried chicken and potatoes. As usual, he didn't notice that she had no appetite.

O'Malley's napkin was tucked into the neck of his long-sleeved undershirt. The rest of his clothing was limited to his police uniform trousers and marled wool socks. His boots and uniform tunic were in the bedroom.

A faint hum filtered up to her apartment from the Galliano Club downstairs. She didn't go to Jimmy Zambrano's funeral nor would she dream of inviting herself to the club. Instead, she'd prayed that the event would keep O'Malley from keeping their standing Sunday evening appointment.

Her prayer went unanswered. O'Malley showed up at the usual time for her weekly humiliation.

"Not bad, Ruthie June." O'Malley swiped his napkin across his mouth and shoved the empty plate toward her side of the table. He had big hands with prominent knuckles. "What's for dessert?"

"Cake." Ruth reached for his empty plate.

Quick as a wink, O'Malley caught her arm and forced her to lean toward him for a hard, painful kiss. He didn't kiss her like that often, only when he wanted to prove that he could.

O'Malley knew about Ruth's past. About her out-of-wedlock pregnancy, the horrible miscarriage in Poughkeepsie, and her stint in prison for indecency and lewd behavior. He knew that her real name was Ruthie June Crosswater.

She paid the price for his silence every Sunday night. They both knew that if she didn't, he'd ruin her. Ruth would lose everything and be run out of Lido on a rail.

The Tapping Toes School of Dance, also on the second floor of the Galliano Club building, was all she had. After those punishing months in Poughkeepsie, Ruth had poured what little she had left into building something for herself, desperate for stability and acceptance. If O'Malley revealed her secret and she lost

Tapping Toes, not only would she be destitute, but the scandal would kill her.

O'Malley ended the kiss with a popping sound. Ruth took a dizzy step backward to regain her balance.

The policeman came around eight o'clock every Sunday night, interrupting his shift keeping the peace on Hamilton Street. After some awkward conversation, he took her into the bedroom. Later, Ruth fed him supper.

At least the bedroom part passed quickly, O'Malley panting like a racehorse on top of her while Ruth's thoughts soared through the clouds to all the places she read about in the pages of *National Geographic* when she could afford to splurge fifty cents on a copy. Paris, Athens, the Nile River, the Great Wall of China.

Ruth opened the icebox and took out the slice of ricotta cake from the Bella Napoli pastry shop. Poured him a cup of coffee from the pot on the stove and returned to the dining table.

O'Malley forked up a big mouthful of cake and nodded as he chewed. "With all the attention on the Galliano Club I drummed up by conking that Procopio fella, your dance business must be doing pretty good."

"Dancing has nothing to do with what happened."

Ruth had been there when O'Malley struck Nick Procopio with his police nightstick, killing the man and saving Luca Lombardo from certain death by strangulation. The sound of those furious cracks still rang in Ruth's memory yet she shuddered to think of the alternative if O'Malley had not been in her bedroom that night.

Luca dead, splayed on the ground. Stiff and cold, his beautiful eyes staring at nothing; the strength revealed in every movement stilled forever. No, it would have been too much to bear.

"You're getting free advertising every day in the *Lido Daily Clipper*, Ruthie June." O'Malley spewed cake crumbs as he talked. "Galliano Club this, Galliano Club that. Lucky Lombardo. Reporters taking pictures of that dago all the time."

He slurped his coffee and started listing his own accolades for saving Luca and hearing the dying confession that led to the discovery of Jimmy Zambrano's body. A big certificate from the New York State Police Benevolent Society. A special Mass in his honor at Saint Brigid's Church. An upcoming banquet hosted by the Bison Club.

When he left to continue his shift, Ruth scrubbed herself raw and wondered how long she could endure.

Ten hours later, Ruth admitted to herself that anyone with half a brain would take advantage of the Galliano Club's burst of notoriety and advertise a business located in the same building. Why else was she caving to O'Malley's blackmail demands, if not to save her business?

After her Wee Tots class, Ruth walked to the offices of the *Lido Daily Clipper*.

As promised, her advertisement appeared in the next day's evening edition on Page Two, with a little border so it stood out amid notices that the new Chrysler showroom was open on Union Street and Victor Records were on sale at Spear's Music House.

Learn all the latest steps now at
Tapping Toes School of Dance
Foxtrot. Waltz. Charleston.
Galliano Club, 2nd Flr
No partner needed. Singles welcome.

The headline on the front page, however, made Ruth wonder if anyone would even see the second page.

CORONER SAYS UNKNOWN WOMAN FROM RIVER WAS STRANGLED

CHAPTER 3

Big wheel

Seeing as Benny Rotolo's cousin Nick Procopio was a confessed murderer, he didn't get a funeral like in Chicago where every gangster got a real wingding at Holy Name Cathedral. Nick's coffin got parked on the sidewalk outside Saint Rocco's.

Benny folded his arms as Father Somebody stood on the steps with the plain wooden casket and moaned out a prayer. No music. No candles or flowers.

Nick's prizefighter of a wife and her pack of wild kids were there, along with a handful of mill workers from Lido Premium. Not one of those lousy mugs took off a hat to show their respect.

Clearly, Nick wasn't on his way to hobnob with St. Peter at the Pearly Gates but to the basement to shovel brimstone. Maybe he'd run into Dean O'Banion and Hymie Weiss, Benny's dearly departed mentors from Chicago's North Side gang. Hell of a party.

Benny didn't wait around when the funeral was done. If he did, Nick's widow Maria Teresa was sure to say something, maybe even hold her hand out for money when she was lousy with Nick's share of the Lido Outfit beer racket. Nick never spent a dime of his share and even kept working at that damn Lido Premium mill. Mostly kept out of the way of the old ball and chain. Home for dinner now and then and a whack at making another kid.

Despite the chill temperature, the Cadillac roared to life on the first try. Benny cruised through downtown Lido, then turned south toward the freight yards. A few minutes later he nosed the Cadillac into a parking slot by Perk's Diner, his headlights passing over the blue neon sign advertising *Fresh Coffee 24 Hours*.

The diner wasn't far from the brothel where Benny lived with his gal Trixie and half a dozen working girls. Benny liked Trixie's bleached blonde hair, hourglass figure and skill in the sack. Trixie liked his dark hair, bedroom eyes and Chicago swagger.

Benny went inside, threw a nickel on the counter for a newspaper, and slid into a booth. A few other fellas were there, shoveling in Bud's greasy stew and sucking down undrinkable coffee.

A stone's throw from the railyard and a scrap heap, Perk's catered mostly to transients like freight workers and teamsters, along with those staggering out of Trixie's with a goofy smile and empty pockets. Fella named Bud ran the joint. Always wore a striped shirt and a paper hat like he was working the lunch counter at Dix's Drugstore. Completed the effect with a cigarette stuck in the corner of his mouth.

"Trixie finally kick you out?" Bud stood by the booth with a scrap of paper and the stub of a pencil.

"Not funny." Benny was in no mood for Bud's attempt at a joke. "Gimme coffee and a slice of pie. Wait, make that two slices."

"What kinda pie?"

"What kind ya got?"

Bud looked over his shoulder at the counter. "Chocolate custard or huckleberry."

"Huckleberry," Benny ordered. No self-respecting Chicago torpedo was ever caught gumming custard.

Bud shuffled off. Benny spread out the evening edition of the *Lido Daily Clipper*. The headline shouted a warning. For a moment, the diner shimmered around him.

"You know anything about that?" Bud slung down the pie and a mug of syrupy coffee.

"What?" Benny had been so absorbed in the article he nearly came out of his seat.

Bud took the butt of his cigarette out of his mouth and tapped ash on the floor. "Nobody's talking about anything else except that naked girl they pulled out of the river the same day they found Zambrano, the dead foreman. Nobody knows who she is."

"Yeah, well." Benny dumped sugar into the coffee cup. "Neither do I."

"It's the most exciting thing that's ever happened in Lido."

"I'll bet."

Bud stuck the cigarette back where it belonged and ambled off.

Benny's attention went back to the article about that gal from the river.

CORONER SAYS UNKNOWN WOMAN FROM RIVER WAS STRANGLED

Lido, New York: County coroner Dr. Simon Lawless today declared that the cause of death of the unidentified woman pulled from the Mohawk River at the same time as Jimmy Zambrano, long-time foreman of the Lido Premium Copper and Brass Rolling Mill, was strangulation.

"She was squeezed by the neck until dead," Dr. Lawless stated to news reporters. "The man's tie around her neck was likely placed there after the fact in an effort to obscure finger marks on her skin. Foul play is assumed."

During the underwater search for Zambrano, divers

were shocked to find the partially dressed young woman. Like Zambrano, she was wrapped and weighted to stay underwater.

Luca "Lucky" Lombardo, one of the two people to hear the confession of Nicola "Nick" Procopio who killed Zambrano, says Procopio did not confess to killing the unidentified woman before dying himself.

Anyone who can identify this unknown dead woman is asked to come to the courthouse to speak with the Lido Police Department.

Of course, there was another damn picture of Lombardo next to the article. The *Lido Daily Clipper* was in love with him, probably because he was a ringer for that Hollywood sheik fella who died a coupla months ago. Valentino.

The pie tasted like sugary lard or maybe reading about Lombardo made Benny sick. The newspaper called him a heroic victim. Benny called him Sheik to his face and a fucking bastard to everybody else.

Now that he was so famous, Lombardo was an even bigger problem than before. Benny should have rubbed him out when nobody cared who he was.

Lombardo was keeping Benny from buying up the Galliano Club and making it into the finest speakeasy north of Manhattan. The club's owner, Vito Spinelli, was ready to make a deal, but Lombardo got in the way every time. Turned down a pile of cash that made Spinelli's eyes pop out of his head and wave around on their stems. Lombardo even refused Benny's offer to work for him when the place became a speakeasy.

With Lombardo in the way, Benny had resorted to an old Chicago trick. Force old man Spinelli to buy beer at inflated prices, get him in debt, and seize the property as "payment." Benny's Lido Outfit had stamped out all the local competition, so Spinelli had to buy beer from Benny at sixty dollars a barrel. As soon as Spinelli defaulted and Lombardo conveniently disappeared, Benny could swoop in and seize the club.

But with Sheik in the newspaper every other day and reporters roaming up and down Hamilton Street, the Galliano Club was paying its bills. Benny would have to wait a little longer. Hard to rub out a famous fella and get away with it, even if Benny was paying Chief of Police Doyle three hundred a week to look the other way.

"Mr. Rotolo?" One of Lido's local yokels stood by Benny's booth. A real *cafone*, from the smell of cow dung that clung to him. The farmer twisted a tweed cap between his hands.

"Who's asking?" Benny eyed the fella. Wool jacket, dungarees, old-fashioned mustache on a head like a pumpkin but a real respectful-like attitude.

"I'm Al Genovese. I've got a farm on Bell Road. Biggest in the county."

Benny swallowed some coffee. "You selling eggs or what?"

"Information," Genovese said. "The kind of information someone like you might find useful."

"Someone like me?"

"A big wheel," Genovese hastened to clarify.

"Okay," Benny said, mollified. "Have a seat."

Genovese slid into the opposite side of the booth.

"Make it quick," Benny said. "I'm a busy man."

"The newspaper's wrong," Genovese said, with a meaningful glance at the *Lido Daily Clipper* next to the pie plate. "Nick Procopio didn't dump Jimmy Zambrano in the river."

"How would you know?"

"The night Jimmy Zambrano went missing I saw Vito Spinelli's Packard on the riverbank," Genovese said, lowering his voice. "Spinelli owns the Galliano Club. I think Spinelli and Luca Lombardo put Zambrano in the river."

Benny's heart thumped against the Colt Pocket Hammerless hidden in a special chest pocket in his jacket. He knew that Nick left Zambrano's stiff behind the Galliano Club but always figured the cops took care of it to prevent scandal from touching Lido Premium, the city's biggest employer.

But if this farmer had the goods on Spinelli, that changed everything. "Oh, yeah? How'd you know it was Spinelli's Packard?"

"From my attic window," Genovese said. "The moon was out and I seen the car real clear."

"He's not the only mug in Lido with a Packard."

"Rich people don't come down Bell Road."

The fella had a point. "You see him?"

"No, I just saw the car drive through the trees. It was right on the river."

Benny wasn't sure if the *cafone* was on the level or not. "All I got is your word. Maybe you're nuttier than a fruitcake."

"I know it was Spinelli's Packard," the farmer said stoutly.

"Go tell the cops."

"I did. They didn't believe me." Genovese leaned forward. "You read the paper. The cop caught Procopio trying to cut Lombardo's throat with a wire, the same way Zambrano died. Both the cop and Lombardo say that Procopio confessed. Lombardo's a big deal now, him and that Officer O'Malley. The cops don't want a different story."

Benny scraped up the last bit of jellied berries,

mulling his options. Genovese believed what he was selling. The fact that the cops didn't want to get involved made the set-up perfect.

The information racket was small potatoes compared to beer and hookers but there was always an exception. Big Vinnie Salerno, a sometime pal from Chicago, always had new suits and expensive dames on his arm. Nobody ever shot at Big Vinnie, neither.

"I know a buddy," Benny said, making up his mind. "He's got this system. Say he's got a friend what's got the goods on somebody but doesn't want to tell the mark direct, just in case they finger him to the cops. So he writes a letter and sticks it in two envelopes and sends it to my buddy Vinnie. Vinnie burns the first envelope then takes the letter in the inside envelope to the post office and mails it to the mark. Different post office, is the trick, see? This way the letter comes from a place the mark don't know at all. It can't get traced. The mark pays, the friend picks up the dough, and Vinnie gets a cut. Everybody's happy."

"Except the mark," Genovese said.

"That's right."

"Do you think your buddy would help?"

"Sure," Benny said. "But Big Vinnie don't work for nothing. Like I says, Vinnie gets a cut and he don't take peanuts, if you get what I'm saying."

"The mark has to pay up big," Genovese said.

"That's right," Benny said again, pleased that Genovese caught on so fast. "Spinelli's got money. He'll pay. What about Lombardo?"

"He doesn't have any money," Genovese said. "But his cousin does. Enzo Russo. Got a farm near me. Just put up a new barn. He's got money."

"You think Lombardo told this cousin about dumping the stiff?"

"Sure. They're real close."

"Okay. Two marks." Benny would have been satisfied to suck Spinelli dry. This cousin was gravy on top. "You ever been in the information racket before?"

"No," Genovese said. "I have cows."

Benny slurped up more coffee and regarded the *cafone* across the table. His cousin Nick might be shoveling brimstone with Hymie Weiss and the gang, but he'd sent Genovese as a parting gift.

"Are you married?" Genovese asked.

"No, why?" Benny replied. "You got a sister?"

CHAPTER 4

At the mill

The steam whistle signaling the end of the work day at the Lido Premium mill cut through the clatter and hum of the machinery on the shop floor. Karol Dombrowski pulled off one heavy suede work glove to fish a bandana out of his pocket and wipe the sweat stinging his eyes. The members of his dipping crew grinned tiredly at each other and went to collect the huge lids for the chemical vats. The timbre of noise changed as forge fires were banked, the trolley-sized wire rollers began shutting down, and the cranes put into rest positions.

"A good day's work." Next to Karol, Henry Blick wore the same ankle-length leather apron as members of the dipping crew to avoid being burned as they cured sheets of copper in the caustic chemical baths.

Blick was Lido Premium's operations manager, usually attired in suit and tie and working in the office building adjacent to the giant mill. But Blick had been acting as foreman ever since Nick Procopio died, returning it to the tightly run ship it had been under

Jimmy Zambrano. Blick's ability to know what was going on at every moment in every corner of the huge mill was uncanny.

The one-eyed former Army officer could perform every function on the shop floor as least as well as the man whose job it actually had been. Blick terrified most of the workers but Karol admired him to no end. He was tough but fair and explained his decisions in a way that no other supervisor ever did.

"I've got a good crew," Karol said, watching his men go through the familiar evening routine. Chemical vats were covered and pressure valves adjusted. The levers and cranks that controlled the passage of copper sheets to and from the dipping station were set to neutral.

The last checks were called out by the crew's safety officer of the day, a responsibility that rotated so everyone knew how to do it. Karol created the routine after realizing that most of his crew's accidents occurred in the morning as they opened vats which had been improperly closed the night before.

"See me in my office before you leave the mill tonight," Blick said to Karol as he removed his apron and hung it up. Mixing with the men heading for their lockers to collect coats and go home, Blick was easy to track as he left the shop floor. As tall as Karol but leaner. His head of close-cropped silver hair rose above the crowd.

Karol felt a prick of unease. The last time he'd been asked to go to the office, it was to answer questions about Jimmy Zambrano's disappearance. There was no reason Blick wished to speak with him in private unless it was to find fault with the way Karol was running his crew.

Frank Conti, the wire crew chief whose station was on the same side of the mill as the dipping crew, passed through the parade of workers heading to their lockers as Karol hung up his own leather apron.

"How did it go with Blick?" Conti asked.

"No problems," Karol said. "We met our quota and then some. How about you?"

Conti shrugged. The wire crew chief was a no-nonsense type with a barrel chest. He was one of the few Italians who didn't give Polish workers—and Karol as the only Polish crew chief—a cold shoulder. "Blick spent the morning with my crew. Ran the Number 3 wire roller as good as anyone."

"He say anything to you later?" Karol asked, wondering if Blick was having a pep talk with each crew chief.

"Nothing." Conti shook his head. "How long do you think this is gonna go on? Blick acting as foreman, I mean."

"The eye getting to you, Conti?" Karol asked.

"Sometimes I see sparks shoot out of it," Conti replied in a way that said he wasn't entirely joking.

Karol grinned tiredly. "Blick's got one eye in front and a dozen looking behind him."

Blick had lost an eye in the Great War and wore an eye patch. His remaining eye was a startling shade of pale blue, or maybe the patch just made it seem that way.

The Italian workers called it *malocchio,* meaning the evil eye. Karol picked up useful bits like that from Luca Lombardo, fellow resident of Mrs. Esposito's boarding house and Sunday evening chess partner.

"Did you hear about the Ferlo kid?" Conti asked. "Finally out of the hospital. They saved two fingers on that hand. Not sure if they'll be good for anything but he's young. He'll be all right."

"Thanks for letting me know," Karol said and meant it.

A few weeks ago, acting foreman Nick Procopio had broken a cardinal safety rule by assigning David Ferlo, a relatively inexperienced worker, to handle a two-man job on his own. Changing wire spools on a catwalk above one of the huge wire roller machines was a dangerous task even with two men. When the inevitable disaster happened, Karol was first on the scene. He saved the young man's life and got a tongue-lashing from Procopio for it. But Conti, who'd been there, knew that Karol had also saved the life of every worker in proximity to the runaway iron spool.

The two men headed for the lockers in the outer corridor. Karol took his time extracting his mackinaw, cap and lunch pail, to avoid being caught up in the stream of men leaving the mill for the warren of narrow streets north of Hamilton Street. Almost all the Italian workers lived in that East Lido neighborhood. Mrs. Esposito's boarding house was there as well.

He finally left the mill and took the path to the adjacent office building. Miss Camden, the secretary, led him down the hall to Blick's office. The other offices were dark, including that of Mr. Fisher, the dapper little accountant for the mill.

"Dombrowski, thank you for coming." Blick gestured for Karol to take one of the armchairs in front of the desk and took the other for himself. Miss Camden left, closing the office door behind her.

Karol settled into the chair, feeling out of place in his stained and sweaty dungarees. The office was large and elegant, with windows on two sides. Blick might be willing to roll up his sleeves and run a wire roller or dip copper all day long, but he was also the nephew of owner Nathan Packham. Everyone knew that Blick would inherit Lido Premium one day.

"It's been some time since we lost Zambrano," Blick started. "Things got a bit slipshod under Procopio, like what happened to young Ferlo. I'm looking for a new foreman who can keep output high but make Lido Premium into the safest mill in the east."

The eye bored into Karol, who nodded.

"I've proposed a new way to approach the foreman position," Blick went on. "In addition to running the shop floor as usual, the new foreman will also be an apprentice of sorts, learning the full scope of the business. One afternoon a week he'll come in and shadow one of the officers of the company. Shipping, sales, contracts, accounting procedures. The goal is to understand all of Lido Premium's business practices as well as I do. Eventually, the foreman could move into a position as deputy operations manager, a position we don't have at present but sorely need. Then the deputy foreman moves up and becomes both the new foreman and the new business apprentice. What do you think?"

"I've never heard of such a thing," Karol said honestly.

Blick leaned forward, speaking with real passion. "We need more people with hands-on experience in office positions to help the board of directors make informed decisions. There must be more opportunities for the men on the shop floor to understand they're part of something more than simply running a wire roller or a copper press. Just as important, I want your safety procedures to become the standard across the mill."

It dawned on Karol that Blick had spent so much time on the shop floor lately because he was studying every process with a view to setting up this new system.

"The new foreman has to be a person who can move between the shop floor and the world of business." Blick paused and the single eye sparked blue fire. "If you'll take it, Dombrowski, the foreman's job is yours."

It took a long moment for Karol to absorb what Blick was offering him. *Him.* Karol Dombrowski, a Polish immigrant who lived in a boarding house. He was being given a chance to become foreman of the biggest mill in the northeast, with the possibility of a step up into suit-and-tie management as well.

Reality smothered the brief thrill.

"The foreman is always Italian," Karol pointed out. "I don't have seniority, either."

The foreman and deputy foreman were always Italians from East Lido, selected for skill, seniority and influence over the mostly Italian workforce. Jimmy Zambrano had held the position for years, giving him enormous status within East Lido.

"Lido Premium is ready for a change," Blick asserted. "Being Italian is no longer essential. The men respect you. They like the way you look out for your crew. You gave Carbone a slot when you could have picked another Pole but you rewarded a good worker instead. You saved Ferlo when Procopio put him up on that catwalk alone. In fact, you and Conti saved quite a few men and they know it."

Karol rubbed sweaty palms on the knees of his dungarees. "What about Conti? He should get the foreman job."

But even as he asked the question, Karol knew why Blick wasn't offering the new position to Conti, an East Lido Italian. It wouldn't be enough of a break with tradition. Conti was committed to the way things were.

As if reading Karol's mind, Blick nodded. "Conti will make a good deputy foreman, if you agree."

Karol rubbed a hand across his mouth, knowing he was on the brink of a huge opportunity but too bound by unspoken rules to seize it.

"Did I misread?" Blick asked. "Are you still intending to join the police department?"

"No," Karol blurted. That dream had died the day he took the entrance examination. "One punch from Officer O'Malley was enough to convince me."

"A punch? During your entrance exam?"

"I'd rather not talk about it, sir," Karol said uncomfortably, wishing he hadn't mentioned anything about his abortive attempt to join the all-Irish police force. The advertisement encouraged all men of good character to apply. Karol had been naïve enough to believe it.

"Would it suffice to say that you were prevented from meeting the police department's height requirement?" Blick asked.

Karol blinked. "How did you know?"

"I was a military officer for far too long," Blick said as a knock sounded at the door. He rose from his chair. "The same sort of tricks are played there, too."

Blick opened the door. An elderly man came in, a gold-knobbed walking stick complementing a black suit with an old-fashioned celluloid collar and a diamond horseshoe stickpin. With a start, Karol recognized him as Nathan Packham, Lido Premium's reclusive owner. Mr. Packham came to the mill once a year to hand out the Christmas bonuses.

Karol leaped to his feet, wondering if he should bow or genuflect or leave.

"Dombrowski, may I introduce my uncle, Mr. Nathan Packham," Blick said. "Uncle Nathan, this is Karol Dombrowski, chief of the dipping crew."

"Hello, young man." Despite a voice that quavered

with age, Packham spoke at freight train speed. He did not extend his hand but leaned on the ornate cane and held a pince-nez to eyes that traveled the length of Karol's frame. "You're certainly bigger than Zambrano, but I must say, I didn't realize you were quite so young."

"Thirty-two, sir," Karol said. Both he and Blick towered over the old man.

"Young enough not to be mired in tradition. Not like me, eh?" Packham gave a chesty cough. "Time to be receptive to Henry's progressive ideas, eh?"

"It's a wonderful opportunity, sir," Karol said.

"Henry says you're the best man for this new business apprentice scheme and I've seen your record. Got us to the finish line for the Beacon Maritime contract. Saved that Ferlo boy, too. Oh yes, I know what goes on in my own mill. You understand you'll be in the office part of the time, getting ready to be Henry's deputy? Can you handle the Italian workers at the same time? There's a lot of loyalty to Jimmy Zambrano in this place."

"I can handle the workers, sir," a voice like Karol's said.

"Well, then, that's fine." Packham turned to Blick. "Present your plan to the board with my concurrence. Once Dombrowski's approved, get the wheels rolling."

"I'd like to hear Dombrowski say he'll take the job," Blick said.

"What's the matter?" Packham demanded, swinging toward Karol and thumping his stick for emphasis. "Don't you want the job?"

"Yes, I do," Karol said. "I accept your offer."

"Excellent." Blick started to discuss salary, which also was subject to the board's approval, but Karol barely heard him. Jimmy Zambrano had hired him fifteen years ago, taking a chance on a young Polish immigrant. Now Karol would become the youngest foreman, the first non-Italian one, with the opportunity to reach even higher.

This must be how it felt to be struck by lightning.

"Then that's settled," Packham said, cutting off his nephew. He limped to the sofa by the window. "Break out the brandy, Henry."

Thunder was still echoing inside Karol's head as Blick opened a file drawer, extracted a bottle of brandy, and poured three glasses.

"To a new era at Lido Premium," Blick said.

"Thank you, sir."

"I hope you're right, Henry," Packham snapped and drained his glass. "All right, gentlemen, that's enough business for today. Goodbye, young Dombrowski. Don't disappoint me."

It was dark as Karol drifted back to Mrs. Esposito's in a brandy-fueled daze. Maybe by the time the board of directors met, he'd believe this was really happening.

CHAPTER 5

Bananas

It took Benny four dollars in long-distance calls, sitting in a telephone kiosk in the post office, to find somebody who'd relay a message to Big Vinnie Salerno. Finally, his butt falling asleep on the hard wooden seat, Benny was put through to Big Vinnie himself in Chicago.

"I got some bananas what need to be cooked," Benny said, showing Big Vinnie that he knew the code.

"Simmered or boiled?" Big Vinnie had a gravelly voice that came through the telephone line loud and clear.

"Boiled. And fast."

Two hours later, a telegram arrived from a wholesale grocery warehouse in Gary, Indiana, talking nonsense about banana prices and shipping bananas and money orders to pay for banana purchases. Substitute the word *mark* for *banana* and the plan was clear as day.

Benny had to tip his hat to Big Vinnie. The fella wasn't no slouch in the business department. His foolproof system used double envelopes, just the way the rumor mill said back in Chicago. Big Vinnie was real particular about the signature, too. Benny didn't know if he was part of the gang or just using their moniker, but it was the kind of attention to detail that scored the big bucks.

Every letter was to be signed like it came from the real gang that sent Benny's ma into fits of sheer terror when he was little and they lived on Elizabeth Street in New York City. He remembered how scared she was, how scared everyone in the tenements were. Every Italian with two nickels to rub together was a target. It was one of the reasons she packed him up and skedaddled to Chicago when he was still a pup.

That gang snatched kids off the street for ransom and chopped up marks who didn't pay. Blew up stores and tenements and businesses. Slit the throats of squealers and lopped off the ears of those who heard too much. Stuck a body in a barrel of sugar and left it on the sidewalk in New York City to liquefy.

As a kid, Benny had nightmares about Clutch Hand, the gang leader with a withered arm. Clutch Hand prowled the streets of Little Italy with the bum arm in a sling made of dirty string. Propped his claw-like hand right below his chin, where everyone could see it.

Following Big Vinnie's directions, Benny's letters were gonna be loaded with more firepower than the

Colt Pocket Hammerless. If Spinelli didn't pay after reading a letter signed by a ghost from the past, it would be because he'd dropped dead of a heart attack.

Benny burped and shoved aside his empty plate. Al Genovese had been real keen to show off his farm on Bell Road and point out Russo's new barn as well. Al's place was all right, although to a city kid like Benny the smell of dung took two bits of shine off the place. The tour had ended in the dining room of the Genovese farmhouse.

"You want more?" Al didn't wait for Benny's answer but shouted for his wife. Her name was Claudia. She had a skinny face, suspicious eyes, and a figure like a washboard. Benny didn't like her.

But Claudia could teach Trixie a thing or two about keeping a fella fed. She dumped another mountain of mouth-watering linguini on Benny's plate, along with a couple of meatballs. The same second helping for her husband. Al topped up their glasses of dandelion wine which tasted like piss but produced a nice buzz.

When the two men were alone in the dining room again, it was time to finalize the details.

"Two thousand dollars," Al suggested.

"Spinelli's good for ten times that," Benny scoffed. Two thousand dollars minus Big Vinnie's hefty chunk, a cut for Al and a bit, so Fishy did the numbers. Those percentages didn't leave much for Benny.

They'd start with five thousand for both Spinelli and Russo, he decided. Enough to shock the system and let the mark know they weren't fooling around. After the first payment, they'd up the stakes and go for big money. Ten thousand. Fifteen. And so on until Spinelli was bankrupt and bleeding and ready to sell the Galliano Club for peanuts.

"When Russo goes under, I'll buy his place," Al confided in a whisper.

The *cafone* was a fast learner.

Claudia cleared the plates away, a scowl on her face. Benny gave her a sullen, appraising look in return and opened his jacket so she could see the outline of the Colt Pocket Hammerless. She didn't come back into the dining room.

Benny and Al got to work. Remembering the conversation about bananas, the letters were written the way Big Vinnie wanted and stuck in envelopes. Benny carefully printed the home address for Spinelli on one and Russo on the other. Each of those envelopes went inside a fresh blank envelope.

When Benny left the Genovese farm, he stopped by the post office for stamps and mailed both envelopes to the wholesale grocery warehouse in Gary, Indiana.

CHAPTER 6

The person I want to be

Luca tried not to stare at Tess, his *Tessa*, as he wrote out the deposit slip. She was finally back in Lido. Everything was going to be all right.

The First National Bank of Lido was a baronial palace of financial decisions where customers submitted transactions to the tellers behind a tall counter running the width of the lobby. On the other side of a wooden railing, more than a dozen men in dark suits were on display in a section cordoned off from their customers. They were too exalted to acknowledge customers waiting in line for a teller, sitting at large wooden desks where they studiously consulted ledgers and adding machines and each other.

The exception was Tess, seated at her desk in the middle of the section. The chandelier above glinted on her spectacles and turned her red hair into flame. She caught Luca's eye and dipped her head at his nod.

Every fiber of Luca's being longed to wrench open the gate, rush to her desk, and crush her to him.

"How are you today, Mr. Lombardo?" Ralph, his

favorite teller, accepted Luca's passbook, the deposit slip and the accompanying ten dollars.

"Fine," Luca said distractedly, watching Tess out of the corner of his eye. She bent over some papers on her desk.

"Saw your picture in the *Clipper* again yesterday."

Luca gave a tight half smile.

"It was next to the article about that poor girl who was found along with Mr. Zambrano," Ralph went on as he calculated Luca's account balance and filled in the column in the passbook.

"I don't know anything about her," Luca said for the hundredth time.

"Of course the rumor is that Nick Procopio killed her, too," Ralph persisted, carefully inking the date in Luca's passbook.

"First they need to find out who she is," Luca pointed out.

"Exciting, isn't it?" Ralph finally slid Luca's passbook across the counter to him.

Not for whoever that poor girl is.

Luca loitered in the lobby. Tess looked his way again and glanced at the clock on the wall above the tellers. He knew what she meant. It was nearly closing time. Luca went outside to wait under the big bank awning.

The bank was on a busy intersection, known as the American Corner, across from the big Western Union office. Traffic cruised up and down. Cars slotted into parking spaces along Liberty Street, Lido's most important boulevard, lined with stores and restaurants and anchored by the grand Strand Theatre. A parade of pedestrians in hats and flapping overcoats went in both directions.

Luca unbuttoned his own coat, revealing his good suit and a green tie that matched his prized fedora, the only thing he had ever purchased new from Nelson's Department Store. He'd dressed well on purpose. It had been almost five weeks since he and Tess last saw each other, five weeks since that fateful quarrel after a romantic evening at the Candyland Supper Club that almost ended with a proposal.

Once again, Luca mentally rehearsed what he needed to say. He would explain everything, wipe away her worries. Make her understand the truth. Well, most of the truth.

And then he'd say the words he had come so close to saying weeks before. *Tessa, will you be my wife?*

The November sun was setting, throwing watercolor streaks of gold and purple across the three-and four-story brick buildings that lined the street. Pedestrians continued to clog the sidewalks of the busy commercial district. Traffic stopped as the trolley clanged its way along the tracks set into the pavement.

"Hello, Luca." Tess joined him under the awning. She was as lovely as ever, green eyes wide behind wire spectacles. She wore a creamy coat that reached to her fingertips. A gray pleated shirt showed below, reaching to shapely calves. Gray leather buckle shoes, gray stockings, gray gloves, and a gray cloche hat to hide her rusty-red curls, as if the somber color suited her mood.

"Tessa." Luca reached for her hand. "I missed you."

"I missed you, too." She eased away from him. "Let's take a walk."

This wasn't at all how Luca had imagined their reunion. He fell into step beside her. "I have things to tell you," he said.

"I have things to tell you, too," Tess replied, then fell silent. She kept both gloved hands on her purse instead of taking his arm, the way they always walked.

The smell of coffee and fried potatoes wafted out of McSweeney's Restaurant as they passed. Luca slowed. "Shall we go in?"

"No, I'm not hungry." Tess kept walking.

Beau Geste with Ronald Coleman was playing at The Strand, which offered the potential for a private conversation if they sat in the back, but Tess just shook her head.

The crowd thinned after six blocks. As their shadows lengthened, Tess led him toward West Park, the posh neighborhood anchored by a round park of the same name. She lived at 112 West Park Circle, with her aunt Evelyn Kennedy Thompson in a big house on the ring road that traced around the park itself.

"Where is your car?" Luca asked. She drove a green Ford coupe.

"I thought it would be better if we walked," Tess said. "Give us some time . . ." Her voice trailed away.

Luca looked sideways at her. Tess didn't meet his eyes.

Brick mansions ringed the park, each detailed with soaring white columns, flickering gas lamps, and opulent landscaping. Franklins and Cadillacs waited in front or under covered drives originally built to shelter carriages and horses.

Instead of making for the house, Tess led him into the park itself. It was almost dark by the time they stopped at a bench by the rose garden. The blooms were long gone and the pruned rose bushes were nothing more than thorny stalks waiting to survive the coming winter.

"We can talk here." She perched gingerly on the bench. "I know we both have a lot to say."

"I need to tell you about that pocket ledger," Luca

said before she drew another breath. "The one I showed you. Jimmy Zambrano gave it to my boss Vito to put in the office safe. After Jimmy disappeared, Vito just left it there. He didn't want to give it to the police because he was afraid of being blamed for Jimmy's disappearance. I found it in the safe and tried to understand what it meant. That's when I showed it to you and you figured out it was a divvy sheet. Crooks dividing up profits."

"I remember," Tess said. "It was all in Mr. Fisher's handwriting. Exactly the same as the handwriting on his loan forms."

Between the gathering night and the long shadows of the nearby pine trees, it was hard to see her expression but Luca plowed on. "That's the truth, Tess. We don't know why Jimmy had it or how he was involved with Rotolo and Procopio and Fisher. I don't know who else is involved, but I'm not part of it."

"That Mr. Rotolo made it seem like you are," Tess said.

"I'm not," Luca said stoutly. "The club buys beer from Rotolo but that's all. He's squeezed out the competition. And don't say the club doesn't need beer. We've got five hundred thirsty members and Vito needs to pay the mortgage. Rotolo wants to buy the club, too. I won't let that happen."

"That horrible Procopio man was involved, too, wasn't he? Is that why he tried to strangle you? Because you have the ledger?"

"Yes."

"Oh, Luca." Tess shook her head in sorrow but kept both hands on the purse in her lap. "Why didn't you tell me all this before?"

"I wanted to shield you from Rotolo." It sounded like a weak excuse and maybe it was, but it was also the truth. "He's a bad man. And then you were so angry, I didn't know what to do so I said all the wrong things."

"Yes, you did." Tess gave him a small, flickering smile.

Luca offered up another lie, another stone from the bottom of his heart. "There's more, Tess. I didn't fall down the stairs at work. I got shot on a boat in the middle of the ocean."

"What?" Her eyes opened wide behind the spectacles.

"Rum Row is a big line of ships--."

"I know what Rum Row is. What were you doing there?"

"My friend Toby Gleason is a rumrunner. We picked up a load of liquor, but the captain turned out to be a crook and was going to let pirates board us and steal it. I fouled their engine. We got away with the cargo but I got shot just here." Luca tapped a spot over his ribs to indicate where the bullet had scored him. "A woman in Montauk stitched it closed. It healed but I have a scar."

Tess's shock was palpable. "Why would you do such a crazy, dangerous thing?"

"For you," Luca said, surprised that she needed to ask. "For us. One risk and I made two thousand dollars. It's enough to get married."

"You did it for us? And lied about it?"

Pride nearly choked him but he had to say it. "I was afraid that if you knew the truth you wouldn't believe me."

"Because you don't trust me?"

"Because I thought you wouldn't love me."

"You did it for us." Tess drew in her breath. "How could I not love you?"

"Do you forgive me?" Luca asked. "Can we go back to the way things were?"

The weeks before she left for Saratoga had been an open door to the life he wanted to share with her, a world of information and opportunities beyond East Lido. Lectures at the library, political debates, long walks through West Park discussing everything and anything. Kissing in the back row of the Strand Theatre.

It was completely dark now. Luca grappled with

telling her more. Not that he and Vito put Jimmy Zambrano in the river because he would carry that secret to the grave, but what he did a long, long time ago.

To his surprise, Tess began to cry. She groped for her purse and pulled out an embroidered handkerchief.

"I'm to marry James Howland," Tess said. She took off her spectacles and pressed the handkerchief to her eyes.

Luca was sure he had misheard. "James Howland?"

Tess took a shaky breath. "Yes, my boss at the bank. I'll be Missus Vice President of the First National Bank of Lido."

"The man with the baseball mustache?" Luca was stunned. They'd joked about Howland and his old-fashioned ways, obvious paunch and feeble facial hair. *A baseball mustache. Nine hairs on a side.*

"Aunt Evelyn and his father arranged it even before she had the cancer. It's why the bank offered me a job. It was all arranged without me knowing. Everyone keeps secrets except me. Honest little Tess, thinking she can make her own decisions."

"Do you want to marry him?"

"It's not about me." Tess made a choking sound. "Aunt Evelyn wants to see me settled before she's gone. Settled with James and his father's money. It's an . . .

an arrangement."

"What about us?" Luca demanded. "She gave me permission to court you."

"Aunt Evelyn thought you'd lose interest when you found out that I won't inherit any money. Or I'd get tired of you. Now she says her permission is revoked."

"*Oddio*," Luca swore, so nonplussed that the English language was momentarily lost in a churn of emotion. This was why they were sitting in the park instead of sharing a booth at McSweeney's. "Is that what you want?"

Tess sniffed hard. "Aunt Evelyn gave me everything. A home after my father died and I was lost and angry. She sold her pearls so I could go to college and travel to Europe. Now she's dying and has asked for one thing, just one thing. She's never asked me for anything before."

It was fully dark now. The pine trees made feathery points against the charcoal sky. A car turned onto the ring road, its throaty hum breaking the quiet. Headlights sliced over the rose garden and moved on.

"We could run away," Luca said desperately. "I have two thousand dollars. We can go anywhere."

"What if this was your family, Luca?" Tess asked, her voice quiet and strained. "Someone you loved and owed so much to, wanting the best for you before they died? Could you refuse?"

Family. The thing he wanted so much yet was destined to never have. First his parents were gone, then Rafaella and their infant. Now Tess. His *Tessa.*

Tess began to cry again. Luca put his arms around her. She sagged against him.

Lights brightened an upstairs window of the house across the street. Another car rumbled around the ring road. Not a star to be seen, each and every one hiding from the sad scene in the barren garden below.

"Tell me one thing," Luca said hoarsely. "If things were different, would you marry me?"

After a long moment, Tess pulled away from the circle of his embrace. "It's no use saying things like that," she gulped. "Things aren't different. I wish Aunt Evelyn wasn't dying. I wish women could make their own decisions. I wish you'd never been shot or been hurt by that terrible man who tried to strangle you. But wishes aren't the same as real life."

She stood, handkerchief in one hand and purse in the other. Her eyes were watery behind the lenses of her spectacles. "Don't walk me home. Annie will see and tattle to Aunt Evelyn."

"I won't let you go." Luca got to his feet, part of him refusing to believe that this was happening. "I love you. Forever."

"I love you, too." Tess gave him a crooked smile. "I always will. You were the one person who made me feel like the person I want to be."

She walked away without looking back, the frozen grass crunching under her steps.

CHAPTER 7

Widows and Orphans Fund

Yawning, Benny hauled on his trousers and a flannel shirt. He walked out, leaving the girl curled up and trembling under the blanket. The upstairs hallway was dark. All the customers were gone. Benny heard a few snores from behind the other bedroom doors, the sound of tired working girls, but otherwise Trixie's place was quiet.

He trotted down the stairs. Lights were on in the kitchen. Trixie was at the table, counting how much she and the girls had made that night. She was swathed in a silk kimono. Wisps of platinum hair peeked from the folds of a turban.

"Hey, doll." Benny bent to kiss the back of her neck.

Trixie pulled away. "Leave me alone."

Despite the pile of cash, there was a sourpuss look on her kisser that meant trouble. Benny sauntered to the icebox and opened the wooden door.

"I don't like you fooling with the other girls, Benny," Trixie said, her words hitting Benny right between the shoulder blades. "You're supposed to be my man."

"Sure, I'm your fella." Benny continued to study the contents of the icebox. "I'm just breaking in the new girl. Helping your business."

"Helping yourself to the business is more like it."

"Hey, didn't I give you a mink jacket?" Benny chugged down some buttermilk and wiped his mouth on his sleeve. "Send all my boys here for a good time? They're big tippers, too. Your girls barely got time to complain anymore."

"You know what I'm talking about," Trixie snapped. "Annunziata doesn't speak English. I don't think she knows that you're my fella."

"She knows I'm your fella," Benny said dismissively. He stuck the bottle of buttermilk back in the icebox. "They all do."

He pulled Trixie into his lap and kissed her noisily. She tried to resist but Benny pinned her to him until she relaxed. "See?" he said against her mouth. "I'm your fella."

Dames like Trixie were always looking for something to worry about, Benny decided half an hour later as she fell asleep against his side. Playing rough with Annunziata tonight was nothing more than blowing off steam.

But Trixie was right in one regard; Annunziata

Genovese was new to the job and she only spoke Italian. Benny made sure that Trixie only sent Polish boys her way. No Italian speakers except Benny.

The information racket was up and running, thanks to Al Genovese's dirt on Spinelli and Big Vinnie Salerno's foolproof system, but it wasn't the instant money-maker he'd expected it to be. Letters went out, but the marks didn't pay. Big Vinnie explained that sometimes they needed to get half a dozen letters before they did. Benny still had to pay him a so-called set-up fee.

Peanuts, given what the beer racket was pulling in, but it pinched Benny's pocket all the same. Not to mention giving Benny a queasy feeling that Big Vinnie might not be the most honest partner a fella could have.

Trixie was still sound asleep, as were the other girls, when he drove over to Perk's Diner for breakfast the next morning. A couple of Bud's fried eggs, a side of hash browns, and a quick read of the morning edition of the *Lido Daily Clipper* set him up for the day. Another hand-wringing story about the unidentified dame who was pulled out of the river with a man's tie around her neck. Benny left the paper in the booth.

He headed outside to see that damned rumrunning mick Toby Gleason leaning against the Cadillac, a smile full of sunshine plastered on his mug.

"Get off my car," Benny snarled.

Gleason languidly peeled himself off the front bumper. "You're a hard man to find, Rotolo. Chief Doyle's been looking for you."

"He knows where to find me," Benny blustered.

"Doyle likes the personal touch. Instead you're sending somebody named Siwak to make your weekly contributions." The smile vanished. "He wants to see you. Better go talk to him, smooth things over."

Benny got right up in Gleason's mug. "Wadda you, his messenger boy?"

"Just a wee bit of advice." Gleason didn't back up. The mick might look like a nobody in a newsboy cap but he was packing heat under his coat, the kind sailors wore. "Head over to see the chief now, before his bad temper gets the best of him."

"Oh yeah?" Benny felt the reassuring weight of the Colt Pocket Hammerless in its special pocket. "I'm no dog to come when some fat old mick snaps their fingers."

"Sure and that's a man's pride talking," Gleason said in that slightly mocking, smooth Irish way of his. "Use your common sense."

"Go on, get outta my face."

Gleason tugged on the brim of his cap in a fake salute and sauntered into the diner.

Benny jumped into the Cadillac and gunned it out of the lot in the direction of the courthouse. Despite the bravado he'd shown Gleason, Chief Doyle wasn't a man to be trifled with.

The cop at the desk in the courthouse lobby swallowed Benny's lie about an appointment and directed him across the black and white checkered marble to the big curving staircase. Once on the second floor, Benny followed the brass signs to the office of the Chief of Police.

He waited an hour sitting on a hard chair while Mrs. Clancy, the chief's gnarled old secretary, alternately pounded on a typewriter and shot Benny baleful looks over the top of her spectacles.

Finally Benny was admitted into Chief Doyle's inner sanctum and the door closed behind him. It was the same as before, a big vault of a place, lousy with velvet draperies and flags and polished paneling, not to mention leather chairs and that damned diploma from the Loyal Order of the Bison attesting to the fact that Gerald Francis Doyle was a member in good standing. The thing was the size of a bedsheet, making it impossible to miss the gold lettering or watermark of a fat cow with a hump.

All the bold signatures on the thing reminded Benny of the way him and Nick and Fishy signed their names in that pocket ledger back in August, establishing the Lido Outfit beer racket.

Lotsa things had happened since then.

"Nice of you to drop by," Chief Doyle snarled, the Irish in his voice adding to the menace. The collar of his police uniform was unbuttoned and loose jowls wobbled against blue wool. His iron-gray hair was slick with pomade. His nose was webbed with red veins.

Without being invited, Benny boldly dropped into one of the leather armchairs. "Always a pleasure, Chief. Thought I'd stop by and see if there was anything I could do for you."

"Aye, boy." Chief Doyle glared at Benny from behind the desk. "You can tell me who killed one of my coppers and left his body on the side of the road."

Benny spread his hands, tensing the joints so his fingers didn't shake, a trick he'd learned from Bugs Moran back in Chicago. Bugs might be crazy in the head but he never showed a lick of nerves. "Why would I know anything about that?"

"Do you believe in coincidences, Mr. Rotolo?"

Was there a right answer? Benny took his chances. "Sure."

"Wrong," Chief Doyle roared. "It's no coincidence that Officer Scully was shot dead on the side of the road right after you pranced into Lido to start your business in the beverage trade. That's what you called it. The fucking beverage trade."

"I run a decent business," Benny protested, his heart going like a triphammer.

Chief Doyle turned the color of a ripe tomato and pounded his fist on the desk. "One of my boys was killed. My boys! What happened? Tell me now or I'll break you like cheap glass."

Benny's memory of plugging that stupid cop at close range was vivid. If damned Officer Scully hadn't been so curious to see what was in the back of Benny's truck that evening, he'd still be alive. "I don't know anything about it," Benny bluffed.

"You've got the nerve to lie to my face." Chief Doyle was practically spitting as he charged around the side of the desk. "Why you little fucking weasel. Lying to me with a straight face."

"Hey!" Thinking fast, Benny bolted out of the chair and swung around it. There had been no witnesses to the shooting. He could brazen it out. "You're calling me a liar with no proof."

Chief Doyle's bulk was no match for Benny, who was at least thirty years younger and forty pounds lighter. After a few circuits around the chair, the old lard bucket was breathing hard. They glowered at each other across the expanse of leather.

"I don't need proof to call you a liar," Chief Doyle said in between sucking inhales. "You killed Scully. You or one of those Polish thugs working for you."

"Why would I need to kill a cop?" Benny put a hand on his heart, wounded to the core but keeping an eye on the chief in case Doyle made another grab for him. The man probably had a grip like the bite of a horse. "We've got an agreement that's costing me three hundred a week. Unless you didn't pass the word to your boys? Do they make their own arrangements? You might have said something about that. Fair warning and all."

"Watch your tongue, laddie," Chief Doyle growled. "Don't go accusing without knowing all the details."

"You might want to take your own advice," Benny retorted.

Chief Doyle retreated to the chair behind the desk. Benny stayed standing, not sure if he'd won the round or not.

"You're a wily one, Rotolo," Chief Doyle said. He produced a cigar from the box on the desk.

Benny knew the chief was smart enough to deal. "Did the good officer leave a family behind?"

"A lovely wife and two fine boys. I had to hand them the flag from his coffin, so I did."

"I could increase my contribution to the Police Widows and Orphans Fund. Not claiming responsibility, you understand, but to help out in their time of need."

The offer hung in the air, shining with potential.

Chief Doyle took his time lighting the cigar, puffing on the tobacco as the flame from his match circled the end. "Very generous of you, laddie. Three hundred a week doesn't go very far. Orphans get hungry."

"Five hundred," Benny suggested.

"Scully was a fine officer." Chief Doyle dropped the blackened sliver of a match in a glass ashtray. "A very fine officer. Pity to think his legacy isn't worth more."

"Six hundred."

"Doesn't buy those poor fatherless boys a bowl of oatmeal for their breakfast."

Benny gritted his teeth. "Seven hundred."

"A thousand, laddie," Chief Doyle snarled, stabbing the air with the cigar. A ragged thread of smoke unspooled from the end. "Not a penny less if you want to keep doing business in my city."

Benny tottered out of the courthouse clinging to the shreds of his dignity, not to mention the remnants of his wallet. There were plenty of uniform-wearing thugs in Chicago but Doyle outclassed them all.

A thousand dollars a week was serious money. Moreover, it was clear that paying off Doyle wasn't the same thing as paying off the Lido police department.

Benny had to put individual officers on the payroll.

Nor did that thousand a week mean Chief Doyle would protect Benny from federal Prohibition Bureau agents.

But that thousand, along with a pound of jittery sweat had purchased some valuable insight.

Chief Doyle didn't know anything about the information racket.

CHAPTER 8

Enter the Finch

Dear Mr. Lucky Lombardo,

News of your recent narrow escape from death at the hands of the Lido Strangler has caused me to reflect upon the brevity of life and how tragic it must be to live without love in times of great trial. And so I offer myself to ease your suffering. My hand in marriage is yours on condition that you forswear intoxicating beverages and attend the Lutheran Church.

If you voted to re-elect Governor Smith in the recent election, my offer is withdrawn.

I look forward to hearing from you immediately upon receipt of this letter.

Very truly yours, Abigail Brinker, New Rochelle, New York

After so many years of diligent study, Luca's English was good but there was always a new word to learn. He looked at Sonny Zambrano, draped over the bar next to a pile of schoolbooks. "What's forswear mean?"

Sonny grinned. "No liquor."

"*Oddio*," Luca exclaimed with a grin. He stuffed the letter back into the envelope. "Tell her no, thank you."

So far, he had received over fifty letters from women who'd seen his picture in a newspaper. Most offered marriage. Some sent photographs, party invitations, a play handbill, even train tickets. To deal with the flood of correspondence, Sonny had been promoted from after-school dishwasher and floor sweeper to dishwasher, floor sweeper, and writer of polite refusals.

The letters did nothing to ease the gutted feeling Luca had ever since the conversation with Tess in the park.

He'd barely thought of anything since, unable to sleep, his mind filled with crazy scenarios. Marching into the bank and kidnapping Tess. Confronting James Howland. Bursting into the house on West Park Circle and demanding that Evelyn Kennedy Thompson allow him to marry Tess. Stupid, desperate ideas that would only hurt Tess and send him to jail.

Once upon a time, Luca would have asked Vito for advice but blue dog days were eating the boss alive. That's what Vito called it when he drank the day away to forget. At first he drank to forget the pain of losing his soldier son who went to France with General Pershing and never came back. Now he drank to forget Jimmy Zambrano.

Vito was in his office right now, ostensibly doing the accounts but in all probability napping away the rotgut that substituted for lunch.

Luca put away the leftover fixings for the sandwich of the day. A joint of prosciutto di Parma had enough dry-cured meat and fat on it for another lunchtime menu, as did the remains of a stick of pepperoni as thick as his fist. A few precious fresh tomatoes, from the stash of green tomatoes wrapped in newspaper and ripening slowly in the club's cool cellar, went into the tiny kitchen behind the bar. If they were mushy tomorrow he'd chop them into a relish with onions and hot peppers.

The whistle calling the end of the day at Lido Premium wouldn't blow for another two hours, giving him plenty of time to prepare for the evening rush. A handful of members, mostly old-timers like Tony Bilotti, played chess or pinochle at their usual tables on the other side of the saloon. A few more members were reading the *Lido Daily Clipper* or Italian language newspapers in the small library. Papers from Naples and Palermo arrived as much as three weeks late, although the ink still came off on the reader's hand. The

Corriere d'America and *Bolletino Della Sera* were published in New York City so were delivered only a day or so past the date on the masthead.

Guido barreled into the bar, bringing a draft of freezing air. The doorman's round face was puckered with worry. "Luca! The policeman is here to see Vito. With Uncle Samma."

Uncle Samma. The all-purpose Italian expression referring to the American government. Luca glanced out the front window.

Two men waited on the sidewalk outside. The taller of the two was Officer O'Malley, big and bulky in his winter wool uniform. A stranger waited with him, an unsmiling man in a double-breasted overcoat and a pale gray fedora.

"*Oddio*," Luca swore under his breath. It looked like O'Malley was helping Uncle Samma get his fair share. O'Malley took money from Vito to ignore club members staggering out with beer on their breath. What were the odds that his new friend was a Prohibition Bureau agent?

"Wait five minutes," Luca said to Guido. "Then bring them into the office."

As Guido disappeared back into the vestibule and Sonny collected glasses from the chess players, Luca rushed down the hall, praying that Vito was sober.

"Boss," he called and pushed the office door open without waiting for a reply. "We got company. Might be a Prohibition Bureau agent. O'Malley's with him."

Vito was sitting at the desk. He blinked watery eyes, the walrus mustache trembling in sudden agitation. His ample paunch pressed against the edge of the desk top. The middle button of his vest was undone and the dark wool gaped, showing a lozenge of striped shirt above a gold watch chain. In front of him, open ledgers shared space with a stack of invoices, an unlabeled bottle and a tumbler with a yellow stain in the bottom that smelled like turpentine.

Vito's eyes followed Luca's glance to the glass. "First one today," he said weakly.

"Sure," Luca said. "You got visitors."

Next to the leather Chesterfield sofa the safe was open, revealing two more unlabeled bottles of poison tilted on top of a jumble of papers and envelopes. Luca added everything from the desk and clanged the door shut as Vito laboriously thumbed a candy out of a roll of Pep-O-Mint Life Savers.

A moment later Guido appeared in the doorway. "Boss, I brung people to see you."

The doorman moved away to let Officer O'Malley and the stranger into the office. The policeman seemed to fill the room as he introduced his companion as

Inspector Ernest Finch of the U.S. Postal Inspection Service.

"Pleased to meet you." Inspector Finch wasn't as tall as O'Malley, and certainly didn't wear a uniform, but he exuded a quietly intense attitude of authority. He had a robust American corn-fed look about him, reinforced by broad shoulders, sandy hair and a cleft chin. "I believe I've seen your likeness in the newspapers, Mr. Lombardo. They call you Lucky, don't they?"

"It wasn't my idea," Luca said, wondering why the Post Office was paying the club a call.

"He's lucky because of me," O'Malley said, seemingly in no rush to explain Inspector Finch's presence. "I saved his skin by cracking that dago's head like a walnut." The policeman was red-faced from the November cold, although his uniform looked as heavy as pig iron. He took a seat on the Chesterfield, making himself at home. "Procopio gave up his filthy murdering secret as he went to meet his maker and Lombardo here got his picture in the newspaper every day since."

Leaning against the wall by the office door, Luca didn't respond.

"I'm sure Mr. Lombardo appreciates your prompt action, Officer." Finch unbuttoned his coat, removed his hat, and sat on the other end of the Chesterfield. "Is there any proof yet that your so-called Lido Strangler was also responsible for the young woman whose body was found in the river along with the other gentleman?"

"No one knows who she is," O'Malley said.

"I see." Finch nodded. "Of course, that's quite out of the Postal Service's purview at the moment."

Vito sat up, as if three Pep-O-Mint candies had brought him to life. "What can the Galliano Club do for the Post Office? Maybe you're selling stamps?"

Finch opened his coat to reveal an impressive silver badge pinned to the breast pocket of his suit jacket. "The Postal Service investigates crimes having to do with the fraudulent use of the mail. It's a federal offense to tamper with the mail or to use the mail to conduct extortion, blackmail or for any other criminal purpose. I'm assigned to the Midwest region."

"You're a policeman?" Luca asked.

"I enforce the law." Finch let his coat cover the badge again. "The Post Office Inspection Service is authorized by the president of the United States to investigate any crime involving the use of the mail. Any crime, any time, any place. If a criminal so much as glues a stamp on an envelope, I can arrest them." He paused. "Do you understand?"

Vito blinked at Luca, as if to ask if the Post Office

could conceivably have an interest in how Jimmy ended up in the river.

"Yes," Luca said, although he really didn't.

"I've come all the way from Indiana to investigate criminal use of the mail here in Lido," Finch went on. "We have reason to believe that you, Mr. Spinelli, are the target of blackmail letters that originate in Gary, Indiana."

"Blackmail letters?" Luca asked.

"To Mr. Spinelli," Finch affirmed.

"Why would somebody want to blackmail Vito?" But even as Luca uttered the words, answers clawed through his thoughts.

Because Vito was flouting the Prohibition Bureau and buying illegal booze.

Because before he was murdered, Jimmy gave Vito the accounting ledger that showed how the profits of Benny Rotolo's bootlegging operation were divvied up and who was cheating.

Because Vito and Luca put Jimmy Zambrano's body in the Mohawk River after Nick killed him and left the body behind the club.

But how would someone in Gary, Indiana know any of that? Luca didn't even know where Indiana was.

Vito took out a handkerchief and mopped his forehead. "I don't know nothing about no letters."

"The sender is a man named Vincent Salerno. He's a known extortionist against the Italian community. He's what you may call a freelance extortionist, helping clients blackmail people who have achieved some measure of financial success. We believe that he's affiliated with the Society of the Black Hand." Finch held out a small square of cardboard, decorated with the crude drawing of a skull with a dripping knife slicing through it, next to crossed slashes similarly oozing blood. "This is his signature."

"*Oddio*," Luca swore under his breath as he took the image from Finch.

Every Italian immigrant knew about *La Mano Nera*, or The Black Hand, the loose confederation of Italian criminals that preyed on Italian immigrants across America. Kidnappings, bombings, murder, horrible disfigurement. With its roots in southern Italy and a network of spies and informers spreading from New York City to every spot where immigrants worked to make a new life, *La Mano Nera* was responsible for some of the most egregious crimes of the last thirty years.

Lack of Italian-speaking law enforcement, immigrants' ingrained suspicion of police, and the group's ruthless terror tactics let it operate with near impunity.

Twenty years ago, New York City Police Lieutenant John Petrosino fought the group with the infamous Italian Squad, but *La Mano Nera* murdered him in Sicily. Petrosino was there to convince authorities to curtail the flow of criminals into the United States.

In recent years, massive investigations and arrests from New York City to Ohio had diminished the organization. A new law allowed any known criminal to be deported within three years of arriving in America, effectively shutting down its primary source of new recruits: criminals seeking to escape punishment in Italy. Petrosino had championed such a law before his death.

La Mano Nera might be in decline, but its legacy of terror was not yet a thing of the past.

"You think they are targeting Vito?" Luca handed back the threatening square of cardboard.

"Yes." Finch slid to the edge of the Chesterfield, trying to catch Vito's eye. "We believe that Salerno sends letters threatening his victim and the victim's family unless they pay for protection. Threats include destruction of property, kidnapping, that sort of thing. His victims are Italian businessmen who have done well and are known in their community. We need proof and we need testimony."

"No letters." Vito thumbed out another candy from

the roll. "I can't help you."

O'Malley finished examining a bit of something he'd found between his molars and commenced to stare at the ceiling.

"What about the name Vincent Salerno?" Finch pressed, looking from Vito to Luca and back again. "Or Gary, Indiana? Familiar?"

Luca shook his head. "How would someone in Indiana know Vito?"

"Salerno's network is very wide. Extortion based on fear of violence is very profitable." Finch tapped the bleeding heart against his thumbnail. "Think of Salerno as the hub of the network. His accomplices are the spokes. They are the ones that find the victims, provide information for Salerno's letters, carry out any necessary encouragement, and collect the money from the victims. They remit a portion back to Salerno. It's a system. Highly organized. Salerno is miles away but his accomplice could be your next-door neighbor."

Luca was feeling worse by the minute. "I see."

"Please think back to the letters you've received in recent days, Mr. Spinelli." Finch was nothing if not persistent.

Vito shook his head.

"I usually see the mail first," Luca said. "The postman gives it to Guido, the doorman, and he gives it to me. I would have noticed a letter from Gary, Indiana."

Until the torrent of lady letters, the mail consisted mostly of bills, advertisements and the occasional letter for Vito from the Lido Chamber of Commerce, the Sons of Italy in New York City, or the San Gennaro Society seeking donations for orphans in Italy.

"See?" Vito stood up. "You came all this way for nothing."

"I appreciate your time, Mr. Spinelli, and yours, Mr. Lombardo." Finch got to his feet, as did O'Malley. "If you receive a letter with a red first-class stamp and a Gary, Indiana postmark, please notify me right away. I'll be working out of the courthouse here in Lido. Oh, and don't discard the envelope. It's vital to our case."

"Sure, sure," Vito said.

Luca led the two visitors through the saloon to the front door. Guido opened it for them, his mouth slack with curiosity.

Finch hesitated on the sidewalk outside the club and turned to Luca. "Mr. Spinelli doesn't appear to understand the seriousness of his situation, but I hope you will. He's a successful businessman. A prime target for Salerno and his nefarious associates."

"Vito Spinelli's an honest man," Luca said. "If he says he didn't get a letter, he didn't get a letter."

The postal inspector handed Luca a small white card. "I need Mr. Spinelli's help. Find me in the courthouse. Room 203."

"Sure," Luca said. The business card had an impressive Postal Service seal and the name ERNEST FINCH engraved in black below it. "I'll tell him."

For Luca's benefit, O'Malley mimed cracking a dago's head like a walnut before he and Finch walked away.

"Is Uncle Samma making trouble?" Guido asked.

Luca didn't reply right away. A pewter sky promised another snowfall just when the last had melted and the streets were clear. Finch and O'Malley crossed Hamilton Street.

"You always give me all the letters, right?" he asked Guido.

"Ah, Luca, you know all the letters are for you." The doorman's face collapsed into a frown of uncertainty. "I do what you tell me, right?"

Luca clapped Guido on the shoulder and went inside. He passed through the saloon, fielding questions about O'Malley and the stranger, and went back down the hall to Vito's office. "Boss?"

The safe was open again. Vito had a bottle in one hand and the tumbler in the other. He drank as if he'd just crossed the Sahara.

"Boss," Luca said louder.

Vito put down the empty glass. "Later," he said and shut the door in Luca's face.

CHAPTER 9

No partner needed

Ruth ran into Luca as she returned from shopping with three precious lemons in her basket to make lemonade for the first ballroom dance class. Of course, Luca offered to hold her shopping as she fumbled to unlock her door. He was always so courteous, so handsome, so observant.

"I'm sorry," Luca said as Ruth's key skittered into the lock. "I never said thank you for coming outside. With O'Malley. When Procopio was here."

At that moment, Ruth wished she'd never met Luca Lombardo, never saw his face, never thought of him at all.

Both she and O'Malley had been in a state of undress that night. In fact, O'Malley had just rolled off her when they heard the sound of Luca and Nick Procopio scuffling under her second-story window. Of course Luca knew what they'd been doing upstairs in her apartment.

Ruth remained immobile in front of her door with 601 ½ lettered on it, conscious of Luca waiting for a response. All she had to do was turn the key, snatch the bag and run upstairs. But she owed Luca an explanation because, like O'Malley, he'd kept her name out of the newspaper. No one else knew she'd been the third witness to Nick Procopio's dying words.

Luca cleared his throat. "If you and O'Malley step out together, it's none of my business. I haven't told anyone."

"O'Malley comes around now and then," Ruth said miserably. There was no use trying to deny it. "It doesn't mean anything."

"It should," Luca said. "When a woman gives herself to a man, it should mean everything."

It would have hurt far less if he'd called her a whore.

She finally got the door open. He handed her the basket, expression giving nothing away.

Ruth ran up the stairs and into the dance studio before the first sob escaped. Crumpled on the piano bench, trembling shoulders reflected in the big mirrored wall, Ruth wept away all her foolish daydreams, all those ridiculous times when she'd fantasized that Luca Lombardo would be her everything. Partner. Lover. Savior.

The street door opened. The pianist, Mrs. Shaw, clumped up the stairs. Ruth pulled herself together and made lemonade. Her first ballroom dance class would start with the foxtrot and end with the waltz. In between the students would enjoy a break for refreshments.

The floor was polished. A table in the corner was draped with a cloth and topped with a punch bowl and cups. Little paper tags waited to be completed with the name of each student.

The pianist, Mrs. Shaw, played scales to warm up. The piano trilled as her fingers traveled up and down the keyboard. Ruth went into the bathroom to check her hair, splash tap water on swollen eyes, and adjust the garters holding up her silk stockings.

Seven couples and one single man trooped up the stairs right on time. Ruth was happily surprised at the crowd. One class and half her rent for the entire month was paid.

There was much talk and laughter as students stepped up to the table where Ruth made name tags out of squares of blush-colored paper. She wrote the names in big letters so she could read the tags while demonstrating from the front of the class.

"Blick." The last in line to get a name tag was the man who had come alone. His face was angular, his hair was short and silver, and he wore a black eye patch. "Henry Blick."

Dropping her gaze from the eye patch, Ruth wrote HENRY on a fresh square.

"My sister Osa insisted that I attend," he said stiffly. "I doubt I will be a suitable student,"

"Everyone has reservations when they learn something new." Ruth smiled warmly. "I hope you don't mind having me as your partner."

Ruth had been quite startled when Osa and Jack Rutherford came up the stairs and into the dance studio. Osa Rutherford was head of the Women's Institute, chair of numerous charitable events, and one of the most fashionable women in Lido. Her name was constantly in the newspaper. Heir to Lido Lumber, her husband Jack was the president of the Lido Chamber of Commerce.

They were the pinnacle of high society in Lido. Their presence in class was better than an endorsement from President Coolidge himself.

"My apologies in advance if I tax your patience," Henry said. His formal manner was refreshingly old-fashioned and charming. "I'm not a dancer."

"No one is at the beginning." Ruth handed him the nametag and a straight pin.

Henry didn't return the smile.

"You might want to remove your coat before we get started," Ruth suggested.

After a few minutes for the group to get settled, she arranged the couples in a circle around the dance floor.

"We'll start our lesson tonight with the foxtrot. I'm sure you all will catch on very quickly. It consists of two slow steps followed by two quick steps, giving you a combination of rise and fall motions."

A murmur ran around the studio. Henry stood soldier-straight, radiating discomfort.

"Now, we'll start with the gentlemen." Ruth moved around Henry so that her back was to the larger group. "Gentlemen, I'm going to pretend to be you. We'll start with the left leg. Walk two steps forward, then step to the left and bring your feet together. Watch me first. Then we'll all do it together."

There was laughter and shuffling as Ruth demonstrated the moves a few times, then moved around the circle helping anyone who kept putting a foot wrong. When all the men could do the step, their partners applauded.

Ruth went back to the front. "Ladies, now it's your turn. Start with your right foot. Walk two steps backward, then step to the right and bring your feet together. We want to create a slow, slow, quick, quick rhythm."

The ladies caught on quickly. Ruth whirled back to the front of the dance floor. "Now we'll put it all together with the music."

Ruth raised her arms to Henry. He clasped one hand

around her waist and took her hand in the other, maintaining a significant gap between their bodies.

"Gentlemen face your left," Ruth said. Henry turned without being told again. "Ladies, face your right. Take two steps forward, then turn to face your partner. Feet go to the side, then together, still maintaining a slow, slow, quick, quick rhythm."

Mrs. Shaw counted the beat and began playing a basic rhythm. The couples circled the room, some getting the hang of it quickly, others took more time. Despite his initial protestation, Henry was an apt, if silent, student and made no mistakes.

Everyone was breathless by the time Ruth announced the break and offered lemonade and cookies from Bella Napoli. The men clustered on one side of the studio. The women gravitated into a gossipy knot.

Osa Rutherford broke away and approached Ruth. She was tall and slender like her brother, with blue eyes that sparkled with good humor. "I'm sure Henry told you that I made him come."

"He picked up the steps very quickly," Ruth said honestly.

"He really needs to be more social." Osa sipped from her punch cup. "He's the operations manager at Lido Premium and works far too much."

"The events of the past few weeks must weigh on

him very heavily." Ruth said. She decided that she liked Osa very much.

"It's a terribly demanding position, which is precisely why we made him come." Osa dipped her head, making Ruth feel like she was being taken into the other woman's confidence, like they were already friends. "Such a fuss he made. But he didn't run out so we're making progress."

Henry did much better with the waltz. Ruth felt light as a feather as they twirled around the studio to the strains of "The Blue Danube." Their profiles flashed by in the mirror, seemingly brighter and more alive than the other couples laboring around the circle. Ruth saw herself, her face flushed and smiling, elbows bent in the perfect position. Her partner maintained a perfect posture, yet his pose was full of physical grace. He held her firmly, safely. The blue eye never left her face, yet his steps never faltered.

Mrs. Shaw banged out the last notes and everyone eased to a stop.

"Well." Ruth felt disoriented as Henry released her. A smatter of applause ran around the circle. "Everyone has done so well tonight. I hope you all come back next week. We'll work on our foxtrot some more and learn some jazz steps."

She got another round of applause. It was clear the

class was a big success.

"You weren't entirely honest with me, Henry." Ruth found her partner again as he retrieved his suit jacket. "You waltz very well."

The corner of his mouth lifted. "I attended West Point, Miss Cross," he said. "Army officers are expected to know how to waltz."

"You were in the Army?" Ruth asked.

"Yes," Henry said. "Twenty-five years."

"You must have been to so many interesting places," Ruth said.

"They were all interesting," Henry said. He made a tiny, restrained gesture to indicate the eye patch. "But they weren't all enjoyable."

Osa swept down upon them, her husband Jack in tow. "Miss Cross, this was wonderful."

"I hope you'll come back next week," Ruth said.

"Oh we will." Osa put her hand on Ruth's arm. "I enjoyed it immensely."

"Yes," Henry said. The blue eye drilled into Ruth. "I believe I shall."

Everyone left. Ruth was alone.

She waltzed herself around the big empty space, imagining Henry Blick's touch.

CHAPTER 10

12 cases of Irish whiskey

The cellar of the Galliano Club had a low ceiling, a dirt floor, and a secret door that led to a corner of the gravel lot behind the club building. It stayed cool all year, even in the summer.

In the winter, like now, the furnace hummed and clanked. The boiler fed the club's radiators as well as those in Ruth's apartment and the dance school upstairs.

A single electric bulb dangled from the cross beams above, throwing shadows across crocks of oil-cured olives salted with crushed red pepper, jars of pickled eggs and onions, and Mason jars of roasted red peppers shelved in neat rows by the stairs. Long tubes of salami, shanks of prosciutto and bulbs of provolone as big as Luca's head hung from hooks under the wooden stair treads, waiting their turn to become a sandwich of the day. Sacks of onions and carrots made neat piles next to the baskets of green tomatoes wrapped in newspaper.

Barrels and kegs of beer were methodically arranged so Luca could switch empty for full and not keep a bootlegger waiting.

Toby Gleason tapped on the door right on time. Luca wedged it open to see the scrappy Irishman in a newsboy cap and navy pea coat. His truck, customized to appear to be loaded with lumber, waited on the gravel.

"Took you long enough," Luca said, although the Irishman was right on time.

"Jesus wept." Toby looked around, a case of Old Bushmills in his arms. "It's a secret cave so it is. Where do you want the whiskey?"

"Over here." Luca directed him to a nook under the stairs.

The two men wrestled in a dozen cases. Once they were stacked, Luca fitted a wooden panel into place, hiding them from view. The panel instantly became nothing more than a natural extension of the stairway support structure. As a further precaution, he disguised the panel by dumping sacks of onions in front of it. "Did you bring the brandy?"

Toby produced a bottle. "Courvoisier cognac, just for you."

Luca handed over sixty dollars from his Rum Row money, more than twice what he made each week working for Vito, and took the plump bottle. The label was in French and the original seal was intact.

"You going to drink it yourself?" Toby asked skeptically.

"I need to bribe somebody," Luca said.

"I'm silent as the grave, so I am." Toby raised his eyebrows. "Does this have to do with Tessa?"

"I'll tell you if it works."

"Ah, Jesus wept." Toby shook his head in mock sorrow.

Luca never thought he'd have an Irish friend and certainly not one who was an irrepressible rumrunner. And he wouldn't, if not for a harrowing adventure together off the coast of Long Island. They'd been two soldiers fighting to survive in a watery trench. Each had saved the other.

They went outside where Toby stood in the shelter of his truck and lit a cigarette. "A pleasure doing business, as always," he said.

Luca looked around the dark yard, remembering his struggle with Nick right under Ruth's window not so long ago. He jammed his hands in the pockets of his mackinaw. "Have you ever heard of a crook named Vincent Salerno?"

"Vincent Salerno." Toby repeated the name a few times. "No. Should I?"

"Maybe." Luca hesitated. "He's in Gary, Indiana."

"Gary, Indiana? Never heard of it." Toby took a

long drag on the cigarette. The tip glowed red in the darkness. "What's he to you?"

"A crook who writes blackmail letters to Italians who have a little money. A policeman from the post office came to see Vito. Says this Vincent Salerno wants to blackmail him."

"And your boss doesn't have any idea who he is?"

"No. A local accomplice picks out who should get the letters, then collects the money when people pay up."

"So somebody local is angling to squeeze your boss?"

Put that way, Luca could think of a few who'd want Vito's money. Benny Rotolo topped the list. "Yes."

"If the police know what this Salerno is doing, why don't they arrest him?"

"They need a letter as proof."

"And some bugger who will testify. Ah, American justice." Toby flicked ash onto the gravel. "If I hear anything I'll let you know."

"Thanks." Luca didn't have much hope but Toby had a surprisingly long list of connections on both sides of the law.

Toby leaned against the door of his truck. "You hear about Rotolo? Rumor has it that he's paying a thousand a week to keep the police off his back."

"A week?" It was a staggering amount of money.

"You'd think with all the extra money they'd find out who the girl is. The one from the river."

"*Oddio*," Luca swore softly. His statement to that persistent *Lido Daily Clipper* reporter had been a mistake. Just when the story about Nick Procopio and Jimmy Zambrano was over, his picture was back in the newspaper, paired with the front-page story of the unidentified woman. "You think they ever will?"

Toby shrugged. "All I know is that Rotolo's beer racket must be doing real good."

"I told Vito and Guido that we should make our own." Luca pointed to the other side of the alley, where the line of maple trees pointed bare branches at the night sky. "There's a shed behind the bocce and handball courts."

"Dangerous business, going up against Rotolo like that." Toby squinted into the darkness.

"Somebody's gotta do it."

"You know how to make beer? I thought dagos only knew how to make wine."

"What do you micks know how to make?"

Toby climbed into the truck. "Trouble," he laughed. "Like you and women."

Luca watched until the lumber panel disappeared, then struck out for the line of maples with the bottle of cognac hidden inside his shirt. Cutting across the sports area to Third Street was easier than walking around the club building. He'd end up in the middle of the residential neighborhood north of Hamilton Street. From there it was only a few blocks to Mrs. Esposito's boarding house.

The night was battleship gray and old leaves crunched underfoot. The two handball courts needed to be swept out. A task for Sonny some afternoon before it snowed again.

He took care not to trip on the raised wooden borders of the long and narrow bocce courts. In the spring, he'd pour new sand on each court and have Guido rake it smooth. Tony Bilotti and the other old-timers would spend afternoons out there, happily quarreling over each toss and taking hours to calculate scores.

Luca checked the padlock on the shed as he passed. Vito had used the Italian word *stalla*, meaning stable, when he showed Luca around all those years ago. The little wooden building was well constructed. They used it as a clubhouse of sorts, a place to store baseball equipment and a shady spot from which to view hotly contested handball matches and bocce tournaments.

It was also big enough to brew beer, he'd pointed out to Vito not long ago, Guido hovering in the office doorway. No decision was taken.

He gained Third Street where a few lights still shone in the windows, and imagined Tess, his *Tessa* waiting for him. Spectacles perched on her nose, sweater wrapped around her shoulders, a book in her hand. When she sees him, her face lights up, green eyes sparkling just for him.

You were the one person who made me feel like the woman I want to be.

Luca kept walking.

CHAPTER 11

A new distribution situation

It was always slightly terrifying to drive through the old Settlers Rest cemetery at night. Owen Forbes Fisher hunched forward over the wheel of his Ford, the better to see the road's outline through an inch of sparkling white snow.

He made it past the gothic mausoleums guarding the outer edge, to the natural berm shielding the graves from the Mohawk River on the other side. The Ford puttered up the steep rise, hesitated on the top, then plunged down the slope on the other side, sliding in the fresh snow like a toboggan. Gravity pressed Owen's chest against the steering wheel, as if the cemetery wasn't enough to remind him of his own mortality.

The Ford fishtailed, then straightened out as the ground grew level. Owen brought it to a controlled stop by the old pumphouse. Benny's Cadillac was there, along with three delivery trucks and the second Cadillac that belonged to Broz Siwak.

Owen cut the engine but didn't get out. One of the unsavory Polish boys that Siwak ordered about came out of the pumphouse carrying a Tommy gun. Owen raised a hand, the boy nodded, and went back inside.

There were plenty of accounting issues to discuss with Benny, notably a new distribution situation for the remaining two Lido Outfit founding partners, but Owen's hand refused to reach for the door handle. He hadn't seen Benny since Nick Procopio was killed.

Hopefully Benny didn't know that Nick went to the Galliano Club that fateful night to look for Owen's lost pocket ledger.

Early on, Owen learned that Benny Rotolo, the so-called president of the Lido Outfit, could barely do basic math, let alone calculate percentages, fractions, or compound interest. This left Owen free to help himself to a certain off-the-top amount to keep his wife Cynthia happy with Gorham sterling silver flatware and ropes of pearls from Van Dyke's, the nicest store in Lido.

When Owen lost the ledger, he paid Nick to find it.

A poor investment. The ledger was still missing.

He could no longer delay the inevitable. Owen climbed out of the Ford. The little revolver he'd taken to carrying was a reassuring weight in his pocket.

The yeasty smell of fermenting beer swamped him as he went into the pumphouse. The warm air was a nice change from the frosty evening. Cases of malt syrup were stacked around the place, while a line of barrels waited to be filled.

Benny was there with Broz Siwak and a round-headed, thickset Italian man. The three were clustered around a makeshift table, sharing some noxious goo out of a pie plate and drinking from unlabeled bottles.

"Hey, Fishy," Benny called, using the nickname Owen hated. "Come here. We got eggplant parmigiana."

"Hello." Owen joined the three men, wary of Benny's jocular mood. The pie plate held something gray and greasy that Owen had no intention of sampling.

"This is Al Genovese," Benny said, elbowing the stranger. "Al, meet Fishy Fisher, my money man."

Genovese whipped off his cap. "Al. Al Genovese."

Owen didn't offer to shake hands with the moon-faced stranger in a common plaid wool mackinaw. The stink of manure clung to him, combining with the cloying smells of eggplant and yeast to create an aura of nerve gas.

"Another driver?" Owen asked Benny.

"Al's gonna help me expand the Lido Outfit."

"Is he now?" Owen couldn't conceal his surprise.

Broz moved away.

Benny winked at Al. "Didn't I tell you that Fishy was a swell money man? No cutting corners for him."

"Can I speak with you in private?" Owen asked.

He led the way to the niche that served as an office, wondering what was going on. Benny was hardly mourning his cousin Nick, instead hauling in some stinky farmer for who knows what harebrained scheme.

"Before we get into the notion of expansion," Owen said when he and Benny were alone in the office space. If he didn't jump in first Benny would control the conversation. "We need to discuss the redistribution of profits, now that Nick is, ah, deceased."

"Yeah?" Benny said.

"It's been a four-way split. One share to each partner and the other share to pay Broz and the boys. Now that there are only two partners, you and I should divide the three original partner shares." Owen hesitated. "Do you agree?"

"You and me should split Nick's share." In his silk suit and mohair overcoat, Benny actually began to pick his nose.

"Exactly." Owen tried not to shiver.

It was freezing in there, cooler than the rest of the snug stone pumphouse because of the giant iron gears that protruded from one wall, legacy of the paddle wheel that had once generated electricity from the river. Icicles dripped from the iron. The stone walls were white with frost.

"What about Al?" Benny asked.

"That farmer? What about him? Why is he here?"

"Al's getting us into the information racket."

"The information racket? What are you talking about?"

"Al's got the inside dope on the fella who runs the Galliano Club. Gonna help me squeeze until he's bankrupt and hands over the place."

"Inside dope," Owen echoed. "You mean blackmail? You and this farmer are going to blackmail the owner of the Galliano Club?"

"Information racket. Blackmail." Benny shrugged. "Whatever gets me that club."

Owen felt his temper rise. "I gave you ten thousand dollars to buy the Galliano Club. I took out a loan on my house!"

Benny snapped his fingers, flicking away a dot of green snot in the process. Owen watched, revolted, as it hit the wall and stuck to the icy rime.

"Old man Spinelli didn't take the deal," Benny said. "I tossed twenty thousand on the bar and he didn't take it."

"Then I'll have my money back."

"Sure." Benny swept an arm around Owen's neck and marched him out of the office niche.

Owen gurgled a protest but was helpless to do

anything except stumble along.

"We'll be right back, fellas,' Benny called over his shoulder as he steered Owen past the brewing tanks and out the door.

The pressure of the arm around Owen's neck didn't ease until they were at Benny's Cadillac.

After being manhandled like that, the last thing Owen expected was for Benny to get a paper sack out of the car and count out ten thousand dollars.

"Thank you," Owen managed.

"I'll take Nick's share from now on," Benny said, closing the Cadillac's door. "Pay me back for what I invested in getting the information racket up and running. You pay Broz the same as before. One quarter for him and his sluggers."

Owen opened his mouth to protest. Benny didn't give him a chance but snaked a hand inside Owen's coat pocket and found the revolver. He pressed the muzzle against Owen's temple. "Wouldn't it be sad to be snuffed with your own little popgun?"

Owen froze with ten thousand dollars in his hands, unable to say a word.

Benny laughed. "Who do you expect to shoot?"

"Nobody," Owen could barely get the word out. "I just want to be like you."

Laughing, Benny shoved the revolver back in

Owen's pocket. "Gonna carry a piece, Fishy, gotta be ready to use it, right? Nick would still be here if he'd shot that lousy flatfoot."

"I know." Owen's knees were so weak he was afraid of collapsing into a heap.

"Al knows what really happened to the Zambrano stiff." Benny grinned. "That's why the Galliano Club is gonna fall right into my lap."

Owen summoned up the nerve to protest. "I don't want any part of this information racket. I signed up for the beer. That's all."

"You're the Lido Outfit money man. Beer racket, information racket. It's all the same."

"Blackmail is a worse offense than bootlegging."

"Look at yourself, Owen." Benny patted Owen's cheek hard enough to hurt. "You got ten thousand dollars, a share in the best outfit in New York, and a gun in your pocket. More cash coming in every week. Keeping the missus happy, ain't you? Pretty good, eh? Am I right? Am I right?"

Owen swallowed hard. There was a gleam in Benny's eye that bordered on madness. "You're right, Benny."

"Remember that, Fishy. It's all or nothing."

CHAPTER 12

Celebration at the Warsaw Club

Every Polish worker from every mill and factory in Lido jammed into the Warsaw Club, all vying for Karol's attention. Shouts of congratulations merged into a rowdy background hum. The air was dense with cigarette smoke from the cheapest brands of tobacco, evidence of the pinched pockets of Lido's Polish community.

Karol shook at least two hundred hands before Anton pushed a beer at him, saying that it was on the house for the new foreman of Lido Premium.

He wasn't about to climb on the tall pedestal his countrymen had erected, but the warmth was genuine, as was appreciation of Lido Premium as a fair place to work. When the rush of backslapping and toasts abated, Karol made his way to the back room to sip a beer and collect his thoughts. It had been an extraordinary day.

"Look who's here. The new foreman."

Karol had expected to see Broz there. He'd recognized the Ford outside, with its fist-sized dent in the driver's door. But this version of Broz didn't suit the old car. Sitting in a corner, his former right-hand man sported a brand-new suit, a brand-new tie, and a brand-new fedora tipped back from his forehead. Broz wore a gold signet ring, too. He was a prize peacock in a coop full of chickens destined for the stew pot.

At the same time, it was fitting that Broz was the first person to offer congratulations. Karol and Broz went way back together.

"Thanks, Broz," Karol said. "News travels fast."

"Come to play the big man, stick a needle in my eye?"

"What happened to you, Broz?" The words came out before Karol even thought to say them.

Broz took out a pack of Lucky Strikes. "Money."

"Enough to stay two jumps ahead of the Prohibition Bureau?" Karol watched as Broz lit a cigarette. The other man had always rolled his own before.

Broz squinted through a haze of smoke. "What's it to you?"

Karol decided to be honest. "We were friends. You should have been there today when Blick made the announcement. I got the foreman job because we turned the dipping crew into the best crew in the mill. You and me. We did it together."

"You got the job because you saved that Ferlo kid," Broz scoffed. "Everybody knows he would have bled to death up there on the catwalk if you hadn't wrapped your belt around his arm and saved him. You wound up a hero and cheated Conti out of the foreman job."

"Yeah, well." Karol took a step back. "Nice seeing you, Broz."

"Wait." Broz stood up. "Yeah, congratulations. You deserve the job."

Karol hesitated. Broz's face was ten years older than it had been a month ago. His eyes had seen bad things.

"There's an opening on the dipping crew," Karol heard himself say.

"Crew chief?"

"Think about it."

Broz's flinty expression momentarily softened into something like regret. "Saint Karol of Lido. Always trying to save us sinners."

"Everybody is worth saving."

"It's too late for that." Broz's flash of emotion was gone. "Nobody gets off the road I'm on."

"There's always a way off a bad road," Karol said quietly. "Come back to the mill. Crew chief is a good job. Nobody will ask questions."

"Everything comes so easy for you, Karol. The rest of us have to do things the hard way." Broz pushed through the crowd and was gone.

The encounter took the wind out of the celebration.

Karol left the Warsaw Club while his fellow countrymen were still celebrating his achievement. Hunched into his coat, a cap pulled over his ears, he walked to Holy Angels.

The church was open, as it always was. Thick pillar candles threw flickering light across the altar. The little chapels on either side were dimly lit by racks of votive candles in glass cups. The faithful could light a candle to Mary on one side and Joseph on the other while archangels Michael and Gabriel looked on.

A few people knelt in the pews by the confessional booth, waiting for their turn to seek forgiveness for their sins. Others knelt at the communion rail, immersed in their penance. Ten Hail Marys, five Our Fathers. It all depended on the gravity of the sins confessed.

Karol took a pew and wondered why things had worked out the way they had. Was he ready to take on not only the foreman job but Blick's business apprentice program, too? Would it really work out the way Blick said it would?

He wanted to do more, be more. Make sure that the Polish community got a fair chance at making a good life in America. That's why he'd applied to be a policeman. American law was so clear, so different from the mayhem in Poland. There, a man hardly knew from one year to the next who owned which parts of it until the soldiers came.

"A pillar for America," Karol had said in his police interview, not realizing that the Irish cops on the force were never going to admit a Polish officer to their closed circle.

Now, he was foreman of the biggest mill in New York, making more money than he ever thought possible and learning the entire business, thanks to Henry Blick.

A woman bundled in a kerchief and a lumpy wool coat made her way up the side aisle to the chapel of Mary. She dropped a coin in the poor box and lit a candle. As the woman adjusted the candle in its votive cup, the flame sent a flickering line of shadow across the hem of Mary's gown.

The woman stood in front of the statue and the rack of votive candles, head bowed and lips moving in silent prayer. Karol wondered what she was praying for. Perhaps someone was ill or had lost a job.

When the woman finally left, Karol heaved himself out of the pew and went to the chapel. Half of the votives were lit, evidence of petitions to Mary. Sickness, heartbreak, loss. *Holy Mary, Mother of God, help me in my hour of need.*

Karol's coins clinked against the others in the bottom of the poor box. He touched the wick of a fresh candle to one already lit and was rewarded with the flare of a new flame. *Holy Mary, Mother of God, help me in my hour of need.*

He stood in front of Mary, mesmerized by the play of the candle flames on Her hem. When Karol finally shook off his reverie, he knelt with those coming out of the confessional to murmur their penance at the communion rail. As his knees protested that they'd already put in long hours at the mill, it seemed selfish to ask for help when he already had so much.

Karol prayed instead for Broz to find his way again.

And then he prayed for the repose of the soul of the woman pulled out of the river.

For her to escape the fate of an anonymous pauper's grave.

For her to have a name.

For strength for her family, wherever they were.

CHAPTER 13

Not for the likes of you

"Well, if it isn't himself," the housekeeper regarded Luca with faint amusement from the open doorway. Her name was Annie Harper, he recalled. Faded red hair in a bun, black dress, black stockings, a white apron with starched pockets.

"Hello, Annie," Luca said. "How are you?"

She made no move to invite him in, despite the whistling chill in the air. "Here to call on Miss Tess, are you? Well, she's not for the likes of you anymore."

Luca ignored the slur and held up the bag containing the bottle of cognac. "I have a gift for Mrs. Thompson."

Annie cocked her head, taking in Luca's green fedora, camel overcoat, and polished shoes with undisguised curiosity. "The newspapers said that fellow from the mill cut you up something fearful. You look fine to me."

"Fully recovered," Luca said. "I'd like to see Mrs. Thompson, please."

A wintry breeze scudded across the porch and whipped his overcoat around his calves. Dry leaves rubbed against the brick façade of the big house.

"Miss Evelyn isn't up to receiving company."

"Five minutes, Annie," Luca said. He opened the bag to show her the bottle. "I know she's ill. This will help her be more comfortable."

"Aye, that it will." Annie hesitated, then held out a hand. "I'll give it to her."

Luca held his ground. "I'll give it to her myself."

An unfriendly staring contest ensued. Luca had the advantage of height and determination.

Annie eventually relented and stepped back so he could pass into the foyer. "Wait here."

She scurried up the wide staircase. Luca heard the patter of her footsteps on the hardwood floor above, followed by a gentle knock and the creak of a door hinge. Muffled voices floated down the banister.

Tess had told him that the house was owned by the Adirondack and Western Railroad. A co-founder of the railroad, her aunt's late husband had written his will so as to give his wife the right to live in the house and dividend income from certain stock holdings, but nothing more. Upon Evelyn's death, everything from his estate would revert to his surviving business partner who was now the sole owner of the railroad. Tess, the child of Evelyn's late brother, would inherit nothing and would lose the right to live in the house.

Annie came back down the stairs. "Miss Evelyn says she'll see you. It's not proper to receive in her bedroom, but she's still the mistress and she insisted."

"That's very kind of her," Luca said.

"Now wipe your feet and off with your coat and be quick about it." Annie all but snatched up Luca's coat and hat. "I've got her propped up on the pillows, but she gets tired fast."

Evelyn's bedroom was doused in shadow. Heavy draperies were drawn to keep out the winter sun. Slivers of light escaped to cast narrow stripes across a patterned carpet. Carved roses tumbled over the suite of dark wood furniture. The bed was a sea of robin's egg blue below an arched headboard that rose almost to the ceiling. The tall mirror of the matching vanity reflected the coverlet. A chair upholstered in the same pale color waited near a shiny tray of glass perfume bottles.

In the weeks since Luca last saw her, the woman propped up in the bed had declined to a shocking extent. Her hair was neatly pinned up and she wore a pink satin bed jacket with a bow at the neck, but nothing could disguise her physical deterioration. Skin the color of wax was drawn tight over her skull. Her lips were bloodless thin lines.

The coverlet was drawn up to her waist. Her legs were nothing more than sticks under the bedding. A claw-like hand rested limply on a closed book.

"Mr. Lombardo, how kind of you to call." Evelyn's voice was a hoarse whisper. The cancer eating her lungs was making good progress.

Luca took her hand and brushed his lips over her skin before unwrapping the bottle. "I brought you a gift."

"Cognac, how marvelous." Evelyn fluttered a finger at the housekeeper hovering by the bedroom door. "Annie, get some glasses. And a chair for Mr. Lombardo. Bring it quite close."

"There's nothing wrong with Mr. Lombardo's arms." Annie's righteous sniff suggested that Luca could fetch a chair himself. "I'll be right back."

Luca brought the chair from the vanity to the side of the bed as the housekeeper produced two glasses and set them on the bedside table. Annie made sure Evelyn could hold her glass before retreating back to the doorway.

"To Tess," Luca said. He lifted his glass.

"To Tess." Evelyn sipped and closed her eyes in appreciation.

"You must know a rumrunner," Annie observed tartly.

"Now, Annie," Evelyn reproved the housekeeper, her voice coming in breathy spurts. "Let Mr. Lombardo tell us why he came. I expect it wasn't just to give a dying woman a nip of cognac."

To Luca's surprise, it was hard to answer quickly. The sickroom brought back memories of his wife dying so long ago in that single room in the New York City tenement. She never called for Luca, only for the baby boy who died of the Spanish flu with her.

Evelyn's circumstances were different. She had a palatial bedroom, the best doctors, and servants at her beck and call. Yet the sense of impending loss was just as brutal. Luca swallowed hard and remembered why he was there.

"I came to ask you for Tess's hand in marriage," he said. "I love her very much and I will make her happy."

Evelyn blinked.

"He's got courage, so he does," Annie observed from her spot against the doorjamb.

Evelyn sipped her cognac. "Does Tess know you're here?"

"No," Luca admitted.

"Yet you think she'll have you."

"Yes."

Annie snorted.

"Tess is engaged to be married to James Howland of the First National Bank of Lido," Evelyn said. "Your request is not remotely possible."

"Tess doesn't want to marry this Howland fellow," Luca said doggedly.

"Tess will do as she's told."

"She doesn't love him."

"That's no concern of yours."

"Everything about Tess is my concern."

Evelyn narrowed her eyes at the doorway. "Annie, please leave us alone. Shut the door, all the way."

"Now, Miss Evelyn." Annie straightened up. "That wouldn't be proper, a man in your bedroom and you all alone."

"I think I'll be quite safe." Evelyn fluttered her finger at Annie again. This time it was a gesture of dismissal.

Annie threw a razor-sharp glare at Luca before backing out of the room. The door latched with a soft click.

Luca got up and refilled Evelyn's glass. She rested it on the cover of the book in her lap. For a long moment, she stared vacantly across the room, as if she'd forgotten Luca was still there.

The room was silent and oppressive, with the competing smells of soap and decay. Luca wanted to fling open the curtains and inhale the winter wind.

"Mrs. Thompson?" His voice came out too loud, too brash.

"Yes, I'm still here, Mr. Lombardo," Evelyn said and eased herself a little higher against the pillows. "You think you're entitled to marry my niece. I should be surprised, but I'm not."

"I love her. I want to make her happy."

"I made a mistake in allowing Tess to step out with you," Evelyn said. "I assumed you would be nothing more than a passing fancy. A novelty. Once she got past the veneer of a gentleman, she'd be repelled by the swart immigrant underneath."

Luca flushed with anger at the insult. "But that didn't happen."

"Even an argument over your unsavory associations didn't deter her." Evelyn flapped a dismissive hand to forestall his explanation. "No, no, I don't want to hear about it. The newspapers have been quite full of your near-death heroism."

"Then Tess has told you," Luca said. "She told you that she wants to marry me."

"Tess is an immature young woman who needs a guiding hand." Evelyn gave a brittle smile. "Wash your clothes? Make macaroni? Raise mixed-breed brats? Surely you see that she is not prepared to live like you people."

Luca gritted his teeth to keep from replying.

"I have to protect her interests and put a stop to her

foolishness," Evelyn went on. "Marriage to James Howland is for her own good. She'll thank me one day."

For her own good. Tess hated that expression. "Stop treating Tess like a child," Luca said, shortly. "She's a grown woman. She can make her own choices."

"Tess will marry Mr. Howland," Evelyn snapped. "The decision is final."

"Who she marries should be Tess's decision," Luca retorted.

"Mr. Lombardo, you are out of line. A gentleman would understand the niceties of the situation. Of course, considering your uncouth origins, I should hardly be surprised. Blood will out, as they say. Well, you bought some time with your bottle of cognac, but we are quite finished. Please go."

"I'll go," Luca said furiously. "But I'm going to marry Tess."

"I positively forbid you from seeing her again," Evelyn rasped. "Your association with my niece is over. Go back to your hovel and stay there."

Sixty dollars had bought him nothing but insults. "I hope you die with a hundred regrets," Luca exclaimed in fury.

The glass slipped out of Evelyn's hand. A trickle of brandy soaked into the coverlet. Luca snatched up the glass before it rolled off the bed.

"You're just like him," Evelyn said and latched onto his wrist with a claw-like hand.

"Who?"

Evelyn stared, but Luca knew his was not the face she was seeing. "So handsome," she murmured. "We walked in the woods. My white dress. Like a wedding. Forever, he said."

Luca had no idea what she was talking about. "Mrs. Thompson?"

They stayed frozen like that, Luca stooped over the bed, Evelyn's talons clamped around his wrist. At long last she blinked and released him.

Luca's anger dissolved into pity. He wasn't sure what to do.

"Open the vanity drawer," Evelyn said. "The one on the right."

There was enough command left in the breathy voice for Luca to do as she bid. The interior of the drawer was a mosaic of jewelry boxes. Most were embossed with the name of a store.

"Bring me the one with the blue stones," Evelyn said.

Luca fished out a bronze box inset with round moonstones the color of a cobalt sky. A tiny key adorned with a faded silk tassel was in the lock.

"Take it with you, Mr. Lombardo," Evelyn said. "It's fitting that you should be the one to carry away my last regret."

Weighty and undoubtedly expensive, the box was the size of a book.

"It wouldn't be right," Luca said. "You keep it."

"Take it, Mr. Lombardo." Evelyn closed her eyes and sagged into the pillows. "Please turn out the light."

The conversation was over. With her eyes closed, Evelyn looked ready for a coffin. Luca was reminded again of Rafaella's last hours. He pressed the light switch and left the room.

Annie intercepted Luca as he came down the stairs with the unexpected gift in his hand. "What did she say to you?" the housekeeper demanded.

"She's taking a nap," Luca said. He held out the bronze box. "Mrs. Thompson gave me this, but I can't keep it."

Annie gave a start. "This is the box for Miss Evelyn's pearls."

"Give it to Tess," Luca said.

With the box tucked under one arm, Annie led him back to the coat closet. "You did your best, Mr. Lombardo. You're not a quitter, I'll give you that."

"Tess isn't married yet," Luca said as he collected the green fedora.

"Best if you start thinking she is," Annie said.

CHAPTER 14

Senate Street serenade

Benny retreated into the shadows darkening the entrance to the office building. He'd picked the spot because the entrance was almost a guardhouse, with stucco walls on two sides and an arch that stretched across the front. Adding to the gloomy façade, all the shrubs flanking the entrance were covered by wooden sandwich boards to protect them from heavy winter snow.

All of the offices in the building were closed, including the dental office, an insurance agency, and a children's bookstore. Traffic on this end of Senate Street, north of Lido's busy downtown area, was sparse. This was mainly a commercial thoroughfare, with numerous warehouses and showrooms for industrial products.

Even if anyone who knew him drove by, they wouldn't recognize Benny in a beat-up old wool jacket, railyard worker cap and shoe polish mustache. Big Vinnie's system was foolproof, but he was in Chicago. Benny was taking all the chances here in Lido.

From where he waited, the loading dock of the Strand Theatre was visible. Just two blocks away, on the other side of the theater, people were having a late supper at the Canal House. Strolling along Liberty Street. Pressing their noses against the windows of Nelson's Department Store, Fulton Florist and Sugartime Toys. Maybe heading for the Strand and the late show.

Benny tugged his hat over his forehead as a Packard slowly cruised along the street. The car passed through the intersection half a block beyond Benny's hideaway, nosed into a spot at an angle to the curb and parked.

Spinelli got out. Stood for a bit, looking around, then jammed his hat on his head and shuffled away from the car.

Sure enough, the old man turned at the corner like he was going to the Strand. If he was smart, he'd follow the directions in the last letter. *Buy a ticket for* So's Your Old Man *with W.C. Fields. Sit in the fifth row. Don't come back to the Packard until the show is over.*

Benny waited ten minutes, then left the shelter of the entrance alcove and strolled along the street like he owned it. Stepped off the curb, sauntered through the intersection and approached the line of angled vehicles.

The getaway car was nowhere to be seen. It was supposed to be there already. A black Ford that belonged to Siwak that Benny commandeered it for odd jobs now and then. It had a dent that made it easy to recognize in a street full of identical black Fords, as long as a fella knew what he was looking for.

Benny went back to his doorway and commenced to freeze his feet. Twenty minutes later the dinged Ford nosed into a slot a few spaces away from the Packard.

Timing was the thing. Benny passed the Packard, reached into the open passenger side window and scooped up the package on the front seat without breaking stride.

A minute later he was in the Ford and the lights of Senate Street were in the rearview mirror.

Al Genovese drove fast but not so fast to get a cop on their tail.

"Jesus, Al," Benny roared at the *cafone* as they headed for Perk's. "Where were you? I was frozen solid waiting for you."

"Sorry, Benny." Al pulled off the street and bounced over the gravel to park by the diner. "It was time for the milking."

Benny was momentarily speechless. No Chicago torpedo ever had to milk cows. Broz would drive the next time.

By the light of the neon sign, Benny began counting. Ten- and twenty-dollar bills were sorted into bundles and secured with rubber bands.

It was all there. Five thousand.

Benny grinned, cows and frozen feet forgotten. Al's dirt on Spinelli was going to be the trick that made the Galliano Club his and fast.

"Next time we ask for ten," he said.

CHAPTER 15

Like sparklers

The maple trees along Bell Road were nearly bare. Just a few scarlet leaves clung stubbornly to their branches. In contrast, towering pines made a soft green backdrop to the fallow fields as the truck rattled toward the farm.

The last snowfall had melted. The day was crisp and sunny.

Luca sat in the truck bed with his cousin Enzo's two oldest children. Eight-year-old Rocco and his younger sister Matilda chattered away to their favorite *zio*, although Luca wasn't really their uncle.

Nearly every Sunday, Enzo and his wife Rosario picked up Luca on their way home from Mass at Saint Rocco's and Luca spent the day on their Bell Road farm, helping with chores and projects that needed an extra pair of hands.

"Let's play the counting game," Rocco announced. "Your turn, Zio. Ninety-two. Eleven. Forty-six."

"Five," Luca answered automatically. Tess always said that five was the perfect number. In the middle of the scale. Perfectly balanced.

He swallowed a painful memory of playing the counting game with Tess, adding a string of numbers one by one to achieve a single digit solution. It became their lovers' code.

The failed plea to Evelyn Thompson weighed heavily. Luca wasn't sure what to do next, only that he could not surrender and watch Tess marry someone she didn't love.

"Is he right?" Matilda asked her brother. Both children wore winter coats, hats and mittens, and snuggled under a blanket in the open truck bed.

"Yes," Rocco said stoutly, then frowned at Luca. "It is five, isn't it?"

By the time the number string was thoroughly dissected, they were there. Like the other small farms in New York's Mohawk Valley, the Russo place grew vegetables for local stores and raised chickens to sell eggs. But the herd of five Holstein cows paid the mortgage.

The cows were well housed, too. During the summer and well into the fall, Luca and Enzo had built a new barn together, first blasting boulders into rocks for the foundation, then nailing boards into walls and mangers. The new structure sat well behind the farmhouse. Room for a dozen cows, a pig pen, and even the tractor Enzo hoped to have someday.

The scent of fresh pine filled the air. The truck rumbled to a stop between house and barn. Luca helped Matilda scramble over the tailgate.

After a cup of hot coffee and a slab of Rosaria's coffeecake spiced with cinnamon and nutmeg, Luca and Enzo went out to the barn. Today there was a pig to butcher. Doing it outside dissipated the stink and made the job a little less grim.

Enzo slit the animal's throat and they bled it into a bucket for blood sausage. With a meat hook in its rear trotters, Enzo used a block and tackle to hoist the carcass upside down and finish draining. The pig cooled quickly in the freezing air and Enzo was an efficient butcher.

Layers of fat went into a pot of boiling water to render for soap. The trotters went into pickling jars that Matilda carried out from the house. By the late afternoon, hams, hocks, racks of ribs, and slabs of bacon were secured in the tiny smokehouse and the fire lit.

Luca and Enzo washed up at the pump behind the barn, yelping at the freezing water and then having an impromptu battle with flour sack towels. They were clean but tired when Rosaria shooed them into the dining room. Luca inhaled the rich scent of Rosaria's tomato sauce, the afternoon's stench of blood and offal forgotten.

Rosaria's *prima piatti* was a huge platter of linguini in rich red sauce. Matilda brought a hunk of parmesan and the grater to the table. Enzo poured dandelion wine for the adults and cider for the children. Grace was said, the pasta served, and not a sound was heard except the clink of forks expertly twirling against china.

When the pasta was finished, Rosaria produced a roast chicken and a tub-sized bowl of potatoes and green beans swimming in olive oil and garlic. Luca plowed through the food like there was no tomorrow. Butchering was hard work and Rosaria's food was better than any restaurant.

"Zio," Matilda said as she picked up a green bean with her fingers. "Mama said that she forgives you."

"She did?" Luca raised his eyebrows at Rosaria.

"Use your fork," Rosaria snapped at her daughter instead of meeting Luca's eye.

"She was mad because you didn't want to marry Mr. Genovese's sister," Rocco piped up.

Matilda ate another bean with her fingers. "Are you going to marry somebody else?"

"Nobody." Luca tried to make a joke. "Nobody cooks as good as your mama and she's already married."

"Claudia Genovese was here the other day," Rosaria said nonchalantly as she added another shovelful of potatoes and beans to Luca's plate. "Annunziata got married to a boy with his own farm."

He should have known that the topic of Annunziata Genovese would come up sooner or later. Rosaria and Al's wife Claudia had tried to play matchmaker. Even if Tess Kennedy hadn't been in the picture, Luca refused to be roped into marrying such a young girl. Al Genovese had even tried to blackmail Luca into marrying Annunziata. It was a relief to know that the girl was settled, even if he disagreed with the notion of marrying her off at such a young age.

"I hope she's happy," Luca said.

Rosaria waved her fork at him. "Claudia said that the boy took one look at her and fell in love."

Dessert was yellow sponge cake sliced thin and layered with vanilla custard and strawberry preserves. Luca ate until he was ready to burst. Rocco and Matilda bundled up to play outside for another few minutes before it got too dark. Enzo unfastened the top button of his trousers and had a second slice of cake. Rosaria checked on the baby, napping in the cradle by her chair, then brought out a bowl of walnuts and a pot of coffee.

"But here's something that's bothering me," Rosaria said as she poured three cups of coffee. "Claudia didn't even know the name of Annunziata's new husband. I asked her, what's his name and she said she couldn't remember. He's the brother-in-law. Who doesn't remember like that?"

"Are we still talking about Al's sister?" Enzo asked wearily.

"In the back of my mind, I don't think they got married," Rosaria said, plunking herself down in her chair. "There was no announcement in the church. No party at the house. The girl just disappeared."

Luca laughed. "Maybe she ran off with some traveling salesman and they're too ashamed to say."

"Sure, go ahead and laugh, Mr. Lucky who doesn't need a wife." Rosaria cut him another piece of cake.

"Pa! Pa!" The back door slammed. Matilda and Rocco jostled each other as they ran into the dining room.

"Pa, you should see this," Rocco said. "The pumpkin patch is fizzing."

"Fizzing?" Enzo stood up and threw his napkin on the table. "What are you talking about?"

Matilda tugged her father's sleeve. "Come see. It's like sparklers."

"Sparklers? We don't have any sparklers." Enzo pushed the girl toward Rosaria. "Stay with your mother."

Luca and Enzo ran out the back door. In the murky twilight, they followed Rocco around the side of the house and into the field ridged with frozen furrows. A cow lowed from inside the barn, informing the universe that she was ready for the evening milking. A second cow took up the refrain.

Despite the lowing, Luca heard the sizzle before he saw the line of sparks racing across the ground. It was traveling straight toward the smokehouse.

"Look, Pa!" Rocco knelt in the dirt. "It's a great big firecracker."

Enzo began shouting, but Luca shot forward on wings of fear. He snatched Rocco around the waist and pulled him off his feet. The next second, the smokehouse erupted with a deafening roar, the ground rose like an angry ocean, and Luca was lofted backward, both arms still wrapped around the boy.

They slammed onto the ground. Luca rolled over Rocco, protecting the child as debris rained down. Chunks of wood, shards of tin, and scraps of raw pig meat battered his back and shoulders. Roiling echoes battered his ears. Luca's mouth filled with frozen grass and the taste of bile. His teeth felt loose and he couldn't catch his breath.

Luca's ears were still ringing as the ground stilled. He slowly sat up, pushing dust and splinters out of his hair. Rocco scrambled to his knees. "Wow, Zio. That was something, wasn't it?"

A moment later Enzo was upon them, pulling at both and shouting to know if they were alive.

"Rocco! Rocco!" Rosaria and Matilda materialized, both screaming the boy's name.

"He's all right," Luca croaked.

"*Madonna santa.*" Enzo left Luca's side and took off running.

The remnants of the smokehouse were on fire, flames leaping into the evening sky, crackling greedily and spreading the scent of burning meat. Sparks blew toward the barn.

Luca caught up to Enzo. Rocco broke away from his mother and joined the men. Without wasting time for words, they grabbed the milking buckets and a canvas tarp from the barn. Enzo furiously worked the water pump, filling bucket after bucket that Luca and Rocco dumped on the flames. Finally, Luca threw the soaked canvas on the burning mess and stamped out the last sparks.

He backed away from the remains of the smokehouse, the stench of burning meat clogging his nostrils. Enzo slumped over the pump. Rocco abruptly sat on the ground. The 8-year-old had worked as hard as either man.

Rosaria, with Matilda clinging to her skirt, came closer. "What happened?"

"Dynamite," Luca said. "I saw the fuse."

Enzo pulled his son to his feet. "Were you playing with the dynamite? You blew up the smokehouse. You could have killed us all."

"I didn't touch it, Papa."

"You knew where I kept it in the barn. Did you think it would be funny? A joke?"

"No, Papa," Matilda sobbed. "We saw sparklers. Rocco didn't do anything."

Rocco's eyes were huge with fright. "I didn't touch it, I swear."

"Don't lie to me," Enzo roared.

He slapped Rocco twice before Rosaria intervened, screaming. "Leave him alone! If he says he didn't touch the dynamite, then he didn't. Go count what's in the barn before you say he's lying."

"In the house, all of you." Enzo strode off toward the barn.

Luca helped Rosaria get the children settled in the house with hot cider, then went out to the barn to find Enzo. The smoldering remains of the smokehouse were black daggers thrust against the starry night sky.

Hung on a nail, a lantern burned in the barn. His cousin had finished with the cows. Steam rose from the pails of warm milk.

"You check the dynamite?" Luca asked.

"I don't need to check." Enzo turned his back on his cousin and poured a pail of milk into a 10-gallon can.

Luca held the can steady as the milk sloshed into it. "Listen, Enzo --."

Enzo cut him off. "You don't have children, Luca. You don't know what they can do."

"Sure, but --."

"I'll drive you back to Lido now."

Rosaria handed Luca a pail of food to see him through the week, always convinced that a man without a wife lived on the brink of starvation. Luca kissed the kids and climbed into the truck. Enzo drove without speaking.

"You need any help to clean up the smokehouse, call the club," Luca said when they pulled up in front of Mrs. Esposito's boarding house. "Vito can do without me for a couple of hours."

Enzo's hands on the wheel were clenched so tightly that the knuckles were white. He didn't cut the engine. "If anything happens to me, take care of Rosaria and the children."

"Why?" Luca asked sharply. "Why should anything happen to you?"

"Just promise me."

"Sure, I promise."

Enzo nodded once and looked away, clearly not intending to explain himself.

Luca got out of the truck with his pail of food and the truck lumbered off.

CHAPTER 16

Speechless

Slumped in her warm dressing gown, Ruth comforted herself with a cup of tea. The ballroom dance class and mesmerizing waltz with Henry Blick seemed like a lifetime ago instead of just a few days.

In his thermal undershirt, wool uniform trousers and suspenders, O'Malley made short work of two bowls of stew.

"You got some paper around here?" he asked, spooning up the last chunk of beef.

"Paper?"

"Need you to write me a speech, Ruthie June. You got a nice way with words."

"A speech? What for?"

"Next Sunday is the Bison Club banquet," O'Malley said. He slathered butter on a biscuit and dunked it into the skim of gravy in the bottom of his bowl. "I'm the guest of honor. For saving Lombardo and getting rid of that killer Procopio. I'm getting the keys to the city. Got to make an acceptance speech."

A speech for her blackmailer. For the man who'd

just taken her like a rutting pig while her thoughts carried her to the exotic places in *National Geographic*. In her mind's eye, Ruth had floated away to the faraway heat of Zanzibar and the Fiji Islands. She watched ships pass through an engineering masterpiece and witnessed the sun sink in flaming glory across the vast Pacific.

"The mayor will be there," O'Malley called after her as Ruth went into the other room to fetch paper and her fountain pen. "To honor me! What do you think of that, Ruthie June? The keys to the city for cracking that dago's head like a walnut. That's what I say when people want to shake my hand. Cracked that dago's head like a walnut to protect the fine citizens of Lido."

Ruth brought her writing tools to the table, on the verge of hysterical laughter at the ludicrousness of the situation. "Shouldn't a speech be more elegant?"

O'Malley shrugged, mouth bulging with biscuit. "Sure, that's why you're going to write it. Go ahead, write something."

"I should write that you're a soulless blackmailer who preys on women. Tell the whole Bison Club. The mayor. Everyone."

O'Malley rose up and struck her across the cheek.

The flat of his hand sounded like the crack of a whip and bounced her head against the wooden slats of the chair. Ruth's eyes filled with tears of pain and humiliation even as she slapped him back as hard as she could. Her nails scoured his jaw, but O'Malley had the advantage of standing while she was seated and it wasn't a telling blow. He smacked her again.

Stars circled her vision. Ruth cringed into the chair.

"Look what you made me do, Ruthie June," O'Malley said, breathing hard. Red lines streaked across his chin. He sat heavily and shoved his empty bowl at her. "Go fetch me some pie."

Ruth's legs wobbled as she went into the kitchen to take a cup and saucer out of the cupboard. By a miracle she managed to pour hot coffee without getting it all over herself. It went on a tray with a slice of apple pie and a chunk of cheddar.

O'Malley forked it up as soon as the dessert was in front of him. "Never forget that you're spreading your legs for a hero," he said, chewing noisily.

Ruth sat and cautiously felt her cheek. Her teeth ached on that side and the inside of her mouth tasted like blood.

As he shoveled in pie and slurped coffee, O'Malley harangued her about the Bison Club banquet. The mayor and the owner of the Lido Premium mill were to sit at the head table with him and his friends. The chief of police, too.

Eventually Ruth picked up the pen and scratched out

some blather, knitting together Governor Smith's re-election campaign speeches, Jack Rutherford's presentation at a recent Chamber of Commerce function, and something Luca had once quoted from a Roman philosopher whose name she no longer recalled. O'Malley told her to include words like *courage* and *motherhood.*

"That's the way heroes talk, Ruthie June."

Ruth handed him the finished pages.

O'Malley folded the speech and put it in his pocket. "I won't be here next Sunday," he said. "You get a wee rest. But I'll be back the next Sunday, Ruthie Ann. Make sure to have more than stew waiting for me. Chicken or steak, I told you. Potatoes. Cake."

O'Malley gave her a bruising kiss before he left. Didn't want her to forget that he wouldn't be back for two weeks.

When Ruth was finally alone, she ran a hot bath. Before she stepped into the tub, she caught sight of herself in the mirror. One cheek was mottled with the imprint of his hand.

She stared at herself, a desperate thought slowly taking shape in her mind. She wasn't bigger, stronger, or braver, but she was smart enough to realize that O'Malley was always too busy inhaling his food to notice that Ruth didn't eat when he was there.

He ate, but she never did.

CHAPTER 17

The pocket ledger

"You still smell like bacon," Karol observed.

"Shut up. It's your move."

They were in Luca's room, with the chessboard and the remains of a pail full of gingerbread and apple pie between them. His friend had come back earlier than usual from his cousin's farm, where there had been an accident that destroyed a smokehouse. In fact, it sounded as if Luca and Enzo, whom Karol had met once or twice, just barely saved the new barn and the cows, too.

Karol considered the board and advanced a pawn. "Do you do the accounting at the club?"

"Sure. Why?" Luca studied the board, then mirrored Karol's move.

"I figure that's going to be the hardest part of the business apprentice program Mr. Blick set up for me."

To Karol's surprise, Luca jerked his head up. "Accounting," he said. "Isn't a man named Fisher the accountant at Lido Premium?"

"Yes." Karol shrugged. "Nervous sort of fellow. I

haven't dealt with him yet."

"Well, watch yourself around him. He's a crook."

Karol laughed. "A crook? Fisher? He wouldn't steal candy if it was stuck in his mouth."

In response, Luca left the chessboard and went to the dresser. Karol watched as he tugged open the bottom drawer, extracted a tin box and pulled out a small book. "Look at this."

It wasn't a regular book but a pocket-size accounting ledger covered in linen with leather-capped corners. Karol opened the front cover and his eye landed on three signatures.

THE LIDO OUTFIT

Benito Rotolo, President
Nicola Procopio, Vice President
Owen Forbes Fisher, Treasurer

Karol looked up at Luca. "What is this?"

"The accounting for Benny Rotolo's beer racket."

"The bootlegger who offered to buy the Galliano Club?"

Luca nodded. "Fisher is in with him. Probably met Rotolo through Procopio. Rotolo and Procopio were cousins."

Karol let out a soft whistle of amazement as he turned the pages. "Mr. Fisher is a bootlegger? I don't believe it."

"It's his handwriting. Tess recognized it from his paperwork at the bank. She said it's a divvy sheet. Shows how bootlegging profits are divided and that somebody is skimming off the top. Him. Fisher."

Karol shook his head in disbelief as he leafed through the little ledger. Half of the pages were filled with tidy columns of numbers. The rest was blank, as if the business had gone bankrupt. "I don't understand any of this."

"You're not supposed to. Tess said she only could figure it out because she did something similar for the bank. But she was sure once she did. Someone is taking a third off the top of whatever is coming in. The rest gets divided in four equal parts. It's Fisher's handwriting. Makes it very likely that he's taking the third off the top."

"Fisher," Karol confirmed. He could not imagine anyone less likely to be in a bootlegging ring.

"Yes."

Karol looked up from the indecipherable columns of numbers. "Then why do you have it?"

"Jimmy Zambrano gave it to Vito to keep in the safe." Luca took a deep breath. "I think Procopio killed

Jimmy because he was looking for it."

"This?" Karol frowned. "Everyone says that Procopio killed Zambrano for the foreman job."

"That's not what Procopio said two seconds before he put that copper wire around my neck."

"Jesus, Luca." Karol closed the ledger in agitation, only to open it again. Such a small thing to have such a big impact on so many. "Who else knows you have it?"

"Only Tess. And now you."

The new business apprentice program at Lido Premium suddenly took on new and ominous meaning. "What about Henry Blick?" Karol blurted. "Is he involved?"

Luca shrugged, releasing another waft of bacon scent. "I only know about the names in the book."

Karol held up the little book. "This has to be the outfit Broz is working for now. You remember me telling you about Broz Siwak? We worked on the dipping crew together for years. Then one day, he quit. No warning, just quit."

"That's bad."

"I saw him at the Warsaw Club and offered him a job at the mill. Almost thought he was going to come back."

"Is he friends with Fisher?"

"Broz? No. Mr. Fisher never mixed with anyone

inside the mill, not like Mr. Blick." Karol shook his head. "It's hard to think of Mr. Fisher doing anything bad. He reminds me of a mouse. A little nervous mouse in a nice suit."

"That mouse is a bootlegger, along with Rotolo." Luca scooped up the ledger and replaced it in its hiding spot. "That makes him dangerous."

"What about you?" Karol pressed. "Doesn't the club buy beer from Rotolo?"

Luca threw himself back into the chair. "Vito doesn't have a choice. There's no competition. Rotolo is the only one selling beer in Lido."

"Where does he get it?"

"He must have a brewery someplace. At least he hasn't tried to buy the club again." Luca straightened his pawns so that each was perfectly centered in its square. "Your move."

Too many thoughts leapfrogged each other, making it impossible to focus on strategy. Karol randomly slid a pawn ahead two spaces. "Is there a connection to the woman from the river?"

"Everyone keeps asking me that. I don't know. She doesn't even have a name yet. Where do you think she's from?"

"No idea."

In short order, both of Karol's rooks were gone. His

queen was vulnerable. He moved a knight to block the threat.

Luca's bishop came out of nowhere and knocked the knight off the board. "Checkmate."

Karol opened his mouth to protest but he'd been crushed in less than fifteen minutes. His king was lost. Foreman or not, he'd played badly while his friend was still buzzing with adrenaline from the events at the Russo farm. "You win."

"Another game?"

"Sure."

They switched colors. Karol was determined to do better this time. "What about Tess? Did you patch things up?"

"She's to marry her boss at the bank." Luca moved the white queen onto the correct square. "James Howland. It's all arranged. I'm not to see her again."

"But I thought --," Karol started.

"So did I," Luca said.

CHAPTER 18

Lunch with Muriel

Tess felt like Alice after drinking the shrinking potion.

Lunch at Buckner's with her future mother-in-law, Muriel Howland, was the first indication of what life was going to be like when she and James were married and living in the Howland's home in the West Circle neighborhood. The ostensible reason for the lunch was to plan the engagement party. Aunt Evelyn was the official host but had turned over the arrangements to Muriel.

"I've already paid for the announcement to be in the *Lido Daily Clipper* after the party." Muriel inhaled a healthy portion of salmon mousse and plucked another cracker out of the basket in the middle of the table.

Tess lost what little appetite she had. A formal engagement notice in the newspaper would make this mess into a genuine 5-reel comedy. She wished Buster Keaton would appear, pummel James into submission in some comedic fashion and reunite her with Luca as "Happily Ever After" flashed on the screen.

But this was real life.

"I'll ask Aunt Evelyn--" Tess started.

"I've already spoken to Evelyn and her doctor." Muriel scraped the last of her mousse onto the cracker and ate it. "He says we should proceed as planned. The invitations are being printed as we speak."

Muriel wore a cunning mint cloche with a dyed egret feather fastened with a rhinestone clip. A matching dress and crocheted sweater spoke of money, good taste, and pride in her ample frame. Even if she did look like a giant Jordan almond, surely all of the woman's clothing came from Van Dyke's.

"I would have liked to choose them myself," Tess said stiffly.

"You can choose your calling cards." Muriel looked around for the waiter. "Ivory or white? I don't ascribe to this modern notion of pale blue. Of course, you must use his middle initial. A name with a middle initial is so much more refined."

"Of course," Tess murmured. She sipped tea and ignored the rest of her mousse as a headache bloomed behind her eyes. James could give himself the middle name of Fiddlesticks and Tess could care less. Not that it mattered. Muriel would have the calling cards designed, ordered, and printed before Tess finished her lunch.

"Then there is the matter of your trousseau," Muriel went on as the waiter removed their appetizer plates and replaced them with lamb chops and glazed carrots. She flapped her hand before he could withdraw from their private dining alcove. "We'll both have the apple tart with ice cream for dessert. Bring it in fifteen minutes precisely, young man."

"Really, I don't need any dessert," Tess said. Her nerves were so tight that the two bites of mousse that she'd eaten were threatening to make an untimely reappearance.

"As I was saying about your trousseau." Muriel sawed off a chunk of lamb. "Evelyn has given me a small budget, so we'll have to do our best."

"She didn't say anything about that to me." Tess pushed the food around on her plate, fork clicking on china in a mournful tattoo. Yet again, things were arranged without telling her.

Muriel started on her second lamb chop, having already dispatched the first as well as the glazed vegetables. "You'll need a going-away suit, of course. A peignoir set for the wedding night and a few party frocks. James adores pink. Or ivory. Either color is suitable for your age."

"Dark colors are more modern," Tess said. She was wearing a navy sweater set today, with her favorite cream cloche with a crystal brooch in the shape of a rabbit on the band. The outfit was very fashionable, according to the editors of *McCall's* magazine. "I'd prefer green or plum."

"Yes, I've noticed what you wear, dear. Those are widow's weeds colors. Evelyn has neglected your wardrobe frightfully. I've heard she even lets you wear trousers."

"What's wrong with trousers?" Tess asked, although she knew it was fruitless.

Muriel pursed her lips, the egret feather quivering in disapproval. "No Howland woman has ever worn trousers. They are vulgar and mannish. It's simply not done."

Tess stared at her food. Prodded at a lamb chop with her fork. Lamb to the slaughter, that's what she was. Just like this bit of meat and bone.

"Excellent," Muriel said breezily, as if Tess had agreed. "We'll find you a suitable wardrobe. Something virginal to suit James."

"I'll wear what I want on my honeymoon," Tess exclaimed.

"Evelyn has given me the purse strings and I've promised to make sure your clothing is what is expected for your new station in life."

Tess bit her lip to keep from screaming in utter

frustration. This is what life would be like when she was married and living in the Howland home in West Park with James, his parents and younger brother Richard.

In a house full of servants, and without a job to lend purpose and independence, Tess would be at the mercy of her mother-in-law. Each day would be an exercise in catering to James and learning how to be meek. Never making a single decision for herself, not even her nightgowns.

She wouldn't even have Aunt Evelyn's shoulder to cry on as she had during those first difficult years after her father died. That thought hurt as much as the notion of being trapped in an endless nightmare with a husband she didn't love and certainly showed no evidence of loving her. She was to be the proverbial bird stuffed into the proverbial gilded cage.

Tess nudged her plate away. "I'm not feeling quite well."

Muriel dabbed at her lips with the napkin. "You've been running yourself down with those dance lessons. Oh yes, Evelyn has told me all about your excursions to East Lido with who knows what type of girls. Shop girls and clerks who are no better than they should be. Of course this has to stop. James can't marry a French can-can dancer. It's bad enough that James has agreed to let you continue working at the bank until the wedding."

"I really need to lie down," Tess murmured. Aunt Evelyn thought marriage to James was a safe harbor, but instead Tess was shipwrecked. She was losing everything by marrying James. Her independence, her job, now even the few hours every week when she flexed her muscles and worked herself into a sweat as Ruth Cross called out the steps.

But worst of all, she had lost Luca. The look on his face when she said goodbye still haunted her.

"My goodness." Muriel suddenly filled Tess's entire field of vision, the egret feather trembling violently as the woman peered intently at her. "You do look dreadfully pale."

Tess stood up shakily as the waiter raced to pull out her chair. She made it to the ladies' lounge. Without a word, she passed the attendant presiding over perfume bottles and monogrammed linen hand towels. Tess darted inside a toilet cubicle, latched the richly paneled wooden door, swept the hat from her head and threw up.

CHAPTER 19

The Red Book

Vito was sound asleep on the Chesterfield. One arm was flung out, the other crossed over his straining vest buttons. An empty bottle of Old Bushmills was on the floor under the outstretched hand.

The boss looked peaceful enough as he slept, mustache fluttering with every shallow snore, but he looked old in a way that Luca had not noticed before. Worn down, with deep lines etched across his forehead and an unhealthy puffiness that melted his jawline into the folds of his neck. His clothing was wrinkled, the creases gone from his trousers and the wool splashed with stains.

On the desk, an overturned glass leaked amber fluid dangerously close to the picture of Ciro Spinelli in his Army uniform.

The Lido Premium whistle blew, a long, sustained cry. Vito didn't stir. Luca backed out of the office and returned to the saloon.

"Is Mr. Spinelli all right?" Sonny asked as Luca busied himself filling a pitcher with beer.

"Taking a nap." Luca sometimes wished that Sonny wasn't so smart. The kid knew exactly what was going on with the boss. Good thing he was also smart enough to keep quiet.

The club filled up with thirsty men from Lido Premium. Karol's tenure as foreman had started with a bang in the form of new safety rules. Some of the men liked the extra responsibility, others grumbled. Luca stored away what he heard to tell Karol.

Guido lumbered into the saloon, stamping slush off his boots as he barreled through a line of beer drinkers. "Luca, look at this!" He brandished a newspaper.

Luca set down his pitcher. "What's going on?"

"Look." Guido slapped the newspaper onto the bar in front of Luca. "Pictures of the dead girl. Itsa bad, no?"

Luca smoothed out the front page of the evening edition of the *Lido Daily Clipper* and saw a trio of large photographs. For once none of them were of him.

The headline was sparse.

PUBLIC HELP SOUGHT TO IDENTIFY DEAD WOMAN

The main photograph was a full-face portrait. The dead woman's eyes were sewn shut by the coroner and the thick thread was visible yet she was still lovely, with high cheekbones, a straight nose, thin arched brows and pale hair long enough to brush her chin.

Another photograph was of her profile. The last showed a hand with a scar about an inch long at the base of the thumb.

"I never saw pictures of a dead woman before," Sonny said and made the Sign of the Cross.

Members crowded around to see the pictures. Luca scanned the accompanying article, which quoted Chief of Police Doyle saying that publishing photographs of the dead woman was a last resort. He called on readers with any knowledge about the woman to step forward to assist in finding out who she was as well as to help find her killer.

Details were provided. The woman was no more than 22 or 23 years old, five feet and six inches tall, and had blue eyes. The only identifying mark on her body was a small burn on her right hand.

The cause of death was strangulation. A man's tie was embedded in the skin of her neck.

When found, she was clad in a silk camisole. Regrettably, there was no maker or store label on either the camisole or the man's tie.

If she was still unidentified by the spring thaw, she would be buried in a pauper's grave in the Lido city cemetery. In the meantime, her body was at the hospital morgue.

"Somebody must be missing her," Sonny said, peering at the newspaper over Luca's shoulder.

"Hey." Luca cut his eyes to Sonny. "This isn't for kids."

"I'm old enough."

"Go do your homework." Luca spoke more sharply than he intended to. What if this was Tess, dead and far away from home? How would he find out what happened to her?

And then he remembered that Tess wasn't his anymore, that she was going to marry James Howland. For a brief second, he was as dead as the unknown woman in the newspaper.

An hour later, Sonny closed his textbook. "Are you going to read the lady letters tonight?" he asked.

As usual, more than a dozen pastel envelopes had come in today's post and now waited by the cash register. Reading the so-called lady letters was now an evening ritual that even macabre newspaper photographs could not preempt. Tonight the letters would be a nice distraction to push both Tess and the unidentified woman out of his thoughts for a few minutes.

Luca wiped his hands on a bar towel. "If any more

come, the postage alone is going to put us out of business." He hitched himself onto the bar top and dangled his legs over the side as Sonny sorted the envelopes.

"Letters!" someone sang out, prompting a round of anticipatory applause and foot stamping. There was general shuffling and chairs scraped on the parquet floor as the crowd in the saloon got comfortable. Pinochle and chess games were halted. A few shouts lured out the pool players to hear the latest. The door to Vito's office stayed shut.

With a comic flourish Luca opened the first envelope. Sonny draped himself over the bar, grinning in anticipation, pencil poised to act as secretary.

Miss Beverly Holcomb of Rochester, New York, offered Luca convalescent care at Pinewood, the Holcomb family camp in Canandaigua. Her letter thoughtfully included a train timetable with the 9:40 from Syracuse circled and *Highly recommended* penciled next to it.

"No ticket?" someone called.

"No ticket," Luca confirmed, earning a chorus of boos.

"She thinks you're a rich man!"

He passed the letter and timetable to Sonny for the customary polite refusal.

Next, Miss Elizabeth Landry from Newton, Massachusetts, requested that Luca send his clothing measurements to determine their compatibility. She hoped that he was six feet, two inches tall, with a waist approximately 38 inches in circumference. If so, he would fit into her late brother's clothing.

"You're too short, Luca," Gio Tulipano shouted. "Too skinny, too!"

"She wants a brother or a husband?"

"Two for one!" Roars of laughter and ribald speculation filled the saloon.

"Wait, there's more." Luca raised a hand to quiet the hilarity and kept reading.

You need not have any reservations about my physical attributes. I am 64 inches tall with a waist measurement of 23 inches. I closely resemble the girl on the cover of the October edition of The Red Book magazine.

Luca put down the letter and frowned at Sonny. "Is that good?"

Sonny let out a long whistle. "Probably. That's a ladies' magazine."

"Maybe I should grow taller, eh?" Luca passed the letter to the young man and picked up the next envelope.

"Hold on, Luca!" Gio raised his half-empty glass of beer to the crowd. "I say we go look at that magazine. Find Luca a wife, no?"

"Alessi probably stocks *The Red Book* at the newsstand," Sonny offered.

That's all it took. There was a mad scramble for coats and hats before everyone thundered outside. Leaving Guido in charge, Luca and Sonny were carried along by the charge down Hamilton Street, more raucous than a Tammany Hall rally for Governor Smith.

Donato Alessi was just closing down his newsstand. "Sure, I got the October one," he said in response to a dozen shouted queries.

The Red Book magazine cost 25 cents. A collection of nickels and pennies was taken up, a copy purchased, and the stampede surged back to the warmth of the saloon.

The magazine passed from hand to hand, accompanied by a chorus of hoots and ribald comments until it reached Luca. The drawing on the cover was of a blonde girl with hair that waved around her ears. Her head was slightly thrown back as she considered something amusing in the distance. She had blue eyes and a strong chin.

"Hubba hubba, Luca," someone crowed. "If she really looks like that, we'll stretch you until you're tall enough for her."

The noisy jokes and laughter petered out as Luca laid the magazine next to the morning edition of the *Lido Daily Clipper*.

"What's going on?" The querulous voice of Tony Bilotti preceded the old man as he struggled through the crowd. Ignoring the stunned reaction of those clustered around the bar, he thumped down an empty glass, dark red sediment in the bottom. "Where's Vito? The service in this place is like nothing."

"Tony," Luca said, tapping the magazine cover. "What do you think? Is it the same girl?"

"What girl?" Tony squinted at him.

"It's the same girl," Sonny said in wonder. "We solved the mystery."

Everyone in the saloon trooped up in turn to compare the images. After an hour, as the beer flowed, strong opinions bounced off the walls and clouds of tobacco smoke hugged the ceiling, the final consensus was that the dead girl from the river and the magazine model were one and the same. A few argued that Miss Landry, the letter writer, was the dead girl.

"The letter is postmarked ten days after the dead girl came out of the river," Luca explained.

"So?" Pasquale Camardo was a stoker at Lido Premium, one of the least skilled jobs.

"If she was dead, she couldn't write a letter, could she?"

"Maybe she wrote it before she died."

"*Malocchio*," Tony Bilotti bleated, ending the discussion. Luca had never loved the old man more.

Despite the striking similarity between the girl on *The Red Book* cover and the portrait photograph in the newspaper, Luca had his doubts. The connection was too tenuous, too random to go rushing to the police. Moreover, contacting the newspaper would mean another avalanche of reporters just when they had finally left him alone.

"You could write to the editor of the magazine, Luca," Sonny insisted. "They'll know who she is." He flipped through the magazine. "Here's the address and the editor's name."

Luca signed what became a letter written by committee, although Sonny actually wielded the pen.

Karl Edwin Harriman, editor
The Red Book
Dear Sir,
I am a resident of Lido, New York, where the murder of a woman remains unsolved. No one

knows who she is. The police are investigating but are stumped.

I enclose a newspaper article with additional details.

Here at the Galliano Club, we have reason to believe that the drawing on the cover of your October magazine strongly resembles this unknown dead woman. Could you please advise if the girl who is depicted on the cover is missing or has ever been to Lido? If not, is she related to anyone who was visiting here within the last few months?

The citizens of Lido would be grateful for your help in this matter.

Sincerely,
Gianluca Lombardo
Galliano Club, Lido, New York

At closing time, a small delegation carried the letter to the mailbox on the corner. Luca sent Sonny and Guido home, locked the front door, and took the magazine and the newspaper down the hall to Vito's office. The door was closed but a telltale strip of light leaked from the threshold.

"Boss?" Luca tapped on the door and pushed it open at the same time. "You missed all the excitement."

Vito was behind the desk with an open ledger and

an empty bottle. His mustache drooped and there was spittle on his lower lip. "First one today," he slurred.

"*Oddio*," Luca swore.

The boss's bloodshot eyes, unbuttoned vest and loosened necktie spoke of a particularly harsh visit from the blue dog.

"What's this?" Vito reached for *The Red Book*. His hand trembled noticeably, the thumb vibrating with a will of its own. "This is what you're reading now?"

"Look." Luca spread out the newspaper, hiding the ledger, and placed the magazine next to the front-page photographs of the unidentified woman from the river. "What do you see?"

Vito wiped the back of his hand across his mouth and mustache. "She's --."

A deafening fusillade of gunfire cut him off. The wall behind the desk shook from the hammering. Luca instinctively dropped to the floor and yanked a drunkenly bewildered Vito under the desk.

The scything clatter went on and on, filling the night with fury.

And then it was over as suddenly as it began.

Luca staggered to his feet, expecting to see smoke and rubble. But the office was wholly intact. The hall beyond was the same as before. White plaster, green paneling, pressed tin ceiling. The pool room and tiny library were dark and empty. The lights in the saloon were still on.

At the end of the hall, the club's back door slowly swung to and fro. The knob was shot away. Splinters were scattered across the floor. Cold leached into the warmth of the club.

Uncertain if the danger had passed, Luca edged to the busted door. The wood was pocked with lead.

"*Madonna santa*," Vito murmured from behind him.

Together they made their way through the destruction to the back porch. The air smelled acrid and burnt. The sound of a speeding automobile faded quickly, but not before they heard squealing tires make a hasty turn on frosty pavement.

Light from the hall bled over the gravel lot, revealing Vito's Packard in its usual spot at a right angle to the back wall of the building.

The Packard's shiny black finish was peppered with hundreds of ugly bullet holes. All the windows were gone, leaving jagged teeth of glass in their place and shards scattered everywhere. Three of the four tires were reduced to rubber ribbons.

Both men gave a start when the Packard abruptly canted to the left, a mortally wounded warhorse collapsing on the battlefield. Heart in his throat, Luca put out a hand to keep Vito from doing the same.

The driver's door drifted open, encouraged by gravity and groaning hinges. The metal edge traced a groove in the gravel, signing the Packard's terms of surrender.

"Rotolo," Luca said. "He still wants the club."

CHAPTER 20

Rat problem

Ruth's nerves were still jangling from being awoken the night before by gunfire in the alley. A disagreement between Vito and a supplier, Luca had explained, but they'd work it out. Standing inside the street door, her back to the stairs, Ruth didn't press for details. She knew it had something to do with beer and that was enough.

Thankfully, Luca didn't take up where they'd left off the last time. If he was still passing judgment on her relationship with O'Malley, it didn't show. Ruth was grateful for his reticence but she hated him for it, too.

She skirted a display of tin washtubs piled on the sidewalk in front of Panetta's Hardware and went inside. The place was warm and cluttered and smelled like the backstage of a busy theater. Musty, with a tang of something oily. Lavender sachets and linseed oil. Enamel paint. Plywood. Copper pipes. Floor to ceiling shelves were full to bursting with everything from spools of rope to sacks of setting plaster. Snow shovels were propped against a corner, next to a pyramid of paint cans.

The only light came through the front windows. Awnings kept the winter sun out, keeping the shop in perpetual twilight.

Mr. Panetta bustled up, short and wide in his canvas apron, hands outstretched to greet his neighbor. "Miss Cross, what do you need today?"

"I, uh." Ruth's courage deserted her. She gazed around the crowded store crammed with shelves and cupboards and tiny boxes of nails and screws. Only a madman or a genius would know where to find anything smaller than a shovel or the washtubs by the front door.

A display box caught her eye, jumbled on the counter with the proprietor's account book, ashtray, and roll of butcher paper for wrapping purchases. *Mulliner's Mucilage.*

Ruth gestured to the box. "I . . . I need some glue."

"Of course, of course." Instead of going behind the counter, Panetta bustled to a shelf. "For paper? Wood? China?"

Hating herself for her cowardice, Ruth grabbed one of the little brown bottles. "This will do."

"Ah, but for paper only." Panetta clicked his tongue in disapproval and held out a white bottle. "Now this. Like a miracle for paper or china. Cardboard, too."

He launched into detailed instructions for mending a mythical broken plate.

"Do you have rat poison?" Ruth blurted in a rush of bravery, interrupting the monologue. "I have a rat problem but I'm not sure how much will do the trick. I'm sure it says on the box--."

"Rat poison? Where did you see rats? In the alley?" Panetta was instantly agitated and appalled, eyebrows jumping and hands flying into the air to punctuate his words. "Thatsa terrible for a nice lady like you. No, no, you can't spend your money on that. Luca should take care of rats. That's his responsibility. I'll tell him right away. Where did you see the rats?"

Ruth gaped at him, unprepared for the sudden drama. "Did I say rat poison?" She gave a nervous laugh. "I meant ant poison. To kill ants. In the kitchen."

"Ah!" Panetta's face lit up with relief and understanding. "Ant poison. Yes, for sure. But if you see rats, you tell Luca. Make him buy the poison."

Ruth left the store with a bottle of miracle glue and a cardboard twist of boric acid. Neither would kill O'Malley even if his next meal was filled with both.

CHAPTER 21

Sign his name good as any man

Cynthia had already gone upstairs to cold cream her face and Owen was almost done with the evening newspaper when someone knocked on the front door.

To his horror, Benny and that odious farmer Al Genovese stood on the front porch.

"Hey, Fishy," Benny boomed loud enough to be heard by the neighbors. "What's shaking?"

"I told you never to come here," Owen whispered furiously.

"Nice kinda welcome." Benny pushed past Owen into the living room, Genovese trotting behind like a circus shadow. "Where's the missus?"

"Never mind Cynthia." Owen reluctantly shut the front door. "What are you doing here?"

"I want Al to sign his name in that pocket ledger book of yours. Make him a proper officer of the Lido Outfit, like we done with Nick."

Owen leaned against the door to stop his legs from folding out from under him. "Why should he sign?" he gasped.

"Alfonse Genovese," the farmer supplied. "I can sign my name good as any man."

No doubt that was the only thing he could write.

"Go get your book," Benny said.

Owen was saved by Cynthia floating down the stairs, lovely and blonde as always in a rosy sweater set. "Mr. Rotolo," she purred, setting eyes on Benny. "How nice to see you again."

Benny turned up the wattage on his smile, damn the man. "The pleasure is all mine." He made a small gesture toward Genovese. "This here is a business associate, Alfonse Genovese. He's looking for business advice from your husband, too."

"Ma'am." At least the farmer had enough manners to take his hat off in the presence of a lady.

"Was Owen able to help you, Mr. Rotolo?"

"Oh, sure. Fishy's the best at his kinda numbers racket."

"Wonderful." Cynthia smiled uncertainly. "Well, I'll let you gentlemen discuss your business affairs in private. Good night."

She went back upstairs, shoulders back and chin held high. With growing despair, Owen knew they'd be having a serious discussion later. The kind of discussion that resulted in him sleeping on the sofa tonight and Cynthia buying more fripperies tomorrow.

It didn't help that Rotolo watched Cynthia's backside until she reached the landing and passed out of sight.

"That's enough," Owen huffed. "We have no business to discuss. I'll thank you to leave my home."

Benny wandered over to the fireplace, picked up a poker and prodded the decorative logs. "Go get the book so Al can sign."

Owen took several deep breaths. "I don't have it."

"Don't have it?" Benny looked over his shoulder, the poker still in his hand. "Why not?"

It was suicide to tell the truth, which was that it had probably been on Zambrano's body when he went into the Mohawk River. Owen's heart thundered so hard he was faint. "I meant that it's not here."

Benny tossed aside the poker, getting ash on Cynthia's rug, and stuck his face in Owen's. "Where is it?"

"It's, it's in my office."

"At the mill?"

"Yes."

"What's it doing there?"

"I have a safe there." The lie made so much sense that he flushed with relief. The lightheaded sensation abated. "It's in my office safe."

"That's real good, Fishy." Benny poked Owen in the

chest. "When I get the Galliano Club all fixed up, I'll have a safe in my office too."

"An excellent idea." Owen nearly tripped over himself going to the front door. "Well, then. No doubt you want to get going."

"Bring the ledger to the pumphouse tomorrow so Al can sign his name. He's done pretty good for the Lido Outfit."

Genovese smiled broadly.

"I'll bring it when I can," Owen managed. "It doesn't do to open the safe very often. I don't want to call attention to things like that."

Benny snorted. "Okay, for now." He plopped onto the white sofa, pulled a scrap of paper out of his pocket and smoothed it on the coffee table, knocking over a china shepherdess and chipping her bonnet in the process. "This is what I want you to put in the ledger."

A simple hand drawn chart, such as a child would make with an unsharpened pencil, showed two rows, one labeled VS and the other ER. The number 5000 was listed under VS. A single column was labeled Money Orders.

"What's this?" Owen asked warily.

"That's the information racket," Benny said. He pulled out another scrap of paper. "When money comes in, you send a money order for twenty percent to my friend. Whatever twenty percent of five grand is."

"A money order for a thousand dollars?" Owen sputtered.

Benny produced a fat roll, extracted a handful of bills, and dropped them on top of the coffee table. "There's gonna be more like that, Fishy. Lots more."

That mad gleam was in Benny's eye again. The room closed in. Owen could barely breathe.

It was a huge relief when Genovese said he had to go home. Benny and the farmer hustled out without mentioning the ledger again, leaving the damning bits of paper with Owen.

Cynthia was not happy, just as Owen anticipated. He let her castigate him before he mumbled an abject apology, collected his pillow and a blanket and went back to the living room.

He lay awake on the sofa in the dark and decided to make up a story about the pocket ledger being destroyed. Miss Camden, the office secretary, was a convenient foil. Perhaps she'd tidied Owen's desk and inadvertently thrown away the ledger. Spilled coffee on it. Even better, she started a fire with a careless cigarette. Maybe Owen could add substance with a little fire in the office and blame it on his pipe. Not enough to actually ruin anything and get on Henry Blick's bad side, but serious enough to be mentioned in the newspaper.

Owen wriggled onto his side, trying to get comfortable. He could solve the ledger problem but the money order demand was another thing entirely.

Postal money orders were cash transactions but still completely traceable. Hopefully, whatever thug was on the receiving end of Benny's blackmail money took precautions, the same way Owen did. No one at Lido Premium had ever discovered the clever accounting that drew money out of the company's coffers and set up the Lido Outfit brewery at the old pumphouse.

"Owen Forbes Fisher, you are a successful man," Owen whispered to himself in the dark. "You are clever. You are capable. You are in the inner circle."

Tomorrow he'd grovel his way back into the marital bed by suggesting that Cynthia buy the champagne bucket she'd been coveting.

CHAPTER 22

Mother will tell you

Tess helped Annie arrange the mountain of white flowers that arrived from Fulton Florist ahead of the engagement party. Jamming stems into Aunt Evelyn's crystal Tiffany vase, Tess recalled Luca's box of pink roses. The roses had probably cost him a week's salary yet Aunt Evelyn had dismissed his gesture with a casual wave of her hand. That evening felt like a lifetime ago.

She wondered what he was doing now.

"Mind what you are doing, Miss Tess."

Tess gave a start and realized that she had kneaded a long-stemmed carnation into a damp blob. Annie clicked her tongue in disapproval and pried it out of Tess's fist.

"Maybe you should finish the flowers," Tess said shakily.

Annie tipped her head to one side. "Go along and change into your party dress. Mind you don't wake Miss Evelyn before it's time."

Tess plodded up the stairs to her room and regarded the simple cream-colored shift that Muriel had picked out when they were trousseau shopping at Van Dyke's. She now had a closet full of dresses that looked like nightgowns and a collection of nightgowns that looked like bedsheets. Her reflection in the mirror wasn't unlike the big portrait of the dead woman in the *Lido Daily Clipper*.

At least two hundred people attended the party that afternoon. Aunt Evelyn looked nearly transparent in an ice-blue dress, her increasingly brittle hair concealed under a matching turban. Breath coming in hushed gasps, she received guests from a wingback armchair in the parlor as Annie hovered behind. Tess's future in-laws, Preston and Muriel Howland stationed themselves on one side of the chair while Tess and James flanked her on the other. James was joined by his younger brother Richard, who had come down from Yale for the occasion.

In contrast to James's hefty build, fleshy face, and sparse mustache, Richard was slim, wiry, and clean-shaven. A champion collegiate boxer, he peppered every sentence with *swell* and a shotgun burst of laughter. It was a *swell* party, Tess was a *swell* girl, he was having a *swell* time. Pops was sure *swell* to increase his allowance.

It was *swell* to be a legacy at Yale. The professors didn't expect too much and *not too much* was his specialty.

Richard laughed loudly at his own wit, clapped James on the back, and feigned a flurry of punches. He was soon bored and wandered off. Tess thought that was *swell*.

Engagement gifts were deposited on a table in the foyer before guests made their way into the parlor to greet their hosts. Everyone was a friend or business associate of the Howland family. The exceptions were a handful of Aunt Evelyn's friends and Mr. and Mrs. Homer Bradshaw. He was the owner of the Adirondack and Western Railroad, partner of the late Uncle Benedict.

Tess watched Bradshaw slyly assess Aunt Evelyn's health. No doubt he would reclaim the house in the name of the railroad as soon as Aunt Evelyn no longer occupied it.

It was hard enough to accept the horrible truth that Aunt Evelyn did not have much longer to live without having to acknowledge the ripple effects. Tess wanted to scream at the unfairness of losing her home. Losing her independence by marrying James. Never working and earning her own money again. Losing Luca.

It was agony to see Aunt Evelyn forcing herself to remain upright in the chair through force of will. She was pitifully thin and obviously in pain. The weight had simply melted off since Saratoga.

Guests spoke gently to Aunt Evelyn but didn't linger. Everyone could see how ill she was.

With a smile pasted on her face, Tess murmured her thanks to all the strangers who passed through the line. Their comments were all variations on *What a suitable match for you, dear,* or *How lucky you are, James. We know your parents are delighted.*

Champagne from the Howland family's private cellar was passed around by Muriel's maids in white pinafores and black bombazine. Guests waited, shallow-bowled champagne coupes in hand, as Preston Howland proposed a toast to the happy couple. It was strange to think that the president of the bank, a remote and humorless authority figure for the past two years, would be her father-in-law. She'd sit at the same table with him for meals. Attempt to make small talk. Be endlessly scrutinized to see if she was a good bargain after all.

James took the opportunity to put his arm around Tess's waist. He pulled her against him even as he held his champagne coupe in the other hand.

Still smiling as Preston droned on, Tess slid nimble fingers over his hand at her waist and pinched the web of skin between his thumb and forefinger. James gave a yelp and spilled his champagne.

"Settle down, James," Preston said archly. Everyone laughed dutifully.

At length a toast was made to the happy couple. Preston pointed at James. Muriel patted Aunt Evelyn's shoulder.

Too late, Tess realized this was some sort of signal.

James grabbed her left hand and put a ring on her fourth finger, driving it over her knuckle. "There you go," he said in triumph.

Tess held up her hand to see the ring. A round diamond gleamed from the center of a filigree basket adorned with engraved flowers. "It's very pretty," she admitted.

"Mother picked it out," James said. "It's platinum."

He leaned toward her, a goofy half-smile on his face and Tess realized that he was going to kiss her. She drew back at the last second. His lips grazed her cheek. The sparse mustache prickled against her skin.

Everyone applauded. More toasts were made, then Muriel invited the assembly to proceed to the dining room for the buffet.

Aunt Evelyn stayed in her chair. Annie appeared with a plate of delicacies. "You run along and get some food," the housekeeper ordered Tess. "I'll take care of Miss Evelyn."

"Are you sure?" Tess knelt by her aunt. "Are you

tired? Do you want to go upstairs?"

"Certainly not," Aunt Evelyn said. Her fingertips were as blue as her dress. "I'm perfectly fine here with Annie."

Tess pressed her aunt's hand. It was ice cold.

James helped her to her feet and escorted her into the dining room with a possessive grip on her arm. "What was that business about?" he whispered.

"What business?" Tess's face hurt from maintaining the fake smile for so long.

"You pinched me!"

"You didn't ask permission before putting your hands on me." Tess shook him off and moved into the buffet line where the server filled her plate. She carried it back to the parlor and sat at the game table by the window. James joined her.

"What if you lost your place at the bank?" Tess asked after long minutes of watching him eat without any attempt to engage her in conversation. "How would you support our family?"

"I'll never lose my place at the bank," James said. "Father is the president." The sparse mustache undulated as he chewed.

Tess recalled joking about the pathetic line of facial hair on James's upper lip with Luca. *A baseball mustache. Nine hairs on a side.* Not only that, but in her lexicon of single-digit numbers, nine was the heaviest, least joyous number.

"It's a hypothetical question, James. What would you do?"

"I wouldn't do anything, because this is silly. I hope you're not going to indulge in silly talk once we're married." James took a bite of creamed chicken and got gravy on the third baseman.

Tess started to feel mean. "What will we talk about when we're married?"

James waved his fork at her. "One doesn't plan conversations."

"Think about it, James. What do we have in common? Do we have the same interests? Opinions on the news of the day? Do we read the same books? What are your thoughts on Marcus Aurelius? I don't even know what you do outside the bank. Do you like sports? Tennis? Baseball? What do you think about the poor girl who was pulled out of the river? Everyone is talking about those terrible pictures in the newspaper but you haven't once mentioned it to me. Who do you think she is? Aren't you curious? I am."

The party quieted as guests settled down to eat. Richard was across the room, balancing a plate on his knee. Tess heard his braying laugh. The food was *swell*.

James continued to fork up chicken and pastry.

"We're getting married, not taking a compatibility test."

"We've never even had a conversation outside the bank. I can't spend the rest of my life talking about loans and collateral."

"You won't be working at the bank anymore." James sniffed the untouched slice of ham on her plate. The entire team twitched.

"Tell me the worst thing you've ever done," Tess said with sudden urgency. "Something you can only tell the most important person in your life."

James frowned. "I've never hidden anything from my mother."

Tess pressed both fists into her lap, her entire body straining for what she knew would never again be hers. "Tell me a secret, James," she said. "Tell me something you don't dare tell anyone else. Something special. A secret just between the two of us."

"You're being a ninny, Tess," James hissed. "Stop it."

"Have you ever taken a risk for love? Would you risk life and limb to build a future with me?"

"I said, stop this right now. People are watching."

"Maybe they can't believe we're so ill-suited." Tess slumped against the back of her chair as despair replaced defiance. "We have absolutely nothing to talk about."

Muriel rang a bell. Two maids wheeled in a cloth-covered trolley bearing a lavish layer cake decorated with red roses. The guests applauded right on cue.

"Mother will tell you the proper things to talk about." James came around to pull out her chair. "It's time for the cake."

CHAPTER 23

Your least apt student

Both Ruth's kitchen and the dance studio were sparkling clean and ant-free when eight couples showed up for Ruth's second ballroom dance class. Henry Blick greeted Ruth with a formal nod before pinning on his name tag.

Another student without a partner showed up. Mabel Hennessey was a schoolteacher whose husband was home with a broken leg. Ruth felt absurdly resentful as she paired Mabel and Henry and began with a review of ballroom holds and the importance of maintaining frame.

Henry easily kept his shoulders back. The rest of the men tended to slouch forward, like they were going to eat their partner's hair.

To help them break the habit, Ruth made them practice holds without a partner.

"Gentlemen, you'll stand with feet together, toes pointing the same direction, not turned out, and knees straight but not stiff." Ruth demonstrated the difference between feet straight and pointing out, conscious of

Henry's eye on her. "Now, feel the weight of your body by raising and lowering your heels."

When the men had all done so, Ruth threw her arms out. "Let's pretend we're directing traffic at the American Corner," she said, earning a laugh. "Don't move your head or shoulders but lift your right elbow and put your hand at your waist. Raise your left hand so that it's level with your head. Turn your hand upward."

Ruth walked around the circle, checking postures. Henry did not need any adjustment.

"Excellent." Ruth beamed. "You've created a protective frame around your partner so that you can control the movements you'll do together and prevent others from banging into her."

With arms in the perfect hold position, she led the men in a circle around the studio floor so they could get used to the position. Their promenade concluded; Ruth had the women join their partner.

"Stand very slightly to his right," Ruth instructed the women as she walked the circle of students. "Keep your head poised and keep looking over his right shoulder. If you continually move your head from one position to another, you'll upset the balance. Now let's practice maintaining our hold."

The couples circled the floor as Mrs. Shaw tapped out a rhythm on the piano. After two circuits all the couples stayed on the beat. Ruth moved on to the waltz.

"We want to achieve continuity and smoothness of movement," Ruth said from the center of the circle. "Some part of the moving foot should always maintain contact with the floor." She slowly brushed the ball of her foot forward against the parquet, then transferred her weight to her toe, executing the ballroom equivalent of tap dancing's ball-change step.

The couples all copied her moves. Soon they progressed to walking through the waltz's rise and fall steps. Like before, Ruth had the men practice their part, then the women, then the couples together in a ballroom hold.

Mrs. Shaw pounded out *The Blue Danube* half a dozen times as the couples whirled around the room. Everyone eventually managed a respectable, if not graceful waltz. As before, Henry steered his partner around expertly. Ruth had no excuse to take Mabel's place. The schoolteacher danced irritatingly well.

At the break, the couples gravitated to the refreshments table for lemonade and cookies. Mrs. Shaw monopolized Ruth for the entire time, with a tale about her lumbago and a swollen foot. Ruth made sympathetic noises and tried to pay attention. Her eyes kept seeking out Henry, tall and lean as he introduced Mabel to his sister and brother-in-law.

They worked on the faster dances after the break, with much breathless hilarity and good-natured competition. The quickstep had all the couples bouncing like India rubber balls. The foxtrot was only slightly more decorous. Mrs. Shaw went through her ragtime repertoire twice before the class was over.

"Thank you, Miss Cross." Henry was the last to leave, trailing Osa and Jack Rutherford out the door.

"Good night, Mr. Blick."

Her students' footsteps faded down the stairs. Ruth was left alone in the suddenly quiet studio. She slipped off her shoes. The soles of her silk stocking were sweaty. The cool parquet floor was a balm to her aching feet as she padded over to the collection bowl. Managing the crowd was a challenge, but the class was much more popular than she'd expected. Ruth decided to treat herself to a new pair of stockings.

The studio door was still open. Ruth was surprised to hear someone running up the stairs. Henry appeared on the landing. "Miss Cross?"

"Mr. Blick." Ruth felt oddly naked in her stocking feet in front of him. "Did you forget something?"

"Miss Cross, I'd like to apologize," he said. "I'm afraid I am your least apt student and my difficulty with the more complex steps is holding back the class."

"Nonsense," Ruth said. "You're doing very well."

"Do you offer private lessons?" Henry asked. "Perhaps this would help me keep pace with the rest of your students."

"Private lessons are two dollars each," Ruth heard herself say.

Henry nodded. "Would Friday evening be possible?"

"Yes, yes." Ruth had to stop herself from gabbling like a fool. "As long as you don't mind practicing to the Victrola. Mrs. Shaw might not be available."

"Thank you." Henry gave her a courtly little bow. "I look forward to it."

"Friday, then. The usual time."

Henry left. Ruth sank onto the piano stool. For one tiny moment, Sunday evenings were forgotten. She allowed herself to feel like a girl again, when a man's touch was rare and thrilling and anything was possible.

The next two days passed both too slowly and in a giddy rush. Ruth taught her Wee Tots class, had a meeting with the mothers making the costumes for the Christmas pageant, and put her hopeful chorus girls through their paces on Thursday evening. Tess Kennedy was no longer a student; Ruth learned from the other girls that Tess was to be married soon to her boss at the bank. Ruth felt a twinge for Luca, whom she'd known was stepping out with the girl, but he was no longer any concern of hers.

On Friday when school let out, thirty kids thundered up the stairs after school for Tap Dance Basics, littering the stairwell with coats and boots and slush from a fresh snowfall. When they left, older children came for Cotillion Dancing, with the usual amount of awkwardness between 12-year-old boys and girls being made to waltz with each other for the first time.

When those classes were over and Mrs. Shaw went home, Ruth had an entire hour to fret, check her hair, and look through her collection of recordings for the Victrola. When she couldn't think of what else to do, she stood at her parlor window and watched Hamilton Street. Finally, a beautiful blue roadster pulled up to the curb in front of her entrance.

"Mr. Blick." Ruth met Henry on the landing. "You brought winter with you."

"So it would seem." His hat and shoulders were dusted with snow.

Henry put two dollars in the collection bowl, hung up his coat and set his hat on the rack. "Do you mind if I take off my jacket?" he asked.

"No, of course not." Ruth spoke easily; all the gentlemen put aside their suit jackets during lessons. Now, with just two of them in the studio, a countering image of O'Malley feeling free to discard his clothes in her presence crept to the surface.

"I have a bad habit of ruining my shirts," Henry said, as he rolled up stained shirt cuffs, revealing forearms striated with lean muscle. "My presence has been required on the mill floor more than customary."

"The past few weeks must have been quite challenging," Ruth offered.

"With a few personnel changes, I believe we are back on stable footing," Henry said. "Unlike myself and the foxtrot."

Ruth gave a nervous laugh. The corner of Henry's mouth lifted.

Without other couples blocking the view, Ruth could use the mirrored wall to good effect. Once Henry saw her perform the steps with no distractions, he immediately saw what to do and mimicked her. Within an hour, he was steering Ruth around the studio in a recognizable foxtrot as George M. Cohan's *Popularity* swelled from the Victrola.

Even more than the first time they danced together, Ruth had the impression of Henry as a man in charge of his body and at ease with himself, despite the ramrod posture and formal way of speaking. She wondered if he had been an accomplished athlete in his youth.

The music ended. They broke apart so she could lift the gramophone needle. "On to the quickstep, Mr.

Blick?"

"Could I request the tango?" he asked. "I had occasion to observe the tango while serving in Argentina and always wished to learn."

Ruth didn't know the tango very well, but she'd seen Rudolph Valentino's performance in *The Four Horsemen of the Apocalypse* and was reasonably sure she could duplicate the steps. Moreover, Henry had paid two whole dollars for the lesson. Ruth was determined to earn it.

"It's a close hold dance," she said. "Lots of knee bends and side slides."

They started with the ballroom hold, shifted position so both looked the same way, then back again. Ruth added the side steps when he was comfortable with the shifting holds, then on to the leaning holds, with her torso balanced against his side. Henry was strong enough to handle all the different positions without lurching or wobbling.

"Now, step forward with your left foot and lean your weight on it," Ruth said as they moved together. "Then step back with the same foot. See how my weight naturally follows." They seesawed as Henry got the hang of the dramatic movements.

Once again, the mirror was enormously helpful. Ruth demonstrated the more intricate steps while Henry watched. Afterward, he executed them as Ruth called out the changes. When he was comfortable with the basics, she threw in something more complex, a turn or small kick.

In short order he was ready for more. Ruth selected suitable music, cranked the gramophone and they swept across the floor in a passable imitation of Valentino and his sultry partner. Ruth tried to keep her wits about her as she leaned against Henry's side or he pressed his cheek against hers.

As the gramophone wound down and the music ended, Ruth saw the clock on the wall. More than two hours had flown by. "I'm afraid that's all for tonight, Mr. Blick," she said breathlessly. "You're doing marvelously well."

"You are an excellent teacher, Miss Cross."

They stepped away from each other. Ruth was very aware of the way the fabric of his shirt clung to his biceps. She didn't know how old Henry Blick was, but he had the musculature of a lanky acrobat.

"You must be wanting to get home and have your supper," Ruth said. She brushed sweaty hair away from her forehead. "Didn't you come straight from your office?"

"I have some refreshments in the car," Henry said. "Would you permit me to fetch them?"

"I, uh, well." Was her tepid lemonade not good enough for him? "Yes, if you like."

Henry headed down the stairs without stopping to fetch his coat from the rack. Ruth went into the bathroom to wash her face, fluff her hair and give herself a little shake. When she came out of the tiny bathroom, she was surprised to see that Henry had spread a checkered blanket over the floor and was unloading a wicker hamper.

"Is this a picnic, Mr. Blick?" Ruth asked, more than a little dumbfounded.

"Of a sort." He took out red and white speckled camp plates and white linen napkins. "Please join me."

Ruth slipped off her shoes and knelt on the blanket, which was already set with flatware and crystal tumblers. The hamper by Henry's side was apparently bottomless as more and more items emerged from it. Bottles of fizzy Saratoga water. Slices of cheese and shaved ham. A loaf of pound cake and two oranges.

"Oranges!" Ruth exclaimed. The fruit was a rare treat, given that New York was so far from where they were grown.

"Do you like oranges?" Henry asked.

Ruth had only tasted an orange once before and that was at a Broadway party. "I think so."

"They're very good for your health," Henry said,

adding smoked salmon sandwiches to the array of food on the blanket.

"This is marvelous, Mr. Blick," Ruth said, surveying the feast spread out on the blanket. "I hardly know what to say."

"You haven't eaten anything yet," Henry observed as he twisted the top off a water bottle and filled her glass.

"Well, I certainly shall."

Everything was delicious. Ruth ate slowly, savoring both the flavors and the surreal experience of an impromptu picnic as a velvety sky filled the studio windows. She sat with her legs curled under herself and the hem of her dress arranged modestly over her knees.

"Tell me about Argentina," she said. "Was it very exotic?"

"It was surprisingly European," Henry said. He sat with his back against the wall. Long legs stretched out by the side of the blanket with his ankles crossed. "Or so it seemed to the young lieutenant I was at the time."

"Was it before the war?"

"Yes." Henry ate some ham. "I was the assistant defense attaché and spent two years chafing."

"You didn't like the job?"

"The position required patience and nuance. I considered myself a warrior, not a diplomat."

"I suppose you've traveled quite a bit."

"I quite enjoy travel," Henry said. "I've been fortunate enough to experience other cultures and appreciate them."

"What places were particularly enjoyable?"

"Japan was more enlightening than enjoyable," Henry said after a pause to consider. "Japanese society is quite restrained and rule-bound, with loyalty to the emperor prized above all. Their notions of honor and fealty are different from ours. I found the lack of individualism quite difficult to accept. Yet the architecture is quite calming and beautiful."

"Do you want to go back?"

"No." The corner of Henry's mouth twitched. "I did not fit comfortably in any abode. Certainly not in their bathtubs. They are shaped like barrels and not suitable for tall people."

Ruth laughed.

"And you, Miss Cross?" Henry reached for his water glass. "Are you fond of travel?"

"Yes, but I've hardly been anywhere so interesting as Japan or Argentina," Ruth said. "New York City, of course. Broadway. I was in *Little Johnny Jones* and a dozen other Cohan shows. I traveled with the Pantages vaudeville circuit in a troupe with three other girls. We saw every small town with a theater and a booking agent."

The blue eye stayed steady on her, waiting for her to tell him more.

"All the theaters were the same but I loved being on the train at night," Ruth confessed. "We'd do four shows a day for two or three days, then it was on to the next booking in the next town. It was a crazy way to live but I loved those late-night train rides. Sometimes I'd see into windows of houses as the train went by. Women in kitchens. Children. Families sitting down to supper. Christmas trees. Their lives were so settled. So different than mine."

Henry picked up an orange and sliced into the rind with a pocketknife. "But you thrived," he said.

Ruth shrugged. "It was hard and thrilling and exhausting all at the same time. You might land a six-month booking and find out that you were on after the ventriloquist but before the man with six monkeys, until the manager got drunk and the whole schedule turned upside down. The audience in Peoria could hate the monkeys but Rochester loved them. Sometimes they liked the songs and hated the comics." Ruth realized that she was rambling and gave a self-conscious cough. "I'm sorry, I'm talking too much."

Henry carefully peeled the orange, assembling bits of peel into a tidy tower on his empty camp plate. "That experience must be how you learned to deal with people so well."

"Me?" Ruth thought about how she'd dealt so poorly with O'Malley. "I don't do anything special."

"You manage your classes very well," Henry said, putting down the pocketknife. "Everyone is ill at ease when they come in, yet within a few minutes you have convinced them that they can dance. Not only convinced, but excited. Everyone in the class wishes to please you and show that your faith in them is justified. I think you are very good at observing people and seeing what they need."

"Everybody can dance, they just have to have confidence," Ruth said. "Dance is so freeing. So many people aren't comfortable in their own skin. Learning to dance helps them feel better about themselves."

"You've very astute." Henry fanned out the orange, creating a giant citrus flower.

"That's very clever," Ruth said, admiring his handiwork. It was time to move the conversation away from herself. "Argentina and Japan. Where else have you been?"

Henry handed the orange to Ruth. "Wherever the Army sent me."

Their fingertips touched and a thrill rippled down Ruth's spine. It was a different sensation than the businesslike ballroom hold. She took the orange. "You were in the war, weren't you?"

"Yes." Henry began to peel the second orange. "Of interest to you, I met Vernon Castle in France, about a year before his death."

"Vernon Castle? What was he like?" Ruth had idolized Vernon and Irene Castle, the couple who had both revolutionized and popularized ballroom dancing. From their base on Long Island, they ran a dance studio and nightclub while making movies and giving live stage performances with their own orchestra. They were hugely popular in Europe as well as the United States. Everyone in the theater knew about Vernon and Irene Castle and the tragedy that befell them.

Born in England, when war broke out with Germany, Vernon enlisted as a pilot in the Royal Flying Corps. He survived the war and was promoted to captain. His unit went to the U.S. for winter training and in February 1918, he took emergency action to avoid a mid-air collision. His plane stalled and crashed. Vernon Castle was only thirty years old when he died. The couple's dance empire died with him.

"He was a good pilot," Henry said. "Castle completed three hundred combat missions and was awarded France's Croix de Guerre. He was doing his duty, like all of us."

"I cried for a whole day when I heard that he died. They were just so wonderful. So creative." Ruth bit into a slice of orange, causing an explosion of juice. She scooped up her napkin to dab at her chin, conscious of Henry's direct, single-eye stare. "Did you always want to be a soldier?"

Henry told her about attending West Point and his military assignments, including France and Russia during the war.

Ruth was dimly aware of an expeditionary force that President Wilson had sent to fight the Bolsheviks in 1918. There had been very little in the news about it.

He looked away. "We were with the British and engaged the Bolshevik forces along the Vologda Railroad. Our front stretched along with our offensive. As winter set in, our position became precarious. The Bolshevik army engaged us along the Vaga River with superior force. We withdrew but it was a running retreat. Our flank was overrun and combat became general."

"I hope you won a medal for surviving such a horrible battle."

"I was cited for stopping the rout and preventing our forces from being pushed into the Arctic Ocean."

"Is that when you lost your eye?" Ruth asked softly.

"As I said, combat became general," Henry pinched

a bit of peel, releasing the sharp scent of orange. "I subsequently retired with the rank of colonel."

"You must have been a very young colonel."

"Yes."

Ruth got the feeling that he had not told many people about the fighting in Russia. "What a silly thing I was then. You were an Army officer fighting a war, while all I was doing was dancing four shows a day."

"Yet perhaps we have more in common than we know. A certain restlessness, perhaps."

"Perhaps." Ruth's heart thumped faster.

Even eating an orange, Henry exuded an almost royal air. "If you could travel anywhere right now, where would you go?" he asked.

"Europe," Ruth said, toying with the last few slices of fruit. "Paris, of course. The pictures are so beautiful. Then Athens. I'd like to see the Parthenon. And Delphi. And Crete. But I'd also like to see the Panama Canal. I've read about it and it seems too fantastic to be real, don't you think? A great big slice through the middle of two continents with tiny trains to pull ships through."

"I admit to great curiosity about the Panama Canal," Henry said.

CHAPTER 24

Bison Club dinner

Owen plunged into the sea of wealth and power surging to and fro in the ballroom of the Elmshore Resort Hotel. The Bison Club had spared no expense to honor Officer Sean O'Malley.

The buzz of masculine voices reverberated off crystal chandeliers brightening forty tables, each ringed with ten chairs. Gold-rimmed plates, antique sterling, and white linen awaited men in black tie and tails or ceremonial police uniforms who milled about, backslapping old friends, greeting new ones, and finally taking seats addressed with engraved name cards.

Thanks to his friendship with Doc Lanigan, Owen was extremely pleased to be at the honoree's table. He had the chair next to Henry Blick, a real coup.

The others at the table were a veritable list of who's who in Lido, starting with Mayor John Peabody. Of course Nathan Packham was there, seated on the other side of Henry Blick. Packham gave Owen a familiar nod as befitting owner to employee, but nothing more.

Jack Rutherford, the head of the Lido Chamber of

Commerce and the current president of the Bison Club, pulled out the chair next to the mayor. Rutherford knew every member, looked like a film star in his evening wear, and made a joke about being Henry Blick's brother-in-law.

The guest of honor barreled in with Doc Lanigan in tow. It was obvious that they'd both been drinking before arriving at the Elmshore. O'Malley wore his ceremonial uniform. Doc Lanigan's evening attire was boyish yet elegant. Their seats were directly opposite Owen and Blick.

Chief of Police Doyle showed up shortly thereafter, in a uniform dripping with gold braid. He brought a guest and made a show of introducing Inspector Ernest Finch from the Postal Inspection Service.

Owen was impressed. O'Malley might be an uncouth Irishman, but the country's oldest and most prestigious law enforcement service had sent a representative to honor him.

Mayor Peabody tapped on a glass with a knife and brought the banquet to order.

Everyone stood for the Pledge of Allegiance and the Bison Club pledge. Four hundred male voices vowed loyalty to family, community, and country. Four hundred breaths ruffled the giant paper gold shields pasted on the walls. Each was embossed with 261, the number of O'Malley's police badge.

Blue and gold crepe paper bunting looped across the ceiling. Bouquets of tiny American flags sprouted from every table.

Standing behind his chair between Blick and Inspector Finch, Owen mouthed the pledges with supreme self-satisfaction. He was two seats away from the mayor and a million miles away from Benny Rotolo.

In the inner circle.

All remained standing as the vicar of Trinity Episcopal Church, who doubled as the club chaplain, gave the invocation. He thanked God for O'Malley's strength and wisdom and begged Him to let the policeman be a role model to children and a guardian of wives and homes. There was a somber chorus of "Amen."

Everyone took their seats. Waiters immediately poured champagne. Thanks to Governor Smith's stance as a "wet," wealthier New Yorkers were getting more and more lax about enforcing the law. Certainly, no one was going to summon Prohibition Bureau agents tonight.

The first toast was delivered by Mayor Peabody, who stood and raised his glass to O'Malley for his heroic lifesaving deed, ridding Lido of a criminal killer, and solving the puzzle of the missing Lido Premium foreman. As applause and shouts of "Hear, hear," rang out, O'Malley guzzled champagne.

Chief Doyle was next, toasting his patrolman with a long-winded accolade to the police department in general and its great task of keeping Lido safe for a future of prosperity and growth. Next came the state senator at the next table who conveyed Albany's great pride in the character of the state's law enforcement officers.

The waiters were kept busy refilling glasses. When the official toasts ended, informal ones circled each table, amid much laughter.

At their table, Doc Lanigan started the round with a call to recognize "Lido's new hero." Everyone drained their glass. After a prompt refill, Jack Rutherford took up the cause with a salute to "Red-blooded manhood." Nathan Packham toasted the fine citizens of both America and Ireland, which prompted Chief Doyle to pound his hand on the table.

Owen couldn't wait for the chance to impress them all. His toast wasn't going to be some forgettable throwaway line like everyone else. He had read the classics.

Inspector Finch toasted Lido's "Valiant men in blue" and then it was Owen's turn.

He stood, wobbling only slightly, and lofted his glass in dramatic fashion. "To Officer Sean O'Malley," Owen declared. "May he always strive to seek, to find, and not to yield."

He got the requisite "Hear, hear" before the men quaffed their champagne. Packham merely gave him a second nod. Owen settled back into his chair, vaguely disappointed with the anemic response.

Blick stood next.

Owen always felt like a stage show conjurer in evening attire but Blick was a cross between a pirate and the king of England, right down to the miniature military medals pinned to his lapel. The black eye patch promised danger while the flinty blue eye scanned the table. Faultlessly tailored tails accentuated wide shoulders and narrow hips. Waistcoats of other middle-aged men might bulge around the middle but Blick was as lean as a cowboy.

Glasses were raised in anticipation. "To wives and sweethearts," Blick said. "May they never meet."

The toast was met with gusts of laughter and celebratory drumming of cutlery on the table. O'Malley and Doc Lanigan in particular howled in mirth.

"Very clever," Owen murmured when Blick sat down again.

"A classic from the British Royal Navy," Blick said.

The corner of his mouth twitched. "Your choice was laudable. I greatly admire Tennyson's *Ulysses*."

"I like your medals," Owen heard himself gush like an admiring schoolboy. "Are they real?"

The single eye raked over him with something akin to pity. "Yes," Blick said shortly and turned to Packham on his right.

Owen flushed and hastily held out his glass for the waiter. Damn Henry Blick and damn Tennyson, too.

The appetizer was shrimp cocktail, served in bowls of cracked ice and topped with wedges of lemon. A dry white sauterne accompanied the shrimp. Owen sampled it and marveled at the quality. First champagne, now white wine. He could only imagine how the Elmshore Hotel acquired such fine liquor and in such quantities in the midst of Prohibition law.

The speeches began after the appetizer. Jack Rutherford stepped up to a podium draped in gold and blue bunting. On behalf of the entire Bison Club membership, he presented a giant loving cup engraved with the name of Officer Sean O'Malley and the date of the banquet. O'Malley nearly stumbled getting up the steps to the podium, then seized the cup by its handles and raised it over his head like a prizefighter.

When the applause died down, the state senator presented the policeman with a plaque and a certificate of appreciation signed by Governor Smith. Not to be outdone, Mayor Peabody produced an enormous gold key to the city.

O'Malley accepted the accolades with barks of laughter at the jokes and smirking humility when the moment called for seriousness. When the presentations were over, he pulled a sheet of paper from a pocket and read a long-winded blather about patriotism, family, and character. He stumbled over several multi-syllable words.

Chief Doyle was the first on his feet when O'Malley finished the oddly impersonal speech, initiating a sustained standing ovation. O'Malley finally tottered back to his seat with his prizes. Dinner resumed. Tomato bisque was followed by prime rib and a stemmed glass the size of a quart jar filled with red wine.

By the time coffee and cheesecake arrived, Owen was seeing two of everything. Doc Lanigan kept laughing and sliding out of his chair. Chief Doyle's face was as red as the stains on the white tablecloth.

O'Malley was a sloppy drunk. His uniform tunic was partially unbuttoned and damp with soup. "I'm a goddamn hero," he slurred, waving his fork and scattering graham cracker crust crumbs. "I got the keys to the city for cracking that dago's head like a walnut."

"Next thing you know," Lanigan said, enunciating his words like they were new. "The dagos will want to join the police."

"A Polack tried to join this year." Chief Doyle dragged a napkin across his mouth.

Blick fixed his attention on the policeman in a way that made Owen want to move to a different seat. "I heard he didn't get in," Blick said. "Why was that?"

"Highest score on the written test," Doyle said and laughed noisily.

"Dombrowski was too short," Lanigan said. He gave a knowing grin. "At least he was when our hero here got done with him."

"Rules," O'Malley chortled. "Rule number one. When you see one dago killing another one, crack his head like a walnut."

From his seat on Blick's right, Packham gave a pronounced sniff. "You saved one life but took another. That's not what we're here to celebrate."

"Mr. Packham, I couldn't agree more," Doc Lanigan said with mock gravity. "We should celebrate that Sean was at the right place at the right time."

"I was there because Miss High and Mighty kicks up her heels for me on Sunday nights," O'Malley said. He leered at the men around the table. "Know what I mean?"

"Women falling at your feet, Sean?" Doyle boomed.

"If a girl's got a past, I can make her fall on her back," O'Malley roared, nearly toppling off his chair. "That dancing teacher shows me a good time."

This time, Blick's attention was a hammer blow. Owen was fascinated by a subtext he didn't understand and the cops were too lubricated to notice. O'Malley convulsed in laughter. Doyle pounded the table. Lanigan laughed until he cried. Packham and Rutherford ignored the raucousness, intent on a private conversation. Inspector Finch looked embarrassed.

Rutherford finally raised his eyebrows in a signal that the banter was unbecoming a gentleman and a member of the Bison Club. Packham pursed his lips in disapproval, but the old man disapproved of everything except money and his one-eyed nephew.

Blick tossed his napkin on the table and stood up. "Let's get some air, O'Malley."

"I'll come," Owen said thickly, curiosity getting ahead of the alcohol coursing through his system.

Together they propelled O'Malley through French doors at the back of the ballroom. They were met by brisk night air, a sky full of stars, and the promise of snow. Beyond the flagstone patio, the Elmshore Hotel's small man-made lake rippled in the moonlight and melted into the dark undulations of the golf course.

O'Malley staggered to the bushes rimming the patio. Presently, Owen heard water plink onto the frozen ground. The scent of urine drifted through the air. Blick faced the lake.

"Good to make room for more, eh?" the cop said when he was finally done. He fumbled with his trouser buttons.

Blick turned that disconcerting single blue eye on O'Malley. "When you spoke about a certain dancing teacher, were you referring to Miss Ruth Cross?"

"Sure." O'Malley finished adjusting his clothing and grinned at Blick. "Get yourself a girl with a past, Blick. If she knows that you know, she'll spread her legs every time."

Owen didn't see what happened but heard a thump. O'Malley doubled up like a boxer going down for the count and spewed vomit into the bushes.

Blick lit a thin cigar and stared at the lake.

When the retching stopped, O'Malley staggered back into the ballroom.

"Who ever heard of an Irish cop who can't hold his drink, eh?" Owen said with a muzzy-headed attempt at humor.

Blick puffed out a perfectly round smoke ring. "Mmm."

Owen brushed a stray snowflake off his sleeve.

Blick continued to smoke and contemplate the lake.

It was too brisk to stay outside. Owen murmured something and went back into the ballroom, leaving Blick to freeze his medals alone.

Inside, a jazz band had the guests in a raucous mood. Chief Doyle and the mayor were telling jokes to a small crowd gathered on that side of the table. Rutherford was glad-handing everyone. O'Malley and Doc Lanigan staggered off to make the rounds. Packham was gone, no doubt to suck a lemon and go to bed on a pile of money.

Annoyed at the way Doc Lanigan was ignoring their friendship, Owen turned to Finch, who seemed reasonably sober.

"The Postal Service must take fraternity among law enforcement officials very seriously," Owen began. "Sending you here to honor Officer O'Malley. I expected you to make a speech."

Finch frowned. "O'Malley had nothing to do with it. Chief Doyle invited me out of pity. Saved me from another meal of corned beef and cabbage at the hotel."

"Then why are you in Lido?"

"To investigate mail fraud," Finch said and tapped the side of his nose. "Keep it under your hat, of course."

"Mail fraud?" Owen exclaimed. "Here in Lido?"

The waiter came by with a tray of cigars. Finch

accepted a thin panetela and went through the sniffing and snipping ritual. When he was ready, the waiter lit the cigar.

Finch inhaled blissfully. "Very serious stuff, mail fraud."

Owen selected the same cigar. It seemed just the thing to add to the gallon of liquor sloshing around in his stomach. "Are the good citizens of Lido steaming stamps off envelopes and reusing them?" he joked.

"I'm on the trail of an extortion artist." Finch exhaled brandy and tobacco fumes. "All the way from Gary, Indiana."

"Indeed." Owen took a cautious puff of the panetela and was rewarded with a bubbling sensation behind his eyes.

"I won't tell you the particulars, of course, but suffice to say that not all stamps are created equal."

"No?" Owen watched as a smoke balloon floated toward a chandelier, wreathing the prisms in vapor. He decided to get drunk with a cigar more often. Damn Prohibition, not that anybody was taking notice of the law tonight.

Finch leaned forward, ready to exchange confidences. "Take a regular two-cent stamp. Red, because it's the hardest color to forge. Now add a tiny dot in a certain spot and pass it to suspected criminals."

He straightened again, smug with accomplishment. "Quite a clever operation if I do say so myself. We passed marked stamps to our primary suspect in Gary, Indiana. We followed those stamps all the way to Lido. And do you know how we identified our extortionist in the first place?"

"No, how?"

"Money orders." Finch blew a smoke ring. "He gets hundreds of money orders from all over the country. Yet he doesn't have a single bank account. Peculiar, wouldn't you say?"

Owen was instantly stone-cold sober.

CHAPTER 25

Fire brigade

Luca passed an unremarkable Sunday with Enzo, Rosaria and the children. No one spoke of the smokehouse and the remaining debris was covered by snow. He got back early enough to see *So's Your Old Man* at the Strand Theatre with Karol. The two friends ate a late supper at McSweeney's, too, a belated celebration of Karol's new job. So far, things at the mill were going smoothly. The anticipated resentment from the Italian workers had yet to materialize. Karol hadn't run into Mr. Fisher, either.

On the way home, they stopped at Alessi's newsstand for the evening edition of the *Lido Daily Clipper*. Another article about the mystery woman from the river was on the front page under the simple headline ***STILL UNIDENTIFIED***.

"You think they'll ever find out who she is?" Karol tucked the paper under his arm.

"She looks like the girl on the cover of a magazine." Luca told Karol about the letter that led to *The Red Book* magazine which was on display next to the bottle of

Liquore Galliano in the Galliano Club saloon. So far there'd been no response from the editor. "It was exciting but we must be wrong."

Back at the boarding house, Luca set up the chessboard in his room while Karol read the article out loud. All the same few facts about the poor dead woman were hashed and rehashed, nothing new added.

"It's all the same story," Karol exclaimed. He turned a few pages, sucked in his breath and muttered something in Polish.

"What's the matter?" Luca rarely heard Karol swear in any language.

Karol folded the newspaper in half and held it out. "Bottom of the page."

Luca took the newspaper. His eyes fell on a studio portrait of Tess looking pale and serious.

KENNEDY-HOWLAND ENGAGEMENT ANNOUNCED

"Howland is a lump of butter with money." Luca pitched the newspaper to the floor. "His father is president of the big bank downtown."

He couldn't stand the look of mingled surprise and sadness on Karol's face, couldn't stand the small room with its cabbage rose wallpaper, couldn't stand the thought of Howland pawing Tess.

A lonely future stretched ahead of him, every day the same as the one before as he made sandwiches and poured beer and plugged in the electric percolator. Losing Tess wasn't so much as a stone in his heart as a boulder crushing his chest until he could hardly breathe.

Luca lurched out of his chair, sending the chessboard flying. Kings and pawns alike sprayed across the floor. He snatched his mackinaw off the hook and threw himself out of the room.

You're not a quitter. But he had no choice but to quit now. Tess's aunt was really going to make her niece go through with it. Become Mrs. James Howland.

Luca blundered away from the boarding house in no particular direction. A dago who spoke English with an accent and lived in a rented room in East Lido was never going to meet with Evelyn Kennedy Thompson's approval, even if he did have two thousand dollars. He would never measure up.

James Howland was the personification of the money and security Evelyn was determined her niece would have.

He was halfway down the block when Karol caught up to him. Neither spoke as the two men trudged along, hands in pockets, their breath curling into the night. There were no streetlights this far from Hamilton

Street.

The rest of East Lido was asleep. The only sound in the darkness was the squeak of the hard-packed snow under their boots.

Walking with his head down, Luca didn't care where they were going. A few lights burned here and there, behind drawn curtains, but for the most part the houses were dark and silent, huddled together along the narrow streets as if for warmth.

"You see what I'm seeing?" Karol elbowed Luca, forcing him to look up.

A flickering orange light mottled the sky to the east.

"*Oddio*," Luca swore. Something was on fire near Third Street, the lane running parallel to the alley behind the club.

They both broke into a run, skidding and sliding, as they headed toward the flames. At the same time, a clanging bell heralded Lido's fire brigade.

As they neared the fire, the bell was lost in a bedlam of shouts and screams. Dozens of people in pajamas, robes, and hastily thrown on overcoats were in the street with buckets of water and snow desperately trying to keep the fire from engulfing nearby homes. Luca and Karol joined in. Soon a ragged human chain was passing buckets up and down as fire licked into the sky, chased by a whiff of gasoline.

Burning wood imploded with a deafening crash and a volcano of sparks. Cries sounded as everyone cringed back. A pumper truck maneuvered its way down the narrow street. The bucket brigade was chivvied out of the way. Karol and Luca watched, both trying to catch their breath in the sooty night air, as the firehose spewed water from the truck onto the remnants.

When the smoke cleared, the line of maple trees still stood. The cement backboards of the handball courts were sooty, but otherwise unharmed.

But the shed belonging to the Galliano Club, where the team's baseball uniforms and equipment were stored and where Luca had thought to brew beer, was gone.

It was long past midnight by the time Luca and Karol stumbled back to the boarding house, both stinking like smoke and too tired to talk.

CHAPTER 26

A very nice luncheon platter

Without the horror of a Sunday night visit from O'Malley, Ruth didn't even mind when her Wee Tots class was followed by a spirited discussion between the mothers over costumes for the dance studio's Christmas pageant. The Wee Tots class would play a flock of sheep.

Eventually it was decided that sheep costumes would be made out of sheeting and cotton balls, no quilting required, with wire ears and a red bow around the neck. Of course, sheep would have worn bows when they came to see Jesus in the manger on Christmas day.

Ruth knew better than to argue with the mother of a Wee Tot.

As mothers and children clattered down the stairs, Ruth heard a heavy tread coming up. She stepped onto the landing to see Henry Blick standing halfway up the stairs.

He wore a gray fedora and matching wool overcoat with the collar pulled up. In the poorly lit staircase, he was a shadow.

"Mr. Blick," Ruth exclaimed. "Class isn't until Wednesday."

"Would you accompany me to lunch today, Miss Cross?" Henry asked. "There's something I'd like to discuss with you."

"Lunch?" Ruth said.

"Buckner's does a very nice luncheon platter," he said.

Ruth nearly gasped at such a thrilling invitation. Buckner's was the nicest restaurant in Lido, but she knew it by reputation only. Her last meal outside the apartment had been a sandwich at the drugstore counter. The egg salad in her icebox could wait.

"What a lovely surprise, thank you. I'll just get my coat and hat."

"I'll wait for you outside," Henry said.

Ruth was dry mouthed with excitement as she ran into her apartment to change. Another man would have assumed he could wait in the warmth of her parlor, not giving her reputation another thought. Henry Blick was a real gentleman.

When she went outside, wearing her best hat and the red coat with the brooch pinned to the shoulder, Henry was on the sidewalk next to a blue roadster with a leather top and a winged hood ornament. He opened the passenger door and helped her in. It was a big vehicle and Ruth had to step onto the running board before settling into the luxuriously padded seat.

She folded her hands in her lap and enjoyed the view as Henry steered the heavy vehicle through Lido to Buckner's in the West Park neighborhood. Once there, it was hard not to gawk at the frescoed walls or the dramatic brass sconces.

The maître d' called him "Mr. Henry," asked after Mr. Nathan's health, and brought them to a skirted table in an alcove draped with damask and tassels, giving them almost total privacy. Ruth didn't know who Mr. Nathan was but it was clear that Henry was a regular at the restaurant.

The menu had no prices. Ruth deferred to Henry when it came to ordering. He asked her if she preferred cream soup or clear. They settled on cream of celery soup to start and trout almondine for the main course. The waiter brought a bottle of French mineral water without being asked.

The soup was ladled from a tureen into shallow bowls rimmed with gold filigree. It was decadently rich, with bits of celery floating in a creamy chicken stock.

"What did you need to speak with me about?" Ruth asked after a few spoonfuls of heaven spent surreptitiously watching Henry Blick. He sat without resting against the back of his chair and skimmed his spoon over the surface of the soup to fill it.

His table manners were impeccable. His fine worsted wool suit was beautifully cut. The jacket was precisely tailored to reveal starched white cuffs and heavy gold cufflinks decorated with a military insignia.

Henry's spoon slowed its journey across the bowl. "I recently heard an individual make unseemly comments in reference to you."

The air went out of Ruth's lungs. She put her spoon down very carefully. "Are you a member of the Bison Club?" she asked.

"Yes."

"Did you hear these remarks at the banquet for Officer Sean O'Malley?" Ruth was so stiff with tension her mouth would barely form the words.

"Yes." Henry buttered a roll, seemingly unaware of her reaction to his words.

"And you want to know if what he said was true." Tears of humiliation stung Ruth's eyes. O'Malley talked himself into her bed to paw and use her, and she'd been stupid enough to trust him. Of course, O'Malley hadn't kept his word.

Henry patted his lips with his napkin. "No, I'd like to put an end to what appears to be blackmail."

Ruth looked down, rapidly losing the ability to control her emotions.

"He implied that he was extracting sexual favors from you, in return for concealing certain details about your past," Henry said. "I believe that falls under the definition of blackmail. Am I incorrect?"

O'Malley wasn't enough. Henry Blick's betrayal was a sharp, stabbing physical pain.

"Is that what you want, too?" Ruth asked. "Sexual favors?"

"Good grief, Miss Cross," Henry said indignantly. "Of course not."

To make her humiliation complete, she had misjudged a perfectly decent man. Ruth began to sob. She fumbled blindly for her purse, but Henry was faster. He pressed a monogrammed square of cotton into her hand.

Ruth cried harder. It took forever to get herself under control again.

"I'm sorry I could not present this news to you in a less upsetting manner," Henry said when she quieted.

"I apologize for making a scene." Ruth pressed his handkerchief to her eyes. She was hurt, broken, and beyond embarrassed.

"Blackmail is a particularly vulgar crime," Henry said.

Ruth's chest hurt with the effort not to break down again. "Especially when it's all true."

Henry didn't reply but the force of his attention gave her strength.

"My real name is Ruthie June Crosswater," Ruth said. "I've been on my own since I was fifteen, dancing for my supper. Vaudeville, Broadway, touring companies. Anything I could get." Ruth felt the tears cascade down again. "A dancer named William Wilson said he was in love with me. We were supposed to get married but our act didn't do well and he said he wanted to wait until we could do it up right. He ran out on me after I got pregnant. I was looking for a job in Poughkeepsie when I got sick and lost the baby. It happened in a public place. When I got out of the hospital, the police arrested me. I spent six months in jail for indecency and lewd behavior."

The silence grew. Ruth squeezed her eyes shut with the effort to keep from crying again.

It was over. She'd given herself to O'Malley for nothing. What little money she had would get her as far away as Newport or Boston. Rich people lived there. Maybe she could get a job as a maid.

"You have suffered a series of grave misfortunes," Henry said at length, his voice gentler than before. He continued to look at her squarely, evincing neither horror nor revulsion nor guile. "Please accept my sympathies."

"O'Malley found out," Ruth gulped. "He said if I didn't do what he wanted, he'd make it public and ruin me."

Henry's lips tightened. "Officer O'Malley has attempted to benefit from your misfortune in a manner I find coarse and unacceptable. Please do not misunderstand my reasons for bringing Officer O'Malley's indiscretion to your attention. It is my intention to negate his claims and ensure that your situation in Lido is not diminished in any way."

"Mr. Blick," Ruth said as tears threatened again. "Everything I just told you is true. Officer O'Malley has the police report from Poughkeepsie."

"Have you seen it?" Henry asked.

Ruth blinked. "Well, no."

"Then how do you know for certain that it is in his possession?"

"He said so."

Henry picked up his spoon again. "Is the soup not to your liking? Would you prefer something else?"

"No, it's lovely." Ruth tried, but her hand shook so badly that the creamy broth slopped back into the bowl. Henry Blick's bland reaction to her sordid past was baffling. Either he wasn't listening, or he didn't understand the severity of her scandal. Both options were equally impossible, which left her with no explanation.

As if he knew what she was thinking, Henry cleared his throat. "You have shared your story, Miss Cross. Permit me to share mine."

Ruth put down her spoon.

"After years as a soldier, I left the army with a chest full of medals, one eye, and lungs permanently weakened by poison gas. My sister graciously gave me a home and my uncle gave me a position. I have attempted to repay them with diligence and honest affection. My financial situation is comfortable. In addition to an inheritance and a generous salary, I have a military pension. I read a great deal of history and I know how to organize a fight. Please let me use whatever small talents I have to help you."

"There's nothing you can do," Ruth said. "I made a terrible mistake and Officer O'Malley took advantage of it. My past will never go away. I'm . . . I'm soiled." *Whore.* She couldn't bring herself to say the word aloud.

"That is not a permanent condition," Henry said.

"It is for some people." Ruth pressed the handkerchief to her eyes again.

"At least allow me to share my plan."

"A plan?" Ruth echoed. "How could you have a plan?" Yet even as she spoke, Ruth knew a soldier would think of something better than rat poison.

"First, we cannot discount the possibility that Officer O'Malley lied to you and has no proof in his possession," Henry said. "With your permission, I will engage the Pinkerton Agency to investigate."

Ruth considered the offer. "All right."

"Second, will you do me the honor of attending my sister's birthday celebration this coming Sunday?" Henry asked. "My brother-in-law has reserved the Candyland Supper Club for a formal ball, with a house party to follow."

Lunch at Buckner's was one thing, but an invitation to Osa Rutherford's birthday party was another matter entirely. It was the social event of the year, celebrated by the wealthiest and most influential in Lido, many of whom had attended the Bison Club banquet.

Henry gave a nod as if he'd read her mind. "Many of the same men who heard Officer O'Malley's claims will attend. When they see us together, his words will be dismissed as fiction. The crass longings of a man whose desires exceed his social standing."

"You can't do that." Ruth gasped at his casual confidence. If Henry was wrong, he'd be ridiculed for carrying on with another man's whore and she'd be mocked all the way to the train station.

"My social position in Lido is unassailable," Henry

said. "I'm quite confident in the outcome."

"Why would you take such a risk?" Ruth asked.

"I have a keen personal interest in your welfare, Miss Cross, although I do not presume that my interest is returned." The blue eye conveyed a meaning that only added to the chaos thrumming through Ruth's veins. "But in the interest of honesty, I confess to a secondary motive. A very fine employee of mine wished to join the police department. Officer O'Malley was instrumental in preventing him from doing so. Mr. Dombrowski's loss is our gain, but he was unfairly treated. It would give me no little satisfaction were Officer O'Malley to experience a fitting retribution."

"You mean I'm not the only one he's . . . he's . . . cheated?"

"It is safe to assume that Officer O'Malley's unsavory behavior has affected a wide circle." Henry poured more water into both glasses. "And is likely to continue."

His forthrightness challenged her to accept his invitation, to trust his plan. To fight back. Ruth felt like she was falling from a great height.

"Thank you," she breathed. "I accept your invitation."

The corner of Henry's mouth twitched. "Excellent. Osa will call on you tomorrow morning to shop for evening wear. My account at Van Dyke's is available to you."

"Van Dyke's?" It would take Ruth a year to earn enough to buy a pair of silk stockings from Van Dyke's, let alone an evening dress. "No, no. I could never repay you, Mr. Blick."

The waiter appeared, deftly removed their soup bowls, and replaced them with plates of fish and potatoes, with a side of greens simmered with sweet peppers that was a Lido specialty.

When they were alone again, Henry cleared his throat. "Possibly I have not made my intentions sufficiently clear, Miss Cross. I find you to be a most captivating woman in all regards. You are both intelligent and vivacious. Undeniably beautiful. My life has already been markedly enriched by your presence and I ardently wish to reciprocate. Shopping at Van Dyke's is a minimal effort, at best, but please accept this small token of my esteem in the spirit in which it is extended."

Ruth opened her mouth, but no words came out. Once again, Henry Blick had stunned her into silence.

It took her some time to find words, any words. "Are you always this direct?" Ruth finally asked.

"I'm fifty-one years old, long past the age when being coy serves a purpose." He paused. "Given that we'll be attending a social function to establish a relationship that refutes Officer O'Malley's claims, may I call you Ruth?"

Ruth wanted to laugh, cry, dance, pray, yet not budge from Henry Blick by even so much as an inch.

She picked up her fork. The rich aroma of the food made her mouth water. Her hand no longer shook. "Yes, you may," she said softly and met the blue eye with a smile. "Henry."

CHAPTER 27

You're the connection

The whiskey was gone.

The niche under the stairs was a dark, empty space. Bags of onions were slumped aside. The wooden panel was propped against the stairs instead of slotted into place.

It was impossible, but all twelve cases of whiskey were gone. An investment of over five thousand dollars, sure to pay off double that amount.

Luca's first reaction was to search the cellar's collection of barrels and kegs. None had been shifted or rearranged. Nothing was hidden in the maze.

He checked the door leading to the gravel lot. It was locked. No one had forced it open; the club hadn't been robbed.

"*Oddio*," Luca muttered. The only answer was that Vito took the cases of whiskey. Only Vito and Luca knew where they were hidden; not even Guido or Sonny had been told.

The club's twelve cases of whiskey were probably in a closet in Vito's house. The boss was drinking the club's finances to death.

Three days had passed since the shooting behind the club. The back door had been replaced but otherwise the damage was mostly confined to Vito's Packard. O'Malley inspected the damage. Said he'd write a report but there wasn't anything the police could do about dago-on-dago crime.

There was no doubt in Luca's mind that Benny Rotolo was to blame for the drive-by shooting. The bootlegger wasn't content with merely selling beer at outrageous prices, he wanted to intimidate Vito into selling the club. The boss had been shaken by the shooting and remedied the situation with Old Bushmills and a new Packard bought with the insurance money.

Luca was all for a confrontation, but Toby Gleason had warned him off the idea, pointing out that Rotolo had guns, money and an army of thugs, while Luca just had two fists and a head like concrete. A smart man would complain to Chief of Police Doyle, seeing as how he was taking Rotolo's money. With the city already smarting from the way Nick Procopio had cast a shadow over its reputation as a good place to live, Doyle didn't need Rotolo's antics appearing on the front page of the *Lido Daily Clipper*.

The conversation with Toby gave Luca an idea. He rounded up the reporters who'd been hanging around and showed them the damage. Gave them a quote from Lucky Lombardo hinting at rivals to the Galliano Club. Maybe the notoriety would make Rotolo think twice about hitting the club again.

Luca slotted the panel into place, hiding the empty niche. Grabbing a gallon of roasted peppers for sandwiches, he headed upstairs, carefully swinging the false pantry into place before closing the door and carrying the jar of peppers into the saloon.

"Good morning, Mr. Lombardo." Inspector Finch waited with his back to the bar, one foot propped on the brass rail, his fedora held idly in one hand.

Luca nearly dropped the heavy glass jar at the sight of the lawman making himself comfortable in the empty saloon. "Good morning," he said and went behind the bar to deposit the peppers on the work counter.

Finch's sandy hair was neatly parted and plastered flat. "I understand the club's not open yet but your doorman let me in."

"I always come early to get things ready." Luca felt very uncomfortable alone with the postal inspector. "Vito's not here yet."

"I didn't come to see Mr. Spinelli." Finch tossed his hat on the bar top. "In fact, it suits me fine that he's not here. I expect he'd tell me he knows nothing about the shooting that happened here a few nights ago."

"He knows," Luca said. "He was here when it happened. We both were."

"Officer O'Malley doesn't seem too concerned." A grimace of disgust crossed Finch's face. "But I am. Mr. Spinelli is being encouraged to pay his blackmailers. Vincent Salerno and his cohorts."

Luca shook his head. "Vito still says he hasn't gotten any letters."

"Mr. Spinelli is lying."

"I only know what Vito tells me."

Finch moved around the saloon, his tweed overcoat swinging gently. He studied the picture of the Galliano Club baseball team. "A club team, I see. Play in a city league?"

"The Lido Industrial League," Luca said.

Finch tapped the photograph. "I see you here."

"First baseman."

"Good record?"

Luca wasn't sure if Finch was asking about the team or him. "We took the pennant last year. Lost it this year to the Teaberry Knitting Mill."

"You're very popular." Finch pivoted to confront Luca. "Lucky Lombardo. Battled a killer. Helped the authorities find the body of a murder victim. Gives you a certain stature in your community, doesn't it?"

Luca waited. The conversation had taken a strange turn.

Finch came back to the bar. "Tell me about Enzo Russo. A farmer. Lives on Bell Road. He's your cousin, isn't he?"

"Yes. Enzo's my cousin."

"Both from Calabria, I believe. The same village. Serra San Bruno."

Twin shivers of fear and uncertainty traced up Luca's spine. Exactly how much did Finch know about the past? "That's right."

"I have reason to believe that your cousin also received letters from Vincent Salerno."

The shivers coalesced into a body blow. Luca put a hand on the bar to steady himself at the thought of *La Mano Nera* going after Enzo. "No, it's not possible. Enzo would tell me if he got a letter."

"Let us drop this façade of ignorance, Mr. Lombardo," Finch said. "Your cousin has received at least one blackmail letter courtesy of Vincent Salerno and his network targeting financially successful Italian immigrants. Either he didn't pay, or he didn't pay enough. The recent damage at his farm was a message that he's out of time."

"Enzo said the children were playing with dynamite used to break up rocks."

"Or maybe your cousin had a reason to lie to you. Victims rarely discuss their predicament with their blackmailers."

Luca shook his head. "I don't understand."

"Vito Spinelli and Enzo Russo. Both received blackmail letters postmarked from Gary, Indiana. Both suffered significant property damage. What else do these two men have in common, Mr. Lombardo?"

Thoughts swirling, Luca could only shrug.

"You." Finch nodded. "You see, one of the first steps when investigating crime is to look for connections. And what did I find? You. You're the connection, Mr. Lombardo. A single man who has nothing."

Luca made a sound of protest. Finch held up a hand and continued. "Oh, I've checked. No family, no property, nothing except your job and a few dollars in the bank. Perhaps your new-found notoriety made you realize how little you have. Those around you have so much more. Perhaps you decided that it was time they gave some to you."

Luca could barely believe what he was hearing. Was Finch actually accusing him of blackmailing his boss and his cousin? Is that what Uncle Samma did instead of catching real crooks?

"Or did your picture in the newspaper create

problems?" Finch lifted his eyebrows. "Perhaps you've got a criminal record back in Italy. Time to collect what you can before you're deported."

Luca froze at the prospect of being charged with Orsini's murder after so many years. All he could do was stand and stare at the postal inspector.

"Is there anything that you'd like to tell me, Mr. Lombardo? Something that would keep both of us from wasting time? Or perhaps I should be asking if you've come into any extra money recently? Should I ask the Lido police to search the premises? The boarding house where you live?"

Luca thought of the money he'd earned rumrunning with Toby Gleason, hidden in his room at Mrs. Esposito's along with the Lido Outfit pocket ledger and his citizenship papers. He forced his jaw to unlock. "I would never do anything to hurt Enzo or Vito. If Enzo got a letter, he would have told me."

"Let's go ask him, then."

"What? Now?"

"Unless you have a reason not to." Finch settled his fedora on his head, his smile and cleft chin accentuating a gleam of smug self-satisfaction.

"All right, I'll go with you." Luca got his mackinaw and deposited Guido behind the bar.

Finch drove a black Ford, the same as every other

black Ford clogging the streets. Neither man spoke on the way to Bell Road, until Finch asked which house and Luca directed him to the Russo farm.

Rosaria came out of the house, the baby on her hip and a flowered apron over her dress.

Luca hopped out of the Ford and waved.

"Luca! What a surprise." Rosaria's face fell when she saw the postal inspector get out of the car.

Introductions were made and Rosaria led them in, inviting the two men to take a seat in the dining room. Luca could tell that she wanted to speak to him in private but was too good a hostess to leave a stranger alone in her house.

Finch handed her a card. "Thank you for speaking with me, Mrs. Russo. Is your husband available?"

Jiggling the baby at the same time, Rosaria glanced at the Post Office seal then focused on Luca. "What's this about?"

"Your husband, Mrs. Russo," Finch said before Luca could answer.

"Enzo went to Camden to look at a cow." Rosaria lifted her chin in pride. "The new barn has room for twelve."

"Do you mind if we wait?" Finch asked.

Rosaria looked at Luca. The baby yawned.

"It's important," he said.

"I'll put the baby down and make coffee." Rosaria bustled into the kitchen.

Luca wanted to run after her and explain but Finch's eyes kept him pinned to the chair.

Rosaria brought coffee and thick slabs of apple cake. Finch complimented her food, Rosaria beamed and launched into a long explanation of building up the farm. The children were next. As Finch plowed his way through the cake, she told him how clever Rocco and Matilda were, how well they were doing in school and how much they adored Luca.

"He's their zio," she said. "Luca is like an uncle to them."

She beamed at Luca who wanted to search every drawer and closet in the house. But surely if *La Mano Nera* had threatened them, Rosaria wouldn't be acting like she hadn't a care in the world.

By his second piece of cake, Luca was reasonably sure that Finch was a liar. Maybe Uncle Samma was angling for something.

"Is he, now." Finch shifted uncomfortably in his seat and drank the rest of his third cup of coffee.

Rosaria jumped up. "More?" she asked and reached for his cup.

Finch held up both hands. "Thank you, Mrs. Russo. I couldn't eat or drink another drop."

"You didn't like my cake," Rosaria said. "You only had two pieces."

"No, no, everything was delicious." Finch flushed. "It's just that I have to get back to Lido soon."

"I'm sorry you have to wait, but my Enzo is very serious about getting the best cows. For milk, you understand."

Finch checked his watch and seemed to come to a decision. "Mrs. Russo, I know we said we were waiting for your husband, but perhaps you could answer some questions for me."

"Of course."

"I've heard that you experienced an accident on the farm recently. Damage from an unexplained fire."

"The smokehouse," Rosaria offered by way of explanation.

"What happened?"

"The children." Rosaria was wary now. "You come to take my children away?"

"No, no, not at all." It was clear Finch had not expected her to leap to that conclusion. "Have you received any alarming letters lately?"

Rosaria frowned.

"Letters asking for money," Finch clarified.

"You mean letters from the bank?" Rosaria snatched Finch's plate away. "You're from the bank or the Post

Office? Make up your mind."

"I assure you--."

"*La Mano Nera* letters," Luca interjected.

Rosaria gasped. "*La Mano Nera*!"

Luca touched her arm. "You'd know if Enzo got a letter like that, wouldn't you?"

"*La Mano Nera*!" Rosaria repeated, a wild stare going from Luca to Finch as she made a hasty Sign of the Cross. "You eat my cake and drink my coffee and ask me about my children and then you surprise me with *La Mano Nera*? What kind of a man does that?"

Finch blinked, clearly flustered by the force of her emotional outburst. "I apologize, Mrs. Russo--."

"No, we don't talk about *La Mano Nera* here. It's like saying you want to die!"

"Please, please, calm yourself." Finch held up both hands. "I simply asked if you received any letters of that nature."

"No, never any letters." Rosaria's hands pummeled the air in extreme agitation as words spilled out. "Everyone knows about *La Mano Nera* but those criminals aren't here. *Madonna mia*, not here. Lido is a good place. A good place for our children and you keep your hands off them!"

"I understand. Truly." Finch was red-faced. "Please calm yourself, Mrs. Russo."

Rosaria lapsed into Italian as the tirade continued.

Luca finished his coffee, letting Finch fend for himself.

"Please." Finch's authoritative attitude finally overrode Rosaria's outburst. "There's no need to jump to conclusions. However, if you or your husband receive any alarming correspondence, please bring it to the courthouse in Lido. The address is on my card."

Rosaria collected herself enough to glower at Finch. "That's really why you came? To ask about letters we don't have?"

Finch apologized again for upsetting her, emphasizing that he had no designs on her children.

Luca kissed Rosaria, promising to come on Sunday like always, and the two men left.

Once again, they rode in silence. Finch set the brake as the Ford stopped in front of the Galliano Club. "Round one to you," the postal inspector said. "But I'll be watching you, Lombardo."

"Maybe you're wrong. Maybe nobody's getting letters."

"Just what I'd expect you to say."

Luca got out. The Ford rumbled away.

He walked into the club to see Benny Rotolo standing at the bar.

CHAPTER 28

The offer still stands

"Well," Benny drawled. "If it ain't the sheik himself. I see the papers are calling you Lucky now. Personally, I don't see the resemblance."

"Hello, Rotolo," Lombardo said. "What are you doing here?"

Benny hooked a thumb toward Spinelli behind the bar. The old man made a lousy cuppa joe even if a shiny electric percolator did all the work. The stuff in Benny's cup tasted worse than Bud's brew at Perk's. "Having a little talk with Spinelli here. Supplier to customer."

Lombardo didn't even take his coat off, but swiveled his head, taking in Broz and two of his boys at a table, all angled to face the door. "We're all paid up. You didn't have to bring your collection boys."

"The boys keep me company." Benny took a sip of Spinelli's dishwater. "As for the beer, the price is going up. Next time it'll be seventy a barrel, not sixty."

"It wasn't enough that you shot up the back of the club?" Lombardo asked, fists clenched.

"Hey, I got no idea who did that," Benny protested.

"I want to buy this place, not rip it apart."

"It's not for sale."

"My offer still stands. Twenty-two thousand, wasn't it." Benny raised his eyebrows in a question to Spinelli. "I could even go as high as twenty-four. What do you say old man?"

Quick as a wink, Lombardo grabbed Benny's arm and turned him around. "Don't try to run me out of business, Rotolo. It's not going to happen."

"Hands off the goods, Sheik." Benny yanked his arm out of Lombardo's grasp as Broz started to come out of his chair. "Last time I checked, Spinelli owned this business, not you."

"Luca, settle down." Spinelli quavered. His walrus mustache trembled. "Seventy a barrel is okay."

Broz sat down again.

"Yeah, Luca, settle down." Benny mimicked the crack in the old man's voice. "If the boss here decides to sell the club, I'll still give you a job. Dishwasher. Maybe trash collector."

"Your business is done," Lombardo said, stone-faced. "Seventy a barrel. Eight barrels."

"Twelve," Benny countered.

"Eight."

"Ten," Spinelli said. "We always get ten."

"Ten." Benny grinned as Lombardo capitulated.

Back in the Cadillac, with Broz behind the wheel and his boys and their hardware in the back seat, Benny felt like celebrating. Spinelli looked bad, as bad as a mug who'd taken a punch and was still standing but knew he was going down for the count. Big Vinnie's threats were the first punch, the hike in the price of beer was the second and the next demand for cash would be the haymaker that put him on the canvas.

The sky was clear and Hamilton Street was lively. Stacks of tin buckets flanked the doorway of Panetta's Hardware next to the Galliano Club. A placard in the window of Fiori's market across the way advertised prices for bullhead and trout. A couple of blocks further down, the big sign for the Bella Napoli Pastry Shop caught Benny's attention. Maybe he should bring back some almond cookies for Trixie, make her stop fretting over Annunziata.

"Drive around the neighborhood," Benny instructed Broz. "I wanna see Nick's old place."

"Sure, Mr. Rotolo."

Benny settled back in the passenger seat. Broz was steady as a rock. Never had to be told anything twice and was a good driver. Ten times better than Al Genovese who constantly fretted about his wife and having to milk his damned cows.

In fact, Al had run out of ways to be useful. He only

had that one bit of dirt on Spinelli and Lombardo. That was used up, so to speak. Benny decided he'd been too quick to bring the *cafone* along. Fishy sure seemed to think so.

Broz turned off Hamilton and they maneuvered up a side street, past the double decker houses that leaned into each other. Sagging porches top and bottom. Two front doors, one for the family on the first floor, the other for the one on the top. Even in wintery weather, every house was strung with laundry.

His cousin Nick's place came into view, looking just the same as it ever did. Benny wondered if Maria Teresa would stay in Lido, being a killer's widow and all. This wasn't Chicago where the widow of a made man would be taken care of. Clothes, shoes for the kids, another husband if she wasn't a dog or a screamer.

The situation here was different. Maria Teresa Procopio was a rich widow. Nick never spent a dime of the money he made from the beer racket and kept working at that lousy mill to boot.

The house was the same old clapboard leaning Tower of Pisa. Clumps of weeds, slimy with melted snow, hugged the foundation. Paint was peeling off the porch. Stakes for tomatoes along one side, evidence of a neglected garden.

Maria Teresa should clean the place up, Benny

thought. Spend a sawbuck or two. Otherwise, if she didn't want Nick's share, she should give it back.

"Something funny, Mr. Rotolo?"

"What?"

Broz was looking at him instead of the road. "You were laughing."

"Yeah, why shouldn't I?" Benny snapped. "Let's get outta here. I got things to do."

"Yes, Mr. Rotolo."

Benny thought about the information racket as they left East Lido. He needed to talk about bananas again with Big Vinnie.

CHAPTER 29

Encroaching suds

The smell was yeasty and sour and something else besides. Burnt cork, Owen decided.

The Polish boys were emptying the industrial vats. It was a slow process to fill barrels with freshly brewed beer. If the beer flowed out too quickly, it foamed up. Obviously, they'd had issues. The floor of the pumphouse was sudsy and slick.

The Lido Outfit was selling green beer as Owen understood it; beer that did not stay in the tank long enough to complete the fermentation process. But by cutting down on time, they increased output.

That was Benny's department. Or rather Broz Siwak's job to make sure they had enough product to meet demand. Siwak seemed to be in charge of more and more lately, not that it mattered to Owen, as long as Benny didn't want to give his lieutenant a bigger cut of the profits. Owen needed every penny to pay off Cynthia's credit account at Nelson's Department Store. He'd recently added to the damage by buying her a Wedgewood trinket dish, the price for getting back in the bedroom.

Owen edged around the tank area, trying to keep away from the encroaching suds trickling toward the far wall. He didn't want to get beer on either his shoes or his coat. It was bad enough that his clothes were going to stink. Cynthia would notice the smell, too. He'd have to give her some lie about visiting the mill and being in close proximity to some odiferous smelting activity.

The murmur of voices coming from the makeshift office niche made him pause. Benny and that farmer Al Genovese were inside, obviously planning their next mysterious information racket activity.

"Two, three days. Tops." Benny's voice carried a jaunty confidence. "Keep 'em quiet and nobody gets hurt. You just got the one thing to do. Broz'll do the driving and his boys will handle the watching."

"You sure about the spot, Benny?" Al sounded doubtful. "What about your girl?"

"Trixie? She'll never know."

Owen stomped his feet as if getting snow off shoes, counted to five under his breath, then came around the end of the partition. Benny's arms were folded and his fedora was tipped to the back of his head. Genovese held his cap in both hands, blinking and twitching; a nervous supplicant if ever Owen saw one. Or smelled, in this case.

"Well, look who's here." Benny seemed glad to be interrupted. "What's new, Fishy? They still working you like a dog at the mill?"

"In the office," Owen said primly. "Not the mill."

"Yeah, well. Me and Al are done here."

"About that money order," Owen began hesitantly as he opened the big account book. Inspector Finch's tipsy confession had gnawed at Owen ever since the Bison Club dinner. He couldn't send the money order but at the same time, he was terrified not to send it.

"You sent it, right?" Benny resettled his fedora.

"Yes, of course." Owen made a show out of finding the right page in the ledger. "But I've heard that money orders are easy to trace. The Post Office actually pays attention to them. And where they go."

"You think somebody's watching you?"

"No, no, not me," Owen protested. "But the person on the receiving end."

Benny thumped Owen in the chest. "This ain't no amateur game, Fishy. If Big Vinnie says his system is foolproof, then it's foolproof."

He walked out, trailed by Genovese. The stench of manure lingered in the farmer's wake.

Owen sagged with relief.

CHAPTER 30

History lesson

Karol kept looking for problems, for simmering resentment ready to boil over. Some workers resented his relative youth and unmarried status. The foreman's salary belonged to a family man. In their eyes, he was stealing food out of the mouths of children.

Others, like Gio Tulipano and those with specialized skills, wondered if their status would be respected under the new regime.

But there was no sabotage, no refusal to implement the new safety protocols, no open insubordination.

Yet.

His biggest surprise was that the business apprentice program was a full-time job in and of itself. After the workday was over, Karol still had studying to do, reading far into the night with a technical dictionary by his side.

Primed by Luca's warning, Karol was more than ready for his tutorial with Mr. Fisher the accountant and was disappointed that nothing of interest happened. Fisher had spoken at length about accounting procedures, showing page after page of neat figures in enormous ledgers a yard wide. The accountant nervously fluttered his hands if Karol so much as tried to touch the paper or leaned too close to the chunky Burroughs adding machine.

All questions were answered with a minimum of information in a peevish voice, as if Karol's queries were tediously elementary. At least three times during the session, Fisher had casually called attention to both his diploma from Syracuse University and a scroll from the Delta Kappa Epsilon fraternity.

The session with Mr. Binford, the Lido Premium historian and the recording secretary for the Board of Directors was much more interesting. They met in the library in the bowels of the office building. It was a small space dominated by an oak library table. Striped wallpaper above oak wainscotting and portraits of grim-faced men. Lined with tomes on manufacturing, mining, and geology.

One bookcase was devoted to company yearbooks, giant leatherbound books the size of a sheet of newspaper. Scrapbooks, really, with all manner of memorabilia pasted onto thick black paper and the year embossed on the leather spine.

Mr. Binford gave Karol a short history of the company, then tottered back upstairs to his tiny cubby of an office, letting Karol pore through the yearbooks.

Lido Premium began in 1820 as the Packham Foundry. Crumbly newspaper articles told the story of copper goods being shipped on packet boats via New York's web of canals and rivers. The names Packham and Blick appeared in every article about the owners of the mill.

By 1880, Packham Foundry was a two-story mill with a tall chimney on the banks of the Mohawk River, powered by a huge paddlewheel. A sepia photograph showed a group of solemn-faced men in heavy overcoats cutting a ribbon in front of the building. The river flowed behind. Compared to the Lido Premium mill on Hamilton Street, the Packham Foundry was a toy.

In 1909, the foundry burned to the ground. Karol read fragile clippings from the *Lido Daily Clipper.* Eight workers died in the conflagration. Ironically chosen for proximity to the river for both power and shipping, the foundry was too far for the Lido Fire Department to reach in time. Workers were trapped inside and overcome by fumes as the fire spread. The mill had no means of pumping water from the nearby river to douse the flames.

Karol made a mental note to double-check the new safety procedures for instructions in case of fire.

He lingered over a photograph on the last page of the 1909 yearbook. A group of men in overcoats and bowler hats stood in front of the remains of the foundry with the river in the background, a sad mirror image of the 1880 photograph.

The fire had eaten the wooden building but the stone chimney and an outbuilding had survived, rising like cairns to mark the last vestiges of the Packham family's investment. The masonry was outlined in snow, and the photograph was faded, but appeared to show a sizable remnant.

The library also contained a collection of maps. Karol flipped through maps of the city of Lido, maps of New York rail and canal lines, and even geological surveys. All hand-drawn black lines and whorls, an old topographical map of Lido made him pause. The paper was thick but foxed and yellow with age. Karol smoothed it out, noting the legend *Adirondack and Western Railroad* printed along the bottom edge.

There was no date, but the map had obviously been drawn before half the streets in Lido were established. Karol recognized Lido's oblong village green, the American Corner intersection, and the circular park that anchored the West Park neighborhood.

Hamilton Street was a thin artery running east away from the center of Lido, but the immigrant neighborhoods on the eastern and southern flanks of the city were missing.

Bell Road and Railroad Street resembled skinny fingers pointing at the Mohawk River. The Settlers Rest cemetery lay between them, perched on top of concentric whorls indicating high ground. The Packham Foundry was marked on the map, along with a road leading to it that circled around the cemetery.

CHAPTER 31

Part of the plan

Ruth changed three times before finally deciding on a simple navy frock for shopping with Osa Rutherford, although she nearly changed again when a big Pierce-Arrow motorcar glided to a stop in front of the Galliano Club. Her red coat felt shabby as the uniformed chauffeur held the door open. Osa wore a cream velvet turban with a jet brooch pinned to it and a full-length fur coat, making Ruth feel even more poorly dressed.

"I'm so glad you accepted Henry's invitation to the party, Miss Cross," Osa said as the Pierce-Arrow purred toward Liberty Street.

"Please call me Ruth."

"Of course." The other woman beamed and invited Ruth to call her Osa. "I'm terribly glad that Henry invited you. He can be so reclusive."

"I was honored to accept."

"Well, you must be very brave," Osa laughed. "Even as a child Henry could be alarmingly forceful. The Army only made it worse."

"I'd love to hear about the party," Ruth said hastily.

Osa was very likable, yet Ruth was very much out of her element. "It sounds very grand."

By the time the Pierce Arrow stopped in front of Van Dyke's display window, Ruth was reeling. The theme for Osa's big gala was "A Night in the South Seas." The Candyland Supper Club was to be transformed with tropical plants, a steel drum band, fountains and even a sandy beach. Potted palms, hibiscus, and jasmine plants were being shipped all the way from California. The band was coming from Jamaica. Jack Rutherford had even ordered a thatched pagoda. Guests would have their picture taken in front of it while wearing wreaths of flowers. It would be just like Tahiti.

Clearly, Jack Rutherford had forgotten nothing. It was also clear that after 25 years of marriage and four children, Osa still adored her husband.

Ruth added envy to the morning's list of conflicted emotions.

The head of Van Dyke's Evening Costumes department, a dramatically slender woman named Mrs. Scott, waited for them in the store's reception area. Osa and Mrs. Scott obviously knew each other well. There was a subtle appraisal of Ruth when Osa introduced her.

"You've a lovely figure," Mrs. Scott said when they were in the Evening Costumes lounge and a maid had taken their coats. "We have any number of dresses that will suit you."

Something not too expensive, Ruth wanted to say but Van Dyke's wasn't the kind of place where price was a consideration.

Seated on a gilt settee and served coffee in bone china cups, Ruth and Osa watched as models emerged from a curtained entrance and paraded across the lounge to show off a selection of exquisite evening dresses. As each gorgeous creature stopped in front of the settee, Mrs. Scott pointed out the details to her audience of two. She noted the type of fabric, the embellishments, and even the type of gloves, silk stockings, and hair accessory to wear with the dress.

One after another, each dress was a confection of silk, velvet, and chiffon. All had a fashionable dropped waist and were sleeveless to accommodate opera-length gloves. A few had shark bite hems with four points that grazed the ankle while others came to mid-calf in front and dropped lower in back. One or two were cut quite short, skimming the model's knees, although the fabrics were as sumptuous as the others.

Ruth dismissed the short shifts. She might have danced on stage in tights in her youth, but short dresses made her nervous. It was too easy to be labeled a loose woman in a short dress.

"No, definitely not," Osa said firmly as a model revolved to show off a pink dress with a chiffon overlay. "It's the wrong color for your hair."

"And of course, not plum," Mrs. Scott said to Ruth. "Mrs. Rutherford will be in plum."

"It's the most darling dress," Osa added. "Just wait until you see it, Ruth."

More models swished by. With each new outfit, Ruth felt Osa's questioning look asking if this was the one. It would be the height of bad taste to inquire about the price, making the decision an impossible one.

And then a dress made for dancing came through the curtains.

Silk velvet the color of charcoal glittered like black diamonds. The fabric rippled with every step the model took. The neckline wasn't the usual curve but a slash that covered the collarbones and fell into a drape that bared the nape of the neck and revealed a silvery satin lining. The dropped waist was accented with more satin and fell into ankle-skimming godet pleats spliced with chiffon in the same tone. The hem opened like an umbrella when the model did a graceful pirouette.

The dress was even more fabulous up close. The chiffon godets were embroidered with tiny flowers that matched the neckline's embellishment. The embroidery was hidden until the pleats flared out. The dress was minimal, but in the most elegant way. Ruth was sure it cost an appalling amount of money.

"Let me show you the matching gloves," Mrs. Scott murmured and produced a pair of opera gloves in a stunning pale pewter tone.

"Is this the dress, Ruth?" Osa asked.

Mrs. Scott draped a long necklace of rhinestone and jet beads around the model's neck.

"Yes," Ruth said.

Ten minutes later, she stood on the dais in front of a mirror as Osa and Mrs. Scott looked on in approval. The silk velvet felt like a cloud against her skin. The pleats fanned out easily, making it the perfect dress for any dance, not just faster steps.

She would waltz with Henry in this dress.

"An excellent choice." Mrs. Scott gestured to the seamstress who waited with a strawberry pincushion hanging from a ribbon around her neck. "Just a few adjustments, I would think."

The seamstress pinned and tucked to make sure the armholes didn't gape. After that, Mrs. Scott helped her don the matching gloves, which reached almost to Ruth's shoulders. Tiny buttons at the wrist ensured a tight fit. As a finishing touch, Mrs. Scott doubled the necklace to create a choker as well as a cascade that reached to the dropped waist of the dress.

"What about a fur?" Osa asked Mrs. Scott.

Ruth whirled away from the mirror, fluttering the pleats, and threw Osa a stricken look. "A fur?"

"We have some lovely jackets in the Fur Department," Mrs. Scott said. "Did you have a style in mind, Miss Cross?"

"I don't need a fur," Ruth said. The dress was far more than she could ever repay as it was.

Osa stood up as if she needed to consider Ruth's dress from a different angle. "Perhaps you could bring a selection to try with the dress," she suggested to Mrs. Scott.

"Of course." Mrs. Scott gave a knowing smile. "Another cup of coffee while you wait?"

"Lovely, thank you," Osa caroled.

The door closed, leaving the two shoppers alone. Ruth carefully removed the necklace. "A dress is enough. A fur is out of the question. It would be far too much to ask of Henry."

"Darling, everyone will be wearing a fur." Osa regarded Ruth's reflection with a proprietary air. "Henry told me to make sure you had everything. He would absolutely slay me if I came home and said I let you put a wool coat over that dress."

"But Osa, this is all so terribly expensive." Ruth was wracked with indecision.

Osa waggled a finger at her. "Ruth, we're going to be friends, but not if you get me on Henry's bad side. He'll say all sorts of dreadful things." She lowered her voice. "'My assumption that you could carry out this minor task has been severely diminished.'"

Ruth gave a nervous giggle. Osa mimicked her brother very well.

"See?" Osa said with a laugh. "You know I'm right."

Mrs. Scott and two minions carried in three fur jackets for Ruth to try. Osa immediately seized on a fingertip-length black mink with a collar and bell sleeves. Ruth put it on over the charcoal velvet dress and the effect was breathtaking. Not even Irene Castle had ever looked this elegant, this glamorous.

"A perfect fit," Mrs. Scott said admiringly as Ruth stood on the dais. "It doesn't need to be altered at all."

"Black mink goes with everything, Ruth," Osa said. "You'll wear it constantly."

Ruth stopped protesting, surrendered the dress to the seamstress, and promised to return on Thursday for a final fitting. The Fur Department would sew Ruth's name inside the jacket. Osa suggested that the store deliver everything to the Rutherford house on Saturday, the day before the party.

Mrs. Scott turned them over to the manager of the

Foundations and Lingerie Department where Ruth selected silk stockings and matching silk robe and pajamas for the house party. Next was Leather Goods for shoes and a matching evening purse.

Osa insisted that they have lunch afterward and directed the chauffeur to Babylon, the newest restaurant in Lido. Like Buckner's it was stylish and expensive, and Ruth had never been there before. Osa asked for a table by the window overlooking Liberty Street. Babylon was certainly the place to be seen if you were anybody in Lido.

The conversation was mostly one-sided. Osa was funny and entertaining as she talked about meeting her husband Jack and shared anecdotes about their children. The two oldest were in boarding school but coming home to attend her birthday party.

Ruth marveled that with a gala event in less than a week, the woman had time to take a relative stranger shopping and out to lunch. They were halfway through the meal when it dawned on Ruth that lunch with Osa was part of Henry's plan. Jack Rutherford had been at the Bison Club banquet, yet his wife was lunching with the object of O'Malley's crude claim.

If Henry's social position was unassailable, Osa's was even more so.

CHAPTER 32

She's gone

Dear Lucky Lombardo,

I run a vaudeville show and we are in need of a new act. Some folks say as a woman I can't run a show but I say they are rong as I got this show and we done very good this year. Now that you are famous, come be in the show as The Dago That Defied Death. Handbills are printed already and look fancy.

If you don't have enough scars, we can make some. Pay would be $30 a week, plus travel and food.

Rite me back real fast. The show is already booked in Bloomington and Peoria.

You won't be lonely neither as I plan to keep you real warm when you aint on stage. 4 husbands so far and none of them complained of the cold afore they kicked it.

Mrs. Harriet Curwell, of Enfield, Connecticut

"That's good money, Luca!" somebody shouted.

"Wonder how much she paid the other husbands," Tony Bilotti grumbled from the back.

"I don't think you should be the dago that defied death," Sonny said loyally. "It's demeaning."

The saloon was packed, jokes and catcalls mingling with slurps of beer and the crunch of pickled onions. All the chairs were angled to face the bar where Luca sat, swinging his legs above the brass footrail.

Headlights of every car that went by on Hamilton Street momentarily reflected a wintery mix of snow and rain spitting across the club's big window. Guido leaned on the vestibule pony wall, grinning with delight at the latest lady letters.

Luca stuffed the letter back in the envelope and slid it to Sonny. "Tell her no. Absolutely no."

The front door opened, emitting a gust of freezing air and swirling snow. Enzo charged in. "Luca? Where's Luca?" he shouted.

Half a dozen men jumped out of their seats at the urgency in his voice.

"Hey!" Luca threw himself off the bar and grabbed Enzo by the shoulders, stopping his headlong charge. "What's wrong? What happened?"

Enzo was wild-eyed, hatless and his coat was misbuttoned. "She's gone. Matilda's gone. You have to help me."

"What do you mean, Matilda's gone? Gone where?"

Chairs scraped as more men got to their feet and

clustered around.

"I mean she's gone. Disappeared. We've been looking for hours." Enzo was shaking. "Rocco and Matilda went outside to do their chores. When Rosaria called them in, only Rocco came. Said he didn't know where she went. We've been searching and calling but she doesn't answer. She's disappeared. God help me if she went to the river."

Luca left Sonny in charge of the bar. As he reached for his coat, so did many others, including Gio Tulipano and Frank Conti. They all jammed into the truck, ignoring the weather and headed back to Bell Road.

For the next four hours, as snow alternated with sleet, they ranged up and down the fields on both sides of the road with lanterns. More members of the Galliano Club joined them, as did several other farmers.

Luca and Enzo ventured some distance along the riverbank but no one had been there before them. The snow wasn't falling heavily enough to obscure footsteps. Yet Luca couldn't shake the fear that the child had fallen in and now it was too dark to see.

"Matilda is only six years old," Enzo said again. "She's not allowed."

"I know," Luca said.

Two minutes later, they said the same thing to each other.

The search petered out as midnight turned into the next day and lanterns ran out of kerosene. Those from East Lido found a way home. Luca elected to stay with Enzo and Rosaria. He climbed the stairs to the attic, sick with fear and exhausted from tramping through frozen brush.

Rosaria had given him a hot brick wrapped in flannel. Luca shoved it to the foot of the bed under the blankets and crawled into the bed fully clothed. Moonlight seeped through the chinks in the lathe walls. He could see his breath dissolve into the frosty air.

Footsteps came up the stairs. "Zio?"

"Rocco? What are you doing up?"

"I can't sleep. Ma is crying. So is Pa. I'm scared."

"I know."

"Can I stay here with you? I don't want to be alone."

"For a minute."

Rocco scampered over the frosty floor and scrambled under the covers with Luca. "I should have gone with her."

"Gone where?"

"She wanted apples. I told her there weren't any left. We picked them all weeks ago. Matilda got mad at me and went outside. I stayed in the barn. When Ma called, she was gone." Rocco sniffed. "Do you think she fell in the river?"

"No, it's too far away." Luca mustered as much false hope as he could. "She knows she's not allowed to go to the river."

"I don't want to go to school in the morning. I want to look for her, too."

"You're not doing anything unless you get some sleep."

Rocco gave in to his tears. "Pa is going to blame me again but I didn't do anything to Matilda. I didn't touch the dynamite, either. I try to be good, like Saint Rocco at church. I've got the same name. I wouldn't do anything like that. Not ever. Honest."

"I know."

Luca put his arm around the boy's shoulders and let him curl up against his side. Rocco was asleep almost instantly, breathing evenly. Luca lay awake, staring at the slivers of moonlight, listening to Rosaria weeping in the room below.

When he opened his eyes, Rocco was gone and dawn filled the musty attic. Luca followed the scent of coffee to the kitchen. Rosaria and Enzo were at the table, both bleary-eyed.

"Any news?" Luca asked.

Enzo shook his head.

"We'll keep looking," Luca said with determination. "She spent the night somewhere."

Twenty minutes later, he and Enzo were in the truck, ready to resume the search. Enzo dropped his hands to his lap without starting the engine.

"We're not going to find her," he said hollowly.

"Don't give up," Luca replied. "We'll find her."

Enzo stared at the back of the house. "No, we won't. They have her."

"What are you talking about?"

"*La Mano Nera*," Enzo whispered.

Luca caught his breath. "You got a letter?"

In response, Enzo reached under the seat and pulled out a handful of paper. "God help me. I did nothing."

Five letters, no envelopes, all signed with the stabbed heart and dripping slashes. "*Oddio*," Luca swore softly. "*Oddio, oddio*."

Each letter demanded five thousand dollars, to be left on the front seat of his truck parked on Senate Street. When he was ready to pay, Enzo was to tie a ribbon to the mailbox post.

The last letter threatened to take the children.

Russo you must pay us 5000 or we will come for your children and stab their eyes and skin them. You will never see them again, only blood and pieces of bodies.

We laugh at fear. If you go to the police no one will

be saved. Remember we know what happened at the river.

"At the river." Luca found it hard to breathe. Surely this was his fault; Enzo was being blamed for putting Jimmy Zambrano in the river instead of him and Vito. "What do they mean? What do you know?"

"I didn't think anyone knew. How could they?"

"Tell me!" Luca shouted.

"When Rosaria was pregnant with the baby," Enzo faltered and hung his head.

"Go on," Luca said harshly.

"She was so big and tired. Her cousin Gina came to help for a few weeks."

"I remember." Luca cast his thoughts back eighteen months or so. Rosaria's cousin Gina Ignoffo was a pleasant, childless woman whose husband owned a butcher shop in Albany.

"Gina liked to take walks down to the river." Enzo's voice was barely audible. "Sometimes I went with her."

"You and Gina." It wasn't a question.

"Twice," Enzo said miserably. "Then she went home and it was done. But when I saw the letters, I knew Gina told her husband and that he wanted revenge. I decided not to do anything. I thought eventually he'd leave us alone. Never, never did I think he would send *La Mano Nera* against us."

How could Enzo have been so stupid? Luca wanted to roar with anger and frustration. "Rosaria doesn't know, does she?"

Enzo covered his face. "May God strike me dead. She doesn't know anything. Not Gina, not the letters. The dynamite was a warning. I blamed Rocco for destroying the smokehouse because I couldn't tell Rosaria. Blamed my own son because I was afraid to tell the truth. And now they have my girl."

"We'll pay the money. They'll let her go."

"Five thousand dollars." Enzo was weeping now. "I don't even have five hundred."

Rosaria opened the back door of the house, obviously puzzled that the truck was still parked by the barn.

"I have two thousand dollars." Luca had spent some of his rumrunning earnings but there was more in his savings account at the bank. "Two thousand three hundred. Maybe it will be enough."

"Where did you get that much money?"

"Does it matter?" Luca directed Enzo's attention to his wife standing on the back porch. "You have to tell Rosaria. Show her the letters."

Enzo turned to him in horror. "No, I can't."

Rosaria waved a hand to ask *what's going on?*

"Get out." Luca reached across the dashboard, opened the driver's side door and shoved the other man out of the vehicle.

"No, I can't," Enzo repeated.

Luca stuffed the letters into his cousin's hand and slammed the truck door in his face.

Enzo leaned against the hood, shoulders slumped under his coat, then slowly plodded to the house. Rosaria waited with her head cocked in curiosity and concern. Enzo didn't mount the porch steps but spoke to his wife from a few yards away.

Luca couldn't hear the conversation but saw a story of betrayal and shame reflected in Rosaria's changing expression.

Enzo held out the letters. Rosaria let out a scream and flew down the steps. She struck Enzo with her fist, whipping his head to the side. He stumbled backward. The letters fluttered out of his hand.

Rosaria hit him again and again. Shoulders rounded in shame, Enzo absorbed the blows until she stopped and began to sob. When Enzo tried to put his arms around her, Rosaria pushed him away and went into the house.

Luca got out of the truck and collected the letters before the wind carried them away.

CHAPTER 33

Her last regret

Tess sat at her desk and watched Luca as he went to the teller. He didn't once look her way, although she did her best to will him to turn his head, catch her eye. Give a sign that he knew she was alive.

But it was as if he was determined not to see her. Luca conducted his business at the window, tucked his passbook into a pocket and walked out.

She couldn't help herself. Tess sprang out of her chair, slipped through the wooden gate and walked as fast as she dared through the lobby, passing a dozen customers waiting in line without bothering to give the standard greeting required of all employees of the First National Bank of Lido.

The cold hit hard as soon as Tess walked outside, making her eyes water. She braved a few running steps, knowing this could be the last time she saw him. "Luca! Luca!"

He stopped and turned. Tess gave a little wave. After a moment of hesitation, Luca walked back to the bank and joined her under the awning.

"Hello, Tessa."

"Hello." Tess wanted to clutch his sleeve, pull him closer. "How are you?"

"Well enough." Luca's face was like flint. "I saw the announcement of your engagement in the newspaper."

"Yes, well." Tess didn't want to talk about that with him. She wanted to know how he was, what he was doing, if he remembered their counting game and the number five and if he still loved her as much as she loved him. "Thank you for coming to see Aunt Evelyn."

"I didn't do it to be nice," Luca said. "I asked her to change her mind."

"I know," Tess said mournfully. "Annie told me. It means a lot to me that you tried."

"Did you get the box? It wouldn't have been right for me to take it."

"Box?" For a moment, Tess didn't know what he was talking about, then she recalled the bronze box Annie had presented to her, along with the heartbreaking news that Luca had called on Aunt Evelyn and been sent away with a gift he refused to keep. "Annie passed it along. I can't imagine why Aunt Evelyn wanted you to have it."

"She said I should take away her last regret."

"Her last regret? Tess never heard Aunt Evelyn say anything like that. "How strange."

Luca bent toward her. "Are you all right, Tess? I mean, are you happy?"

"I miss you, Luca." Tess bit her lip. "Did you really not tell me things because you thought I wouldn't love you?"

"Yes." Luca looked her straight in the eye.

Tess met his stare. "Did you tell me everything? Really?"

"Nothing else mattered after your news."

"But there was something else, wasn't there? What was it?"

Luca shook his head. "It doesn't matter anymore. You're going to marry Mr. Howland."

Tess didn't want to talk about James Howland. She found herself grasping for something, anything to say. "I won't be working here much longer. I won't see you the next time you come to make a deposit."

"Today was a withdrawal."

"I thought perhaps you were making a payment for Mr. Spinelli." Tess was talking just to keep him there, but she couldn't help herself. "Against that new loan."

"What loan?"

"Mr. Spinelli took out a big loan. Was it to make repairs? I saw in the *Clipper* that someone damaged his car. A shooting. I always thought that Lido was so quiet but not any more."

"The loan. How much was it for?"

"Seventeen thousand dollars."

Luca gave a start. Clearly this news was an unwelcome surprise.

"I'm sorry. I thought you knew. He took out a loan using the club building as collateral. The address jumped right out at me. Six hundred one Hamilton Street." Tess babbled on so Luca wouldn't walk away. "Just like Mr. Fisher did with his house, remember? Although he paid that off, you know. Brought a paper bag full of cash into the bank. Ten thousand dollars."

Luca bent even closer. "What happens if Vito can't pay?"

"The bank would seize the club," Tess breathed. He was almost close enough to kiss. "Sell it at auction to recoup the amount of the loan."

As if conjured by an eavesdropping magician, James appeared at her elbow complete with pretentious black suit, plastered hair and feeble mustache. "Tess? What are you doing out here? It's cold."

"I was speaking to a customer," Tess said, jerking back. "This is Mr. Lombardo."

"Miss Kennedy was very kind to answer my question." Luca tipped his cap to her, his face hard and blank again. "Thank you very much. Goodbye."

Tess clenched her fists as he strode off.

"Come along, Tess," James said testily. He put a hand on her arm. "It's freezing out here."

"Your familiarity is a liberty that I find offensive," Tess whispered furiously and yanked herself away. "In all matters regarding my employment in this bank, you will refer to me as Miss Kennedy."

"You won't be working here much longer," James said.

Tess marched back into the bank and sat at her desk. Her throat was on fire and everything on her desk was blurry. She sat for another hour, doing absolutely nothing, then left for home. The doctor was coming to see Aunt Evelyn again. Surely this time, he could do something useful.

The doctor came and went, prescribing more laudanum. Aunt Evelyn was exhausted by the ordeal of being poked and prodded. Annie made her as comfortable as possible as Tess walked the doctor to the front door.

"I hear you are getting married," he said before leaving. "I hope it's soon. Your aunt doesn't have much more time."

Tess plodded up the stairs to her bedroom, unbuckled her shoes, took off her spectacles and threw herself on the comforter. Aunt Evelyn was dying. Soon, Tess would be married to James while Annie and Cook either found new positions or went back to Ireland. Tess overheard them commiserating in the kitchen one evening. Their plight was bad but at least they were free to make their own choices.

The doctor's words echoed what Tess thought when she saw Aunt Evelyn now. Frail and practically translucent, her aunt slept most of the time. When she was awake, she coughed.

What did Aunt Evelyn think about as death approached? *Her last regret.* That didn't sound like something Luca would make up.

The bronze box was in the bedside table, put there the day Annie handed it over and promptly forgotten.

Tess scrambled over the bed and extracted the box. It was heavy and the bronze metal was cool under her fingers. She put it on her lap and turned the tiny key.

A handful of envelopes nestled in a creamy satin-lined interior intended for jewelry. Tess slipped on her spectacles again and looked through them.

Each envelope was addressed to Miss A. Harper, Post Office Box 78, Lido, New York. The return address was simply c/o General Delivery from various cities across the country. The postmarks were dated from March to November 1902.

Why on earth had Aunt Evelyn tried to give Luca a box of Annie's letters from 24 years ago? Either the laudanum was robbing Aunt Evelyn of the ability to think straight or these weren't Annie's letters.

Curiosity won out. Tess opened the oldest envelope and unfolded a letter written in a bold, masculine hand.

Pittsburgh, PA.
3 March 1902
My darling Eve,

We got to the campsite today and there will be a courier going into the city so I must write quickly. The first thing I did as we passed through Altoona was to go to the post office and your letter was there like a gift from the heavens. To read that you love me still and always will, to savor your words and caress the lock of hair you sent, gave me the strength to go on. This separation is only temporary.

You deserve every happiness. BT will never give it to you. As you say, he is a cruel man incapable of love except for his railroad. The very thing that brought me to you.

We are meant to be together forever, of this I am certain. Our love, our intimate love, is eternal love. I am the luckiest man on earth to have the arms that once held you and for which you yearn. This time apart will be as nothing when we are together again.

Good night, my dearest Eve. I am as always, your

faithful lover, Max

"Good gracious," Tess murmured, her cheeks on fire. "Intimate love."

She refolded the letter and tucked it back in the envelope. The next letter to *darling Eve* was even more suggestive. And detailed. Max apparently had an excellent memory.

Did Aunt Evelyn have an affair with the mysterious Max while married to Uncle Benedict? Did Annie help by being the conduit for their correspondence?

By 1902, Evelyn Kennedy had already been married to Benedict Thompson for several years, having wed the older man when she was nineteen.

Uncle Benedict had died when Tess was about seven or eight years old, years before she went to live with the widowed Aunt Evelyn. Her father, Evelyn's brother, went to the funeral. No one ever talked about Uncle Benedict again, only about his will or the railroad. There weren't even any pictures of Benedict Thompson in the West Park Circle house.

Tess read the letters in chronological order. They were all similar, with Max writing from different places his railroad work took him. Over and over, he declared his love to darling Eve as well as his certainty they would be together again soon. Sometimes his letters were a direct response to a missive from her, which must have been as passionate as his, but apparently riddled with worry that BT would discover her infidelity.

The last letter was postmarked November 1902.

Comstock, CA

5 November 1908

My darling Eve,

The enclosed will be more than enough to bring you to me in California. Find a reason to go to the Wells Fargo office in Syracuse. The enclosed is a bearer bond so they are obliged to pay the face value plus interest. This is the safest way to ensure that you have ample funds without dealing with a bank transaction that would come to BT's attention. Once you have the funds, buy a train ticket in your own name to Philadelphia and another to Chicago using the name we agreed on. Once in Chicago, purchase a ticket to Salt Lake City. From there travel on to Sacramento. Send a telegram at every stop. Remember the ruse that you are taking a governess position in Sacramento.

It is a long journey, my love, but the train will carry you all the way to my open arms. Just follow the plan and all will go smoothly.

Once you are here, we'll sail for Hawaii. If BT accuses you of desertion as grounds for divorce, what of it? The only thing that matters is that he relinquishes his hold and agrees to dissolve the marriage.

We will build a life of unending happiness. Each morning when you awaken, I will swear my love to you. No obstacle can keep us apart. I long to touch you, to hold you, to cradle you in my arms and never let you go. I pledge my life to you.

Hurry to me, darling Evelyn. Your devoted lover, Max

By the time Tess replaced all the letters in the box, her heart was aching. She left her room and nearly collided with Annie tiptoeing out of Aunt Evelyn's bedroom with a tray of uneaten food.

"Annie," Tess started.

"Close the door," Annie interrupted. "She's asleep again."

Tess shut the door to Aunt Evelyn's bedroom as softly as possible. "I need to talk to you."

"Your dinner is on the dining room table."

"Yes, fine," Tess said distractedly and followed the housekeeper down the stairs. "I found some old letters in that box you gave me. The one Aunt Evelyn gave to

Luca? Letters from a man named Max."

Annie gave such a start that she nearly dropped the tray, plates and flatware rattling together.

Tess caught the rim and kept the tray from crashing. "They're addressed to you but they were written to Aunt Evelyn."

Annie refused to relinquish the tray. "Go eat your dinner."

"If you don't tell me who Max was, I'll go back upstairs and wake up Aunt Evelyn and ask her."

The housekeeper gasped. "Don't you dare."

Tess gently released the tray. "I'll be in the dining room."

She picked at her supper of roast beef and glazed turnips while Annie made a pot of tea. Once the housekeeper was with her, hands clasped around a delicate teacup, Tess couldn't wait any longer for answers. "Max. Who was he?"

"Max Lauder," Annie said after an uncomfortable pause. "He was a foreman on the railroad, laying tracks for Mr. Benedict's Adirondack and Western Railroad."

"Was Aunt Evelyn in love with him?"

"I suppose."

"What was he like?"

"German." Annie grimaced. "Rough. A laborer. He made Miss Evelyn laugh, I'll give him that."

"He asked Aunt Evelyn to divorce Mr. Benedict and run away with him, didn't he? What happened?"

Annie gave a fretful sigh. "Miss Evelyn had been married to Mr. Benedict for four or five years by the time Max came along. Even a blind man could have seen that the marriage was a bad one, Mr. Benedict hardly ever here and the entire house on pins and needles when he was. Max took advantage of that."

In her mind's eye Tess saw a younger, healthier Aunt Evelyn fleeing her stiff, snobby husband for the big blonde man who made her laugh; for the chance at "intimate love" that he promised. "He sent her a bearer bond so she could meet him in California," she said.

"No, he never did," Annie told her.

"The bond was in his last letter."

"No, it wasn't."

"She must have been devastated." Tess imagined the crushing blow. A letter that promised freedom, but not the means to escape.

"Miss Evelyn didn't need that bond anyway," Annie snapped. "She came to her senses. What would her family have said? Cast her right out, they would have. She had no business gallivanting off with a common laborer. Live in some shack while he pounded spikes and laid rail."

"And that was it, she never saw him again?"

Annie put down her teacup and glared at Tess. "Miss Evelyn made a mistake when she was no older than yourself and I'm ashamed to say that I helped by fetching those letters. At least it went no further than it did. Miss Evelyn was a respectable, married woman, with a position in society to uphold. When it was all over, she knew it was for her own good."

"Lord, I hate that expression," Tess said bleakly.

They drank tea in silence. The opulent dining room, with its blue and green wallpaper and damask draperies, had never seemed so oppressive. Even the magnificent crystal chandelier seemed to weigh on Tess, a many-faceted sword of Damocles over her head. One wrong move, one wrong judgment from Muriel Howland, and her head would be split in two.

If Max had sent the bearer bond, would Aunt Evelyn have traded her privileged life as Mrs. Adirondack and Western Railroad for Max's promise of unending love?

Tess toyed with her spoon, lost in thought. What sort of letters had Aunt Evelyn written to Max to make him believe so strongly in their future together? Why did he send the letter but not the bond?

"What happened to Max?" she asked at length. "Did Aunt Evelyn ever try to find out?"

"We heard he died in a railroad accident," Annie sniffed. "Put paid to that."

"How awful."

Annie began clearing the table.

"Do you think they would have been happy?" Tess asked. "Aunt Evelyn and Max, I mean. If they had run away together?"

"Nonsense." Annie nearly spat. "He was some foreign roughneck. Who knows why she ever took up with someone so far beneath her."

Tess sighed and surrendered her empty cup. "Maybe he made her feel like the person she wanted to be."

CHAPTER 34

Ransom run

The night was bleak, the air was bone-chillingly damp, and Luca was tight with nerves. The packet of money, wrapped in oilcloth and secured with twine, weighted the inside pocket of his plaid mackinaw. As Enzo drove, Luca knew that he had to put Tess out of his mind and concentrate on the job ahead. Forget the sadness on her face when that giant lump of butter she was going to marry interrupted their conversation.

Enzo's breath was coming in shaky whistles as the truck nosed into an angled parking space along Senate Street. The truck's headlights illuminated the building ahead and the sign painted directly onto the brick. *FLORENCE OIL STOVES Your Silent Partner in the Kitchen.*

"Silent partner," Luca said aloud. They needed more than a silent partner tonight. They needed luck.

Enzo cut the engine.

"An hour," Luca said. "We'll have her back in an hour."

His cousin nodded mechanically; hands still locked

on the steering wheel.

Luca jabbed him with an elbow. "Cut the lights."

Enzo gave a start and turned off the headlights.

Luca climbed out of the truck and looked around. Senate Street was the back door to Lido's bustling downtown district. It wasn't an avenue of fancy shops, restaurants and entertainment like Liberty Street, but rather a spot for businesses that serviced other businesses. Both sides of the street were lined with three and four-story buildings with few windows. From the signs, Luca guessed they were used as both business offices and warehouses.

Hays-Manville Rigid Asbestos Shingles

Berton Lithographic Company. Complete graphic arts services

Leather Supplier to Nettleton Shoes

Pruitt Brothers Upholstery for Home and Office

Luca reached back into the truck, rolled down the window and set the packet of cash on the seat before closing the door. Somehow, they'd scraped up the full amount of five thousand dollars, Enzo managing to beg and borrow the extra that was needed.

"It's time," Enzo said hoarsely, waiting by the front fender. In the glow of the streetlight, the marks Rosaria's rage had left on his face were all too apparent.

Luca had to force himself to leave the truck and the precious packet of cash. He knew that it was even harder for Enzo. The letter had given explicit instructions to walk away from the vehicle in the direction of Liberty Street. Wait in the Strand Theatre until the last show was over.

They'd discussed hiding where they could see who took the money, then following them to Matilda. It was a fruitless idea from the start and they both knew it. Matilda's life was too precious to ignore the instructions.

The block to the nearest intersection was long and poorly lit. A narrow street ran perpendicular between Senate and Liberty Streets. They passed a particularly gloomy building with shrubbery hidden under plywood frames to keep the snow off. A discreet sign advertised a bookstore, dental office and an insurance agency. *The Prudential Has The Strength of Gibraltar*.

The sidewalks were clear of ice. Their footsteps were loud until a few cars trundled by. A truck advertising *Florence Oil Stoves* in the same lettering as the building clattered into a garage behind them.

"Somebody is making a late repair," Luca observed for no particular reason.

Hands deep in the pockets of his buffalo plaid mackinaw, Enzo walked slowly and didn't reply.

There were a few other people walking along the street this late at night. The dull iron tracks running through the street meant that there was a trolley stop ahead. Lights shone in scattered windows. Luca imagined orders being filled and after-hours bookkeeping tasks.

He wondered if he and Enzo were being watched.

The intersection was quiet. They turned up the side street. Two blocks ahead, Liberty Street was alive with lights and traffic. The Strand Theatre wasn't far. Luca had enough change in his pocket to pay for their tickets, although the notion of watching a comic 2-reeler while waiting to see if *La Mano Nera* would deliver Matilda was a cruel one.

He remembered Rosaria's last words before they left the house on Bell Road. "Don't come back without my daughter." Left unspoken was that if he didn't find Matilda, Enzo needn't come back at all.

Enzo stopped and backed up until he was pressed against the nearest building. He cocked his head toward Senate Street as if listening.

Luca stopped, too. "What's the matter?"

Enzo held a finger to his lips. "I heard something," he whispered.

The side street was deserted. No one had followed them when they turned. Holding his breath, Luca strained to hear something besides ordinary night sounds. Automobiles on Senate Street. Distant voices of pedestrians chiding each other to get out of the cold. The far-off clang of a trolley bell.

Without warning, Enzo launched himself down the side street and skidded into the intersection. "WHERE'S MY DAUGHTER?" he bellowed.

Luca tore after him, just in time to see a shadowy figure by the truck with a hand raised to reach through the open passenger side window. It was a man, wearing a black jacket and a hunting cap pulled low over his forehead and ears. As Enzo charged toward the truck, the figure sprinted away.

Enzo gave chase, but he wasn't built for speed. Luca overtook his wheezing cousin, barely conscious of the sidewalk beneath his feet, his entire body focused on *La Mano Nera* getting away.

His quarry was fast but Luca was driven by desperation. Ten steps, then twelve and he was almost close enough to snag the black jacket.

Luca stretched out his hand. The man ahead of him swerved into the street out of reach and raced along the trolley tracks. The surprise move cost Luca precious momentum. He veered into the street, too, gulping air, boots drumming like thunder.

An engine roared out of the night. Something hard and unyielding hit the back of Luca's legs and windmilled him into the sky. Senate Street tilted past in a blur of brick and tarmac and *FLORENCE OIL STOVES*.

Arms automatically cradling his head, shoulders hunching to take the impact, Luca hit the sidewalk and ended up in a messy tangle next to a storm drain.

A black Ford skidded to a stop in the middle of the street. The jacket and hunting cap disappeared inside. A moment later the vehicle was gone.

No headlights.

No Matilda.

CHAPTER 35

Close call

"Nice job," Benny panted as he tried to collect himself. "Did you see who that fella was?"

Broz shook his head as he drove. "No, Mr. Rotolo. I only saw the back of him."

Benny found his hip flask and took a long pull. "Jesus, that was close."

He screwed the cap back on the flask and risked a look behind the Ford. A bend in the street took the spot along Senate Street with the angled parking spots out of sight.

Broz turned on the headlights. Like always, he drove fast and skillfully.

The whiskey in Benny's flask calmed him down enough to think about what went wrong. He had missed getting Russo's money by a matter of seconds. Russo couldn't follow directions the way Spinelli did, even when it meant getting his kid back.

It was Al Genovese's fault for picking Russo as a likely mark in the first place. Didn't he realize that Russo was a stupid hardhead? First, Russo ignored letters until Benny was forced to up the stakes. Then he didn't come alone, like he was supposed to, but brought a champion runner.

The whole fucking fiasco on Senate Street was Al's fault.

Not only that, but Al's dirt on Spinelli and Lombardo dumping Zambrano in the river was played out.

Another swallow of whiskey helped Benny weigh the odds. Overall, the information racket was still a good thing. Russo would pay up or get his kid's body dumped on the doorstep. Spinelli was leaking cash like a spaghetti strainer. Nick's widow would pay up, too.

Chief Doyle still wasn't wise to what was going on. Nobody was.

Pretty soon Benny would not only be the new owner of the Galliano Club, but the goddamned king of East Lido.

CHAPTER 36

Waiting game

"Where's Vito?" Luca asked as soon as he walked into the club.

Guido was behind the bar. The doorman looked harassed and overwhelmed. "He went home already."

"Did you find the girl?" Tony Bilotti rasped from the cluster of old-timers at their usual table on the other side of the saloon.

Luca took off his coat. "Not yet," he said.

"Two whole days?" Tony shook his head mournfully. "Either she fell in the river or someone took her."

"We'll find her." Luca wasn't about to say anything about Enzo's letters from *La Mano Nera*.

He fetched his apron, sent Guido back to the vestibule and considered the mess on the work counter. Half-made sandwiches, irregular slices of bread, a spreading puddle of red pepper and onion relish. The percolator was unplugged. Soggy coffee grounds clumped on the bottom. Guido had dumped the coffee into the pot instead of the little filter basket.

Cleaning up was a welcome distraction, although he was sore from the encounter on Senate Street and the long walk into Lido from Bell Road. Coming back to the farm after the abortive attempt to hand over the money was a nightmare of tears and recriminations. He'd spent a sleepless night in the attic. Rosaria had alternately wept and paced in the room below him. Enzo retreated to the barn.

The morning was worse as the three considered what to do next. Put out the signal again? Make another attempt? Or had they lost the opportunity? Perhaps they should wait for another letter.

Luca left when the argument fractured into accusations of betrayal and shouts and screams. Neither Enzo nor Rosaria noticed him leave.

Guido swept the vestibule. Luca layered salami and provolone on proper slices of crusty bread and topped the filling with the rescued remains of the jar of relish. Everyone who came in knew that Matilda was missing.

Luca offered sandwiches and the same stock answer. Everyone on Bell Road was still looking for the child. They'd find her. He was waiting for Enzo to call.

"It's going to snow again," someone said. "Wherever the girl is, she won't be outside tonight."

When the midday rush was over, Luca stacked plates for Sonny to wash later. He checked the phone in

Vito's office to make sure it was in working order and left the door wide open so he'd hear the ring.

As the club quieted again, his thoughts ran in a vicious circle. *Where was Matilda? Had they hurt her? Was she frightened?*

The old-timers sipped their red wine and began a new chess match. Someone went into the library to read old newspapers from Naples and Palermo.

The front door banged open. To Luca's amazement, Maria Teresa Procopio pushed her way past Guido and his broom. "Where's Spinelli?" she demanded loudly.

Guido lumbered around her, blocking the woman from charging across the saloon. "This is a club for men," he said breathlessly.

Luca vaulted over the bar to confront her. "What do you want?"

"Spinelli." Maria Teresa had apparently recovered from the loss of her husband, Nick. The bloodshot eyes and grief-stricken expression from Jimmy Zambrano's funeral were gone, replaced by a fashionable gray hat and mouton coat. "I need to talk to Spinelli."

"He's not here." Once again, Luca was struck by Maria Teresa's resemblance to his dead wife Rafaella, albeit thirty years older.

"Then I'll talk to you," she said. "Everybody knows Spinelli doesn't move without you."

"Look, whatever you--."

Maria Teresa looked past him. "Get out," she snarled across the saloon at the old-timers.

They all scuttled into either the pool room or the library. Guido fled to the vestibule.

Satisfied that the saloon was now empty, Maria Teresa sat in the nearest chair and slapped down an envelope. "What do you know about this?"

"*Oddio*," Luca breathed and lowered himself into the chair across the table. The postmark was from Gary, Indiana.

Signora Procopio You are a rich widow. Unless you want to join your husband, pay 10,000 dollars. Watch for instructions in 5 days. If you tell the police we will send you all to hell and make you dead with knives and fire. We are not afraid of anything and delight to cut and stab again and again. We will burn you just like we burned Spinelli's place. We are watching you. Beware.

The letter was signed with a heart stabbed with a knife and dripping slashes.

"What's Spinelli doing about this?" Maria Teresa demanded. "They set the fire by the bocce courts, didn't they? Because he didn't pay?"

"I don't know." Even as he said the words, Luca knew that he did. Vito must have sold the cases of whiskey from the cellar to pay *La Mano Nera* but it wasn't enough. No doubt more demands were made, until Vito took out the loan from Tess's bank.

It was just as Inspector Finch warned. The blackmailers would ask for more and more until the club went bankrupt and Vito was forced to sell.

Luca pushed the letter across the table back to Maria Teresa. "Vito hasn't shown me any letters like this," he said truthfully. "But there's a man at the courthouse who's looking for people with letters from *La Mano Nera*. His name is Finch. He's a policeman for the Post Office."

"What good is he to me? Did he keep them from burning down Spinelli's stable? No." Maria Teresa stuffed the letter back in her pocket. "I heard about Russo's girl going missing from their place on Bell Road. Did *La Mano Nera* take her?"

Luca said nothing, more concerned with Matilda's safety than this woman's ire.

"So gangsters snatch our children and burn our homes." Maria Teresa stood up. "All you say is go talk to strangers. Lucky Lombardo. What does it matter to somebody like you? You have nothing. No home. No family."

She swept out, nearly trampling Guido as he tried to open the street door for her.

You have nothing. No home. No family. The words stung because they were true.

Luca unfolded himself from the chair, feeling every bump and bruise earned last night, and went into the library. "Go home," he said to the men behind the newspapers. "The club's closing early tonight."

"What's going on?" Tony Bilotti demanded.

"Bad weather's coming," Luca said. "Go home, all of you."

He delivered the same message in the pool room and to Guido. As the last whistle blew at the mill, Luca locked the front door and turned off the lights in the saloon.

Vito's office was dark. Luca hesitated in the doorway, hating what he had to do. Vito Spinelli had given him everything. A job. Respect. A place in the community. A sense of belonging that Luca never had before, neither as an orphan in Calabria nor as a young immigrant in New York City's tenements with a sick wife and a baby on the way.

Over the years Vito had never replaced Luca's own father, nor had Luca replaced Vito's son Ciro who died in the Great War, but the two had become the nucleus of the greater Galliano Club family.

We stay together, we'll be all right. Like family, no? Vito had said those exact words when he gave Luca a key to the door and the combination to the safe so many years ago. Since that moment, Luca had done everything Vito asked of him and even more that Vito had not. He'd been honest, loyal and protective.

Yet tonight, he would be a thief.

Luca switched on the desk lamp, throwing a circular pool of light over the messy surface littered with receipts and newspapers and the sticky residue of spilled whiskey. Working methodically, he combed through it all. No envelopes or letters signed with a bleeding heart.

The desk drawers yielded more old invoices, bills and receipts. Letters from distant relatives in Italy. A rock-hard bit of fruitcake. Two dirty glasses. Old notebooks with scribbles in both English and Italian. A scrapbook of clippings about the club's baseball team.

Nothing unexpected.

Luca moved on to the safe by the Chesterfield and dialed the combination from memory. Left, right, left. Back to zero. The dial didn't click. The handle didn't budge.

He dialed the combination again, with the same result. By the fourth try, Luca knew the truth.

Vito had changed the combination without telling

him.

Luca sat back on his heels. The table-height safe was a mass of iron. The chances of being able to pry the door open were slim to none.

Perhaps Vito had written down the combination. Luca combed through the desk again, then moved on to the shelves with their motley collection of old ledger books, yellow *National Geographic* magazines, and assorted club trophies. He took down the pictures on the wall and peered behind them in hopes of finding three numbers penciled on the back.

Nothing.

Luca threw himself into the desk chair and rubbed his shoulder, gingerly feeling the worst bruises from his tumble on Senate Street. The clock on the desk said he'd been hunting for over two hours. In the sepia-toned photograph next to it, the late Ciro Spinelli held his campaign hat, youthful and proud for all eternity. The young soldier had short curly hair, puttees wrapped around his calves and two medals on his Army uniform.

On impulse, Luca plucked the photograph off the desk and turned it over. The backing was thick butcher paper. Luca eased his thumb against the edge. Under the paper was the cardboard reverse of the photograph itself.

Numbers were inked in the bottom corner. *12 20*

18.

Luca automatically added the three digits. The solution was five.

Tess's favorite number. He took it as an omen.

The safe opened on the first try. Three unopened bottles of Old Bushmills sat on top of the usual collection of accounting ledgers, manila envelopes, and folders for club business.

The bottles of whiskey clanked together as he emptied the safe. Sitting on the floor, he combed through Vito's business correspondence, tax records, and banking papers. Life insurance policies from the San Gennaro Society for Vito and his wife were printed on heavy parchment and watermarked with an etching of the Italian society's patron saint. Letters of appreciation from Saint Rocco's Church for annual donations.

Luca found the deed to the club building, letters from the Lido Building and Loan Co-operative insurance company regarding recent damage and canceled checks for everything from heating oil to imported prosciutto. A book of coupons to pay a new loan from the First National Bank of Lido.

One envelope held a flimsy yellow telegram dated December 20, 1918 that told Ciro Spinelli's parents that their son was dead. Another contained a raft of letters from lawyers. Each one said, with varying degrees of politeness, that Ciro Spinelli was a battlefield casualty and that his body would not come back to Lido for burial. Ciro would lie where he fell.

Concealed in an accordion folder marked "Receipts," a dozen white envelopes each bore a red stamp canceled with a postmark from Gary, Indiana. They were all addressed to Vito, not at the club, but to his home address. Had he brought them to the club to conceal them from his wife?

Tearing the envelopes in his haste to read what was inside, Luca still had the presence of mind to sort them in chronological order based on the date of the postmark. Heart in his throat, he unfolded one letter after another. The threats were all similar, written in by-now familiar block printing, and signed with the stabbed heart and dripping slashes of *La Mano Nera*.

Spinelli don't risk it. You owe for your crime. The price is now 10000 dollars. If you don't pay we will burn everything you got and your wife GUTTED. You put Zambrano in the river like a COWARD and LIAR. What you did will be EXPOSED. Pay up or die with a million stabs in your heart. They will spit on your grave.

The letter fell out of Luca's suddenly nerveless fingers. There was only one person who thought he saw Vito's Packard at the river the night that Jimmy Zambrano was killed.

Al Genovese.

Al Genovese, who had tried to blackmail Luca into marrying his kid sister Annunziata with the same accusation.

Al Genovese who lived on Bell Road and could have easily damaged Enzo's smokehouse and stolen Matilda.

Al Genovese was the local accomplice.

The realization was staggering. Luca left everything on the floor, uncapped a bottle of Old Bushmills and took a throat-searing gulp.

Al Genovese obviously thought Luca had confided in Enzo after Jimmy Zambrano's body went into the Mohawk River.

Luca mentally kicked himself for not making the connections on his own. He'd been too shocked by Enzo's stupid mistake with Rosaria's cousin Gina to question the reference to the river. Too distraught over the missing child.

All the farmers along Bell Road had dynamite for clearing fields. It would have been a simple matter for Genovese to blow up Enzo's smokehouse.

And even easier for Genovese to snatch Matilda. They were neighbors. She was playmates with his children. She would not be afraid of him.

The whiskey burned Luca's throat and turned shock into resolve.

Right now finding Matilda was the only thing that mattered. Luca would deal with Al Genovese now and Inspector Finch later.

He needed reinforcements.

CHAPTER 37

He's bad news

"Jesus, Fishy," Benny said. "Snap out of it. All you got to do is divvy up the cut and send the twenty percent."

Spinelli had paid up again and the pickup went real smooth. But Fishy was staring at the dough like it was poison.

They were in the office niche but the conversation was still punctuated by the rumble of barrels rolling across the uneven stone floor and the slosh of water into the big vats for another batch of beer. Broz was snapping out instructions in Polish. Benny didn't know what Broz was saying, but he liked the way the Polish boys hopped to it.

"Postal inspectors are very powerful law enforcement officers," Owen said. "You and Genovese are headed for trouble. I never wanted to be part of it. I told you that."

"Here." Benny plucked a C-note off the table and tucked it into Owen's coat pocket, grinning as his fingertips encountered the accountant's pistol. "Buy something extra nice for the missus."

Owen shrank back. "I mean it, Benny. I don't want Genovese around here anymore. You never consulted me about him and I don't trust him. He's . . . he's bad news."

"He gives you any grief, just show him your popgun." Benny patted Owen's cheek hard enough to sting but not enough to be a slap. They both knew the accountant was never going to use it. "That'll teach him."

The groan of an engine straining to come over the berm at high speed drowned out the glug of water being poured into the vats. Tires screeched to a stop outside the pumphouse. Just as Benny reached for the Colt Pocket Hammerless and Owen hastily stuffed the cash into a canvas bag, Broz called a greeting.

A moment later, Al ran into the niche. "They know, Benny, they know. You got to help me!"

"Oh my God," Owen squeaked.

"What are you talking about?" Benny grabbed the front of Al's coat. The *cafone's* eyes were wide circles of fright in a face chapped red from the cold night.

"They know, they know." Al was close to blubbering like a stinking baby.

"Who?"

"Lombardo." Snot dribbled out of Al's nose.

"Lombardo and two goons. I don't know who they are."

"Lombardo's nobody." Benny gave Al a little shake.

"He had the letters we sent to Spinelli," Al moaned.

Benny swore. "What did you tell him?"

"I made Claudia open the door and say I wasn't home."

"And then you raced straight here?"

"Yes." Al nodded compulsively. "I came straight here. You got to do something, Benny. I'm cooked!"

"You idiot." Benny gave the stooge another shake, hard enough to make his teeth rattle. "You came straight here. They musta followed you!"

"No, no. I waited until they left."

"You're sure?" Benny realized that Owen was listening to every word. Hands still bunched in Al's coat, Benny dragged the farmer outside.

It was snowing like the devil. The delivery trucks were covered in a sheen of sparkling white. Benny's Cadillac glowed like a lumpy ghost in the thin moonlight. Al's truck was the only vehicle without a layer of snow. The top of the berm was scored by swerving tire tracks but in another half hour they'd be obscured by the fat flakes.

"Now give it to me straight," Benny said. "What does Lombardo know?"

Al gulped. "Lombardo knows all about your pal Big

Vinnie. How the letters get mailed. Said there's some big deal from the Post Office investigating all the mail postmarked from Gary, Indiana."

"Did the wife tell him to scram?" Benny asked. Al had just become the kind of problem the Lido Outfit didn't need.

The door to the pumphouse banged and Owen was suddenly in their midst. "I knew it!" the accountant cried. "The authorities know all about your little blackmail scheme. We're all going to wind up in jail."

"Jesus, Fishy," Benny snapped. "Shut up."

But for once Owen wasn't cowed. "I told you," he screeched. "I met that postal inspector and he's getting ready to arrest all of us. What's to keep the men who came to your house from talking to him? How do you know they haven't already?"

"Benny, I ain't going to jail for you." Al knuckled his eyes, voice close to breaking. "I got kids. Cows. My wife is gonna kill me."

Benny let him go, thoroughly disgusted.

"Finch is relentless, I tell you," Owen raved at Benny. "He's here, all the way from Indiana. He knows all about the letters. The stamps were marked before they even got pasted onto the letters!"

Al gave a sob.

"Shut up," Benny said savagely to the farmer and

jabbed a finger at Owen. "This fella from Indiana doesn't know nothing."

"I'm not going to jail because of you and your so-called information racket," Owen cried. "I'm a member of the Bison Club!"

"What am I going to do?" Al clutched at Benny.

"Get out," Owen screamed and pointed his little popgun at Al.

CHAPTER 38

Tire tracks

"Turn around," Karol said.

"He's got to be ahead of us." Toby peered over the wheel at the empty street.

"No," Karol said. The old topographic map from the Lido Premium library unfolded in his mind's eye. "He turned."

"Where?" Toby asked. "There's no cross street."

"See that break in the trees? Turn there." Karol wiped condensation off the inside of his end of the windshield.

"Jesus wept," Toby swore. "It's not a street."

"Turn!" Karol exclaimed. "He's heading for the cemetery."

"At least you're big enough to push the truck out of the snow if we get stuck," Toby grumbled and hauled on the wheel. The truck skidded into a turn, the slick road and heavy false rear panel combining to make the going treacherous. Sitting between the other two men, Luca nearly fell into Karol's lap.

"Tire tracks!" Karol could just make out fresh lines

in the snow as the windshield wipers batted back and forth.

Toby swore again as he downshifted. The headlights picked out the tracks but the snow would soon cover them. The truck battled through the night as the ground sloped up. The stones of the old graveyard rose on the right, exactly where the cemetery was on the map.

"I know where we are," Toby said. "The river is on the other side."

"I saw an old map," Karol said. "What's left of the old mill is between the cemetery and the river."

"You think Genovese is holding Matilda there?" Luca asked.

"It's a ruin," Karol said. "There's not much left. A chimney and some old stones. I saw a picture."

"*Oddio*," Luca swore. "If he put her in a chimney, I'll kill him."

"I'll help," Toby growled, hunched over the wheel.

"Stop the truck," Karol said. "It can't be much further. They'll hear us coming."

Toby coasted to a halt. The truck idled roughly as the windshield wipers continued the fight. "What do you want to do?" the Irishman asked.

"Follow him," Luca said immediately. "Hide the truck and follow the tracks on foot."

"Jesus wept. I'll never get her started again." Toby

swerved off the track, aimed for some scrubby pines and cut the engine.

The three men got out of the truck. Their boots were muffled by the freshly fallen snow. Karol fastened the top buttons of his mackinaw and pulled his scarf over his ears. The brim of his cap kept the snow out of his eyes, but just barely.

He led the way, using Genovese's swiftly fading tracks as well as his memory of the map as guides. The route took them around the cemetery. Snow turned the headstones into eerie humps of white. Something fluttered by Karol's head and he ducked, causing the other two men to reflexively do the same.

"Something brushed by me," Karol whispered.

"Bats?" Toby glanced around.

"Crows," Luca muttered. "Winter crows."

A large black bird perched an ancient stone, causing a tiny cascade of snow. As it regarded the three men, the bird stretched and flapped wings as long as Karol's arm.

"You think it's some kind of gatekeeper?" Toby didn't move.

"It's a crow. Just a crow." But Luca's voice was strained as if he, too, wondered if the birds were a message from the dead.

Karol shook off the thought. "Come on," he said.

The tire tracks ended on a rise, as if Al Genovese had driven over a cliff. But a faint glow rose from the other side. Snatches of talk carried over the rise, voices muffled by snow and distance.

"Here." Karol elbowed the other two toward a mausoleum on the extreme edge of the cemetery. Level with the berm, the granite structure was a miniature castle with a deep Gothic arch framing each side and the word BLICK chiseled above.

One at a time, they edged their way to the arch on the side overlooking the cliff and crouched in the shadow of the overhang.

The ruins of the old Packham Foundry were below them, no more than six or seven car lengths away, a scrapyard of strange shapes conquered by time and nature. Cloaked in snow, the brick chimney rose like a ghost from a broken casket.

The biggest remaining structure was a windowless stone cottage. Several vehicles were parked in front, including Genovese's truck.

Swollen with winter snow and wearing a rime of ice on either shore, the river silently swept past the eerie landscape. A tangle of fallen trees and mounded debris cluttered the riverbank.

The door to the cottage was open, illuminating three men confronting each other in the falling snow.

"Genovese," Luca breathed.

"Rotolo," Toby added.

"Mr. Fisher," Karol said. "He's the one with a gun."

CHAPTER 39

Dressed in armor

Wearing the charcoal velvet dress, opera gloves, and matching headband, Ruth came down the curving stairway of Osa and Jack Rutherford's house. The chiffon godet pleats furled and unfurled with every step. The dress from Van Dyke's was armor against the scandal that waited for her at the Candyland Supper Club, a horned beast poised to chew her up and spit out the pieces along some lonely railroad track.

The rhinestone and jet bead necklace twinkled in the glow of the chandelier. Ruth's russet curls were tucked into the headband and held in place with rhinestone clips.

The crowd of partygoers milling through the foyer watched her descend. Henry was there, tall and lean and elegant in white tie and black tails. A cluster of medals adorned his lapel.

The corner of his mouth tipped up and his gaze stayed on her all the way down the stairs. "You look radiant," he said as Ruth reached the bottom.

"Thank you, Henry," Ruth said softly. "No matter

what happens. Thank you for everything."

There was so much more she wanted to say but couldn't. Thank you for having a plan to save me, even if it doesn't work. For wanting to save me.

"Are you ready?" he asked.

"Yes."

She met a dizzying number of people, many of whom would return for the house party after the ball. Most were family members. Ruth heard the names Blick, Packham, and Rutherford over and over.

Henry and Osa had two brothers, both doctors who lived in Syracuse. Younger than Henry, they seemed delighted to meet her, as were their wives who gushed over her dress. Henry came in for some gentle ribbing with comments like "Caught at last, Henry," and "About time, old man."

Henry didn't refute them. Ruth felt her face grow warm and said as little as possible.

After a cavalcade of cousins, Henry introduced her to Mr. Nathan Packham, the uncle who owned Lido Premium. "I've come to rely on Henry's judgment," Packham said, leaning on an ebony stick and eyeing Ruth through an old-fashioned pince-nez. "I find it faultless yet again."

Ruth and Henry went to Candyland in the Pierce Arrow with Osa, Jack, and the two sons who were home from boarding school. Jeffrey and Arthur were twins with their father's handsome features and good nature. They went to Choate, an exclusive boarding school and planned to attend Cornell College next September.

She felt a momentary pang for Sonny Zambrano, who worked in the Galliano Club after school. The boy had a fire inside that the Rutherford boys, as pleasant as they were, would never have, but they'd go to college while Sonny's highest achievement would probably be to replace Luca behind the bar.

Then Ruth became conscious of Henry's leg against her thigh in the cramped car and her mind went blank.

A newsreel photographer captured guests' amazed expressions as they entered the Candyland Supper Club. Attendants in white sailor suits escorted them into the ballroom where a ship with sails towered to the ceiling. The orchestra was arranged on the deck, members clad as admirals. The dance floor, painted turquoise with white ripples to simulate dancing on waves, spread out below.

Across from the ship, a moonlit beach, complete with a thatched hut and enough sand to build ten castles, invited play time. Along with huge paper stars, a crescent moon hovered above dozens of skirted dinner tables. Giant arrangements of tropical flowers, bowls of pineapples, and potted palms were everywhere.

As they marveled at the decorations, girls in grass skirts and coconut brassieres circulated with trays of lime and soda water cocktails. Others offered wreaths of fresh flowers to wear as necklaces. Ruth accepted one. Henry declined.

A master of ceremonies announced Osa as the guest of honor and read a dozen telegrams from notable people wishing her happy birthday and many happy returns of the day. One message was from Mrs. Coolidge, the president's wife!

"They're both well-known advocates of the Red Cross," Henry murmured in Ruth's ear.

Jack made a speech, as did a delegation from the Women's Institute, and then the two sons entertained the crowd with an original poem written in Osa's honor that had every mother present dabbing at her eyes.

The orchestra played as the meal was served, guests seated at an enormous horseshoe-shaped table that anchored the center of the ballroom. Ruth was so nervous she could barely swallow a mouthful, although one delicious course after another was set in front of her. Henry ate with the same beautiful manner on display at Buckner's, with no trace of anxiety or trepidation at the hoax he and Ruth were enacting.

At the end of the meal, a huge cake was wheeled in, the orchestra struck up *Happy Birthday*, and a sailor popped out of the cake with a dozen long-stemmed red roses for Osa. Jack pretended to be jealous and intent on vanquishing his rival to win Osa's hand. The result was a hilarious chase around the ballroom while the music played faster and faster and Jack and the sailor tried to keep up. The clever and unexpected bit of slapstick had everyone in stitches.

After cake and coffee, couples moved onto the dance floor. Ruth and Henry sailed through a foxtrot and quickstep. A waltz began next. Ruth was in heaven as they danced again, closer this time. The godet pleats swirled around her calves, more elegant than any Broadway costume.

They moved together seamlessly, faultlessly, in complete harmony. Her nerves eased.

When the music stopped, Ruth realized that they'd taken over the dance floor. The other couples, including Osa and Jack, had stopped to watch them. Ruth and Henry left the floor to a round of spontaneous applause.

Mayor John Peabody, a handsome man about Henry's age, whom Ruth recognized from the newspaper, tapped Henry on the shoulder. "May I, Blick?" he asked. "This may be the most enchanting creature in the room and I defy you to monopolize her all night."

"Mayor John Peabody, may I present Miss Ruth

Cross," Henry said.

"Miss Cross. A pleasure to meet you." The mayor had a high forehead, chestnut hair, and a web of laugh lines around his wise hazel eyes. "The Tapping Toes School of Dance?"

"Yes," Ruth said. "How did you know?"

"We don't have many women business owners in Lido," he said, holding out his hand. "I can manage a serviceable totter around the floor if you keep your expectations quite low."

Henry gave Ruth an encouraging nod. The mayor had been at the Bison Club banquet.

She smiled at Peabody, hoping her lips didn't tremble. "I'd be delighted."

Peabody whisked Ruth away to the center of the dance floor. He was light on his feet and easy to follow. It helped that he stuck to basic steps. Ruth was quite sure he would never try anything as exotic as the Argentine tango.

"So Miss Cross," he said. "How is business at Tapping Toes?"

"Doing quite well," Ruth said. "We're getting ready for the annual Christmas pageant. I do hope you'll come."

"I wouldn't miss it for the world." He steered her away from the orchestra where it was quieter. "How did you and Henry meet?"

Ruth felt herself tense. So the mayor would deliver the first salvo. "He and Osa and Jack attend my ballroom dance class."

"Dear Lord." Peabody gave a laugh. "Teaching Henry Blick to dance. I do believe you are the bravest person in all Christendom, Miss Cross."

"He's done very well," Ruth said loyally.

"I sense that you are a very kind woman."

She waited for him to say something else, to say that he knew that she was a fraud and O'Malley's whore. When he just kept smiling and guiding her around the floor, Ruth asked if she could ask him a question.

"Of course," Peabody said.

"Would you consider Henry Blick to be an honest man?"

Peabody raised his eyebrows. "I've been friends with Henry Blick since we were toddlers imprisoned in the same playpen while our mothers drank tea and complained about their husbands. I consider him to be the best, truest man I know."

"Thank you," Ruth managed. Henry had very far to fall if scandal came for them.

After the dance, Henry and Peabody retired to the smoking lounge. Osa commandeered Ruth for a cozy chinwag with the ladies of the Women's Institute. To a woman, they were agog that Lido's most eligible bachelor had given his heart away. Ruth parried their questions as best she could. As at their lunch together at Babylon, there was no doubt in her mind that Osa knew absolutely nothing about the real purpose of Ruth's presence at her birthday party.

When the conversation segued into a rehash of recent Women's Institute projects, Ruth excused herself and went in search of the smoking lounge.

There, the orchestra music was a pleasant backdrop to deep throated male conversations and clouds of tobacco smoke. Ruth noticed two women among the tuxedos, both enjoying cigars.

French doors lined the far wall. They were all slightly ajar, letting in fresh air.

Henry wasn't among the circle of smokers. Following the murmur of male voices, Ruth went to the French doors.

He was outside, on the other side of the glass, deep in conversation with Mayor Peabody. Wreathed in cigar smoke, the two men leaned against a low rock wall frosted with brittle ivy. Both had tumblers of whiskey and wore serious expressions.

"O'Malley was the man of the hour," Henry said. His voice was just loud enough for Ruth to eavesdrop. "I didn't want to make a scene."

"He was drunk as a skunk," Peabody observed. "No one took him seriously. To a lout like O'Malley, any woman who has been on a stage has a past."

"I'm taking it seriously," Henry said. "O'Malley forced his attentions on Miss Cross. She spurned him and he's taking his revenge."

Ruth marveled that Henry could lie with no hesitation at all, especially to such a close friend. He was so composed, so in control of this ruthless sea of sparkling society and hidden secrets. Her secrets.

Ruthie June Crosswater's secrets.

Peabody tapped ash onto the frozen grass. "What can I do?"

"I'd appreciate it if you had a word with Chief Doyle."

"Give O'Malley another patrol area? And a warning to stop making baseless accusations?"

"At the very least."

"Consider it done." Peabody looked sideways at Henry. "Just how serious are you about Miss Cross?"

Henry took a long pull from his glass. "It was my assumption for many years that I would die a bachelor. After meeting her, that assumption is no longer valid."

"Well, knock me over with a feather," Peabody said happily. "Put me down for either the silver fish slice or the punch bowl, unless Osa has already claimed those on the gift registry."

Henry laughed but all Ruth heard was a buzzing in her ears as she backed away. He was taking their little hoax too far.

He found her in the ballroom a few minutes later. Ruth could barely meet his eye. They swirled around the dance floor for the last time.

In the small hours of the morning, they piled into the Pierce-Arrow for the ride home through a snowy landscape. Ruth fought to stay awake and pretend nothing was the matter. She ended up on the living room sofa picking at a plate of ham and eggs from the buffet set up in the dining room. Everyone was buoyed by the success of the evening and a few were happily drunk. The Packham and Blick families were nothing if not tireless.

The next thing she knew, Ruth was cradled in Henry's arms as he carried her up the curving staircase.

"What's going on?" she mumbled sleepily.

"You fell asleep," Henry said. He carried her effortlessly.

Without thinking, Ruth twined her arms around his neck and pressed her cheek into his shoulder. Henry smelled like soap and tobacco.

He gained the top of the stairs and went down the hall to the guest room before gently depositing Ruth on her feet in front of the door. The hallway was lit by a carriage light. A series of murky landscape paintings on the wall absorbed the glow, leaving them in shadow.

"Henry." Ruth let her hands slide to his chest and lightly touched the line of bright ribbons and medals on his lapel. Jack Rutherford and the other men had loosened their ties and discarded their waistcoats as they tackled the buffet, but Henry was as starched and polished as he was at the beginning of the evening. "I heard what you said to Mayor Peabody."

"O'Malley will be reassigned and warned to stay away from you."

"No, the other thing."

"Ah," Henry said.

"You shouldn't have said that. You went too far. What if this all goes dreadfully wrong?"

"I saw no reason to hide my true intentions from one of my closest friends. Nor from you." A line of worry creased his forehead. "Unless you find me an unsatisfactory life partner."

Ruth dropped her hands. "Wait until you see the report from those Pinkerton detectives. It's going to tell you terrible things about me. You'll feel differently."

"The report is highly unlikely to affect my esteem for you."

Below them, other guests passed through the foyer;

talking and laughing and completely unaware that Ruth's heart was in mortal danger.

"May I kiss you good night?" Henry asked.

Ruth nodded.

His kiss was unhesitating, yet not rushed. Gentle, yet with intent.

When they broke the kiss, Henry traced a thumb over her cheek. "I have to work in the morning," he said. "Greer will take you home when you're ready to go."

Ruth nodded, unable to say a word.

Henry reached past her to open the guest room door, switched on the light, and eased her inside. "Good night."

The latch clicked and Ruth was alone in the guest room.

She plastered herself against the door and listened through the wood until Henry's footsteps faded away.

CHAPTER 40

Never thought he had the nerve

Benny didn't think Owen had the guts, but the accountant's hand was steady as he held the popgun.

Al raised his hands like he was being collared by the police. "Tell him, Benny," Al begged, eyes as big as soup plates. "Tell him it's not my fault."

"Real interesting situation we got here," Benny allowed. "You got anything to negotiate with, Al?"

"I thought we was partners, Fishy," Al sputtered, eyes on the muzzle.

"Partners?" The word shot out of the accountant's mouth. "I said I didn't want any part of your blackmail shenanigans."

The snow was slacking off. The pearly white ground was marred with their footprints. Benny saw Broz and his fellas start to sidle out of the pumphouse. One of them had a Tommy gun. Benny gave his head a tiny shake. They went back inside. The door stayed open.

"I had the dope on Spinelli," Al said, voice all whiny. "You saw the money. He paid up. You're in it as much as any of us."

"Blackmail!" Owen shrilled, the gun still pointing at Al's midsection. "I never consented to be part of your blackmail scheme. I sat next to that postal inspector at the Bison Club dinner! He knows everything!"

"He can't," Al beseeched, looking from Owen to Benny and back again. "Benny said the plan was foolproof. Tell him, Benny."

"Lombardo and his buddies are looking for you, not me," Benny observed. He felt the weight of the Colt Pocket Hammerless in its secret pocket but didn't want to pull it out. Not yet. Not if Owen could do the job alone.

Al was actually crying. "Don't let him shoot me."

"The marks are after him," Benny murmured to Owen out of the side of his mouth. "He's a squealer. Unless you do him, we're all going to jail."

"I can't go to jail," Owen said. "I'm a member of the Bison Club."

Benny shook his head. "Not if we all get arrested because Al here is a squealer."

Now if Al had kept his trap shut, he might have come out of this in one piece but the *cafone* let out a sobbing roar and charged. The popgun went off with a bark that was swallowed by the snow. Benny stepped back as Al swayed, his face smeared with surprise. Owen fired point-blank again and again, his arm jerking with the recoil until Al crashed to the ground and the gun just made clicking noises.

The echo of the last shot faded away. Owen blinked and stopped pulling the trigger. He lowered the empty revolver and stared at the man lying on the ground at his feet. "Is he dead?"

"Sure, he's dead. You done him good." Benny worked the toe of his shoe under Al's pumpkin-sized head and shoved so that Al looked blankly at the accountant. "See?"

"I didn't mean to," Owen said in a gasping sort of way.

"Sure you did." Benny's ears still rang but he felt like skipping home and banging Trixie to celebrate. "You done us all a favor. Took care of a problem. Just like the way it's done in Chicago."

"I couldn't go to jail," Owen said mechanically. "What would Cynthia say? My fraternity? The Bison Club? I'm on the Membership Committee. Or I will be soon. I've just been nominated. Henry Blick's on that committee so you see how important it is. I have to be on the Membership Committee. I can't go to jail. I haven't blackmailed anybody."

Benny saw it before in Chicago. A fella pops another fella and is so jazzed he can't stop talking. He pried the empty popgun out of Owen's hand. "Stop jawboning. Clean-up time."

The door to the pumphouse was open. Broz and the fellas had watched, of course. Benny gestured at them with Owen's empty gun. "Our money man knows how to take care of business, understand? If he goes down, everybody goes down. Broz, you make sure the boys understand."

"Sure, Benny."

Benny wasn't worried. Broz had his Polish boys under control. Besides, this wasn't the first time they'd seen a stiff.

A fast plan and Broz climbed into Al's truck. He maneuvered so that it was pointed at the river. He and the boys wrestled Al's body into the front seat and left him slumped against the dashboard with the engine running. Snow mixed with the puddle of blood where the body had lain, soon pink in the murky moonlight.

Owen stopped yammering about his club and turned into a store mannequin.

Benny got behind the wheel of the big delivery van to do the honors and show that the boss wasn't afraid of nothing. After some fancy backing and sliding, the heavy vehicle was aligned with the tailgate of Al's truck. The snow was barely sifting down now, but Benny still needed the wipers to make sure he knew where the riverbank ended and the water began.

With the clang of cold metal against cold metal, the van tapped Al's back bumper.

After a couple of tentative pushes, Benny backed up, then floored the accelerator. With the boom of a cannon, the heavy delivery truck rammed into its target. Al's truck rolled forward. The river came up fast. Benny felt the front tires lose traction and jammed his foot on the brake just in time.

Al's truck shot ahead, hung in the air and did a nosedive into the river. The heavy engine pulled the truck down and the back end flipped skyward, spraying bits of hay and a wave of water over the nose of the van.

Benny flinched and threw the engine into reverse and clawed back from the brink.

The swollen black river gave a huge, gurgling belch as Al and his ride disappeared into a watery grave. Broz's men hollered at the spectacle.

Owen still hadn't moved. Benny got out of the van and pressed the empty popgun into his hand. "You don't want to be caught with this. Toss it in."

"You mean . . ." Owen trailed off.

"Go on." Benny gave the accountant a shove. "Every made man loses the gun that traces him to a stiff."

Owen obediently picked his way to the water's edge and threw the gun. The plop was a whisper compared to the loud bang and gurgle of Al's truck going over the riverbank.

"Good job, Fishy." Benny swatted the other man's cheek. "You're a real torpedo now. A made man."

"Genovese can't sign his name in my ledger now," Owen said like it was important.

CHAPTER 41

Witness to murder

Headlights swept across the cemetery, but their beams didn't touch the mausoleum. Nonetheless, Karol pressed himself against the mausoleum's hard granite.

He'd done hard things in his life, saw men hurt and maimed in industrial accidents, but he'd never witnessed a murder before. He felt guilty for doing nothing to prevent it.

Crouched next to him, Luca's face was like marble. Toby had a flask in his hand.

Fisher's car topped the rise and coasted down toward the cemetery. Spitting snow from the rear tires, the car trundled past the snow-covered mausoleum. Karol glimpsed the accountant hunched over the wheel, snow visible on the shoulders of his coat.

Al Genovese's tire tracks had been obliterated by the snow, but Fisher apparently knew the way well enough to navigate his way back to Railroad Street. The accountant's Ford continued along the curving track until it disappeared from sight.

Luca started to rise out of his crouch. Karol put a

warning hand on his friend's arm as another engine roared to life.

"Jesus wept," Toby swore. "Haven't we seen enough."

Headlights again cut the night sky. An engine protested the frozen ground on the other side of the rise.

Rotolo's big Cadillac popped into view. Chains on the rear tires jangled like sleigh bells in the clear night air and propelled the big vehicle over the lip of the rise and down the other side.

"If it isn't himself," Toby murmured. "Rotolo."

Three more vehicles followed the Cadillac over the lip of the rise and through the cemetery. Pressed against the freezing block of granite, Karol set his jaw to keep his teeth from chattering. Luca and Toby were shivering.

The sound of the engines faded away. A single vehicle remained in the clearing. The stone cottage was silent. The old chimney glittered in a patch of weak moonlight. The inky river flowed as before, remorseless and indifferent.

Karol unfolded himself and nearly fell over. His feet were frozen and his knees could barely unbend after so long in a cramped position. Luca and Toby muffled their groans as they, too, found it hard to stand.

"Ah, Jesus wept," Toby beseeched the heavens.

"Freezing my balls off, I am."

The Irishman took a long pull from his flask, then handed it around. Karol's eyes watered as the whiskey hit bottom. Luca coughed.

"We have to go to the police," Karol said. "Report a murder."

"If we go to the police they'll kill Matilda," Luca reminded him.

"Rotolo pays Chief Doyle a thousand dollars a week." Toby prodded Karol's chest with a chilly finger. "That's more than the girl is worth right now. Instead of rushing off to be Mr. Upstanding Citizen, think about the opportunity. 'Tis a gift, so it is."

"Opportunity?" Karol echoed. "A man's dead and a child is missing. Where's the opportunity?"

"Your Mr. Fisher has put himself in a difficult position, hasn't he?" Toby passed the flask around again.

"He killed a man!"

"And a laddie who knows should be able to ask him a favor and expect to get it."

"You think he knows where Matilda is?" Luca gulped whiskey and gave the flask to Karol.

"Sure and isn't he also in a position to pay handsomely for the privilege of telling?"

Karol's jaw dropped. "Blackmail him?"

"Genius," Luca said.

Karol stared from Toby to Luca in amazement. "You're not serious."

"Matilda first, then we get Vito's money back." Luca rapidly outlined a plan.

Another swallow of whiskey and Karol found himself in awe of his friend's blithe disregard for the law, not to mention his confidence that the plan would work. He could tell that Toby was equally impressed.

"Remember, we can't trust Fisher," Luca summed up. "He's already cheated Rotolo."

Toby pocketed the now-empty flask. "Meaning he could cheat us, too."

"It's a chance we have to take," Luca said.

"Not necessarily." Karol could hardly believe it, but he could plug the hole in Luca's plan. He outlined his idea and watched a grin spread across Luca's face.

"Brilliant," Toby said in admiration.

Karol never would have agreed to such a wild plan if it wasn't for the dented car in the clearing. One man was dead, but perhaps another could find salvation.

The impromptu conference over, only their footsteps and labored breathing broke the silence of the cemetery as Karol led the way over the berm, all nearly falling as they skidded down the other side.

No one jumped out of the old Ford or opened the

door to the stone cottage. Karol wished he had a light to look around. The murder had taken place right where he was standing. Tire tracks and footsteps had churned away the evidence.

Snow was still falling, spare flakes swallowed by softly lapping water. He wondered if Al Genovese's ghost was watching from the river.

Toby tugged at the door to the stone cottage. It opened with a slight creak.

Inside, Karol was struck first by the pungent smell of yeast, then by the sheer scale of the operation. He saw industrial vats, the same as in the mill, as well as dozens of wooden barrels and malt cases stacked against the wall as high as his head.

"If I was going big time into the beer racket," Toby said, walking deeper into the gloomy space with hands jammed into the pockets of his pea coat. "This is exactly the setup I'd want."

A man stepped out from behind a partition, a Tommy gun held at waist level.

"Hello, Broz," Karol said.

CHAPTER 42

Breach of promise

Tess smoothed sweaty palms on her jade green silk dress and knocked briskly on the door to the vice president's office. When James responded she slipped inside and stood with her back to the door.

James looked up from the loan application on his desk. "What is it?"

"I'm breaking off our engagement," Tess said, exactly as she'd practiced.

"What?" James frowned.

Tess darted forward and dropped the pretty diamond ring on his desk near the nameplate proclaiming *James R. Howland, Vice President*. "Here's the ring. I hope you find someone who genuinely wants to marry you. Someone else. Not me."

"Don't be a ninny." James scooped it up and brandished the ring at her. "Put this back on."

"I can't," Tess said. "I'm not going to marry you."

"Of course you are." James came around the side of the desk. "Put the ring back on. I won't stand for this sort of nonsense."

"Listen to me, James." Tess stood her ground, although her heart pounded. "We are not getting married. The engagement is off. I will return all the gifts we got at the engagement party and send out letters of apology. Whatever your mother thinks is the right thing to do. But it's over."

"Give me your hand," James commanded.

"Are you listening? The engagement is off."

"It's not off until Mother says so."

"Can't you even accept that we're not getting married without bringing your mother into this?" Tess exclaimed. "I'm sorry if I hurt your feelings but we both know we don't care for each other. We don't even like each other. If we got married, we'd both be spectacularly unhappy."

"I'll sue you for breach of promise," James warned.

"Go ahead. You know I haven't any money. All you'll get is twenty dollars and your name in the newspaper."

The color rose in James's face. Every ballplayer on his upper lip stood at attention. "I'll ruin you. Your aunt, too."

"Leave Aunt Evelyn alone." Tess had been nearly incapacitated with nerves before coming into the office but now she was just mad. "Marriage means the rest of our lives and I want to love a man who loves me. We both know you don't. Why should you? I don't love you."

"Romantic nonsense," James spat, his face now beet-red. "We're getting married. The banns have already been posted at the church. The invitations have been sent out. Monsignor Parnell is coming and everything. You can't call it off now."

"Would it be better if I left you at the altar?"

"You wouldn't dare."

"That's why I'm telling you now." Tess grabbed the door knob. "You needn't bother firing me. I've cleaned out my desk. I'll get a job somewhere else."

"Not in another bank you won't. My father will make sure you never work in Lido again. No respectable man will ever touch you, either."

Tess was done. There was nothing left to say. "Goodbye, James."

"Leave now and you'll regret it for the rest of your life," James swore. "My father will make sure of it."

"Not your mother?" Tess heard herself ask.

She yanked open the door and waded into a sea of stunned faces. All of the account managers apparently heard every word. She and James must have been shouting.

Tess put on her coat and hat. Her hands shook, making the simple task of slotting buttons into buttonholes an agonizingly slow exercise. She found her handbag and gloves and picked up the small box containing the items which had personalized her desk. A miniature of her father. The marble cup from Florence used for pencils. Her favorite pen and leather blotter.

The nameplate reading *Miss Tess Kennedy, Account Manager* stayed where it was. She'd never really had the same job as the other account managers. They just let her pretend.

Tess threaded her way through the desks and passed through the wooden gate to say goodbye to the tellers. There was a ripple of noise in her wake as chairs swiveled and account books closed. She didn't look back, yet knew James was standing in his office doorway, staring daggers at her.

It was a long walk alone across the lobby, buffeted by surging waves of disapproval. Tess held her chin high, jutted her jaw and put one foot in front of the other, intent on preserving some modicum of dignity.

"Have a lovely evening, Miss Kennedy," the doorman murmured.

"Thank you," Tess said loudly.

He opened the door. Tess marched through.

Outside, the sky was a lovely shade of violet. The air was nippy, with the promise of more snow. The sidewalk in front of the bank was gritty with sand. Pedestrians passed by, galoshes buckles jingling. Traffic trundled through the intersection at the American Corner. The Western Union office was brightly lit. A boy selling newspapers shouted the headlines. *Tornado Hits Maryland, School Blown Away!*

Tess hurried toward the lot where the Ford coupe waited. Faster and faster until she was running and running and laughing and gulping big breaths of freedom.

CHAPTER 44

You mean to blackmail me

"Owen Forbes Fisher, you are a successful man. You are clever. You are capable. You are in the inner circle."

Owen stared at himself in the mirror. His eyes were red and his skin sallow. His hand shook as he parted his hair. How many times would he have to repeat his mantra this morning before he was convinced that he'd done the right thing by getting rid of that smelly farmer?

The tragedy at the pumphouse filled his thoughts. Benny whispering in Owen's ear. The bark of the gun. The shock on Genovese's face. How Broz's boys laughed like loons when the dead man and his truck disappeared into the inky depths of the river.

Owen Forbes Fisher, you are a successful man. You are clever. You are capable. You are in the inner circle.

It was no use. The mantra wasn't working. The inner circle was more elusive than ever. Everett Farnum had been forced to resign from the Bison Club simply for getting a divorce. If Owen was arrested, not only would he go to jail, but he'd be booted off the Membership

Committee.

Cynthia would leave him and go back to her Medusa of a mother.

His mother-in-law reminded him of Benny, both frighteningly effective in sly, needling ways. What had Benny called him after the shooting? A torpedo.

"Owen Forbes Fisher, you are a torpedo," he whispered to his reflection. "A made man."

Owen liked the way the word felt on his tongue. *Torpedo. Torpedo.* A torpedo was someone with the power to give and take life.

He stiffened his spine and left the comb on the edge of the sink. Nobody told a torpedo where to put his hair comb.

Owen kept up the inner pep talk as he drove to the mill. The morning was as gloomy as last night, with a dirty sky that obscured the sun and cast a pall over Hamilton Street. The giant brick smokestacks blew out a thin stream of fog. Owen hustled inside the office building as the mill whistle blew. Already seated at her desk, Miss Camden got a greeting that was a bit too loud and jaunty.

At the end of the hall, Blick had a pen in one hand and the telephone held to his ear with the other. He gave Owen an absentminded nod, but was obviously busy, which was a godsend. Had the man barked out, "Tell me what you did last night, Fisher," Owen would have been reduced to the status of a terrified choirboy caught sticking gum under the pew and blurted out a full confession.

Even a torpedo was no match for Blick's cyclops stare.

The day passed without incident. Owen made a lot of noise with the adding machine to keep Miss Camden at bay.

Busy, busy.

The police didn't show up, asking for Owen. Nor did Cynthia call to say the police were at the house.

By the time the last whistle blew, Owen was convinced that he was in the clear. If some Italian farmer was missing, no one was going to look for him at Lido Premium. Nothing linked Al Genovese to Owen Forbes Fisher, a Syracuse University graduate, certified accountant, Trinity Episcopal congregant and member of the Bison Club. They had nothing in common.

Blick left on time for once, merely giving a wave in passing. Owen decided to stop by Fulton Florist and get Cynthia a bouquet. Not an apology for leaving the comb on the sink, of course, but as a token of his esteem. Maybe she would call him *darling* again.

It was well past sunset and the mill complex was mostly deserted as Owen set out across the parking lot.

He was nearly to the door of the Ford when a man approached.

"Mr. Fisher? Can I have a word?"

"Ah, Dombrowski." Owen recognized the brawny new foreman. "What can I do for you?"

"I need to talk to you about last night."

Owen staggered as the ground under his feet shifted and the night sky tilted. "Excuse me?"

"I know where you were last night," Dombrowski said.

"You're mistaken," Owen managed. He whirled around and came face to face with a stranger in a navy pea coat and newsboy cap.

"Not so fast, laddie." A strong Irish brogue mocked him. "We want a wee word, so we do."

Owen spun away and nearly collided with a third man. This one wore a wool cap and plaid mackinaw like many of the Italian mill workers but had a face like a film star from one of Cynthia's magazines.

"This is Luca Lombardo," Dombrowski said, like he was introducing old friends. He pointed to the Irishman. "Toby Gleason."

With his back against the Ford's rear bumper, Owen was hemmed in by the three men. "I'll have your job for this, Dombrowski," he quavered. "What do you think you're doing?"

"You killed a farmer named Al Genovese last night," Lombardo said, a slight Italian accent softening the shock of his words. "Near the ruin of Packham's old mill. Your friends put his body in his truck and pushed it into the river."

Owen tried to breathe. His heart was beating so fast his whole body shook.

Lombardo went on. "Al Genovese was a blackmailer and a kidnapper. He took my cousin's little girl and now he's not around to give her back. So I'm asking you. Where's Matilda Russo?"

"I don't know what you're talking about," Owen gasped.

The Italian was quietly relentless. "Yes, you do. Genovese went to you and Rotolo when he got scared. But he was going to ruin things for you. Caught selling beer isn't so bad. Blackmail and kidnapping are another. You'd go to jail forever. So you got rid of Genovese. Shot him in the chest. That's murder."

Warm urine ran down Owen's leg. He could hardly breathe. How did they know what happened?

"Come along, laddie," the Irishman said and poked Owen in the chest. "Think hard. I'll bet you remember Genovese talking about snatching a girl. Where did he take her? Who's keeping her fed?"

"I'm not involved," Owen whispered, cringing

away from the stabbing finger. "Please let me go."

Lombardo gripped Owen's arm and pulled him close. Their noses nearly touched. "You know where she is," the man said in a terrifyingly flat voice. "Either you tell me now or we go to the police."

None of the three men had anything like Rotolo's braggadocio or even a gun, yet their power was absolute.

"Trixie," Owen mouthed. "They talked about Trixie's place."

"Trixie who runs the whorehouse near the freight yards?" the Irishman interjected. "They took the girl there?"

"Benny said Trixie would never know." Owen took a sniveling, shaky breath as Lombardo's grip relaxed. "That's all I know. There. You have what you wanted. Let me go."

The three men exchanged a look.

Lombardo reached inside his coat and pulled out a linen-covered pocket ledger.

This time, the earth beneath Owen's feet turned to quicksand. "That's mine," he croaked.

"I know," Lombardo said. The flicker of a smile across the movie star face suggested that he welcomed Owen's dismay. "You sent Nick Procopio to look for it, didn't you?"

Owen finally recognized the Italian. O'Malley had saved him from Procopio's garotte. "You're from the Galliano Club," Owen said. "Your picture was in the newspaper."

Lombardo opened the ledger and read from the flyleaf. "The Lido Outfit. Benito Rotolo, Nicola Procopio. Owen Forbes Fisher." Lombardo flipped a few pages. "All your handwriting, isn't it? You're skimming a third off the top."

"No," Owen croaked.

"This ledger is a divvy sheet," Lombardo said. "Forensic accounting, they call it. You are cheating Rotolo. What would happen if he got his hands on this little book?"

Three witnesses to the murder of Al Genovese who also had the pocket ledger and its damning evidence. Slowly and painfully, Owen put the pieces together. "You mean to blackmail me," he managed.

"Genovese stole more than twenty thousand dollars from my employer," Lombardo said. "I want it back."

Owen couldn't catch his breath. His chest was on fire, his pants were wet and his legs were so weak he could barely stay upright. "Please. I told you what you wanted to know. Just give me the ledger."

"Listen to me, Mr. Fisher." The ledger disappeared inside Lombardo's coat. "Every Friday evening, you're going to give Karol your weekly earnings from Rotolo's beer racket. Don't think you can cheat us, because we know how much is coming in."

Tears pricked the back of Owen's eyes. "I need that money."

"You got a choice, Mr. Fisher," Lombardo went on. "Either you hand over the cash every week or Rotolo gets the ledger. If he doesn't understand, I'll explain it to him. In detail. If that doesn't convince you, we'll go to the police and let them know where to find Al Genovese. Rotolo or the police. Your choice."

"He'll kill me if he finds out," Owen gurgled.

"Makes the decision an easy one, so it does," the Irishman said cheerfully.

CHAPTER 45

Ruination

A new policeman appeared on Hamilton Street on Monday afternoon, less than 24 hours after Osa's birthday party. Officer Sullivan introduced himself to Ruth and other business owners, merely saying that O'Malley had been reassigned.

Henry suggested a celebratory supper after the next ballroom dance class. Ruth wore the mink jacket, her best navy silk dress and a cream hat with a frill of netting that drew attention to her russet curls.

They went to Buckner's. This time their table was in the dining room proper, not the discreet alcove.

The meal was delicious and the conversation effortless. Ruth and Henry talked about everything. Her plans for the Christmas pageant. How well the new Lido Premium foreman was doing. The latest lack of news about the identity of the young woman pulled from the river. Turmoil at the League of Nations.

Germany was admitted to the League in September. Spain left in protest. The United States had never joined. Without America, the future of the organization was in doubt. Meanwhile, Leon Trotsky was expelled from the Soviet Politburo. Henry was intensely interested because Trotsky had been the Soviet war commissioner and built up the Red Army.

It was quite late when the blue roadster cruised to a stop in front of Ruth's door. The Galliano Club was closed. Without the club's lights and hum of lively voices, Hamilton Street was empty and glum.

Henry opened the car door for Ruth and escorted her across the sidewalk. They saw the broken glass in her street door at the same time. Henry tried the knob. Unlocked, the door swung open.

"I know I locked it," Ruth said in a small voice."

"Let me go first," Henry said.

He helped her leap across the glass-strewn entryway. Ruth hopped onto the first stair and followed him up to the second-floor landing. The doors to both her apartment and Tapping Toes were open.

The mirrored wall in the dance studio was gone. Not even a few shards remained on the wall. Bits of broken mirror created a sea of glitter waiting to slice her fingers to the bone.

The Victrola was smashed, along with every record. Chunks of black celluloid rode the sea of shards.

Henry went into the apartment. After a moment, Ruth collected herself and entered as well.

The parlor was wrecked. The armchair lay on its side. The settee cushions were scattered across the room. Horsehair stuffing sprouted from slashed upholstery.

The side table was overturned. Her precious photograph of the cast of *Little Johnny Jones* was out of the frame and ripped into ticker tape confetti. The dining room chairs were on their sides. The kitchen cupboard was empty, crockery smashed on the floor.

The aura of violence lingered.

Dazed, Ruth moved into the bedroom. Her feet kicked up small clouds of white feathers. Pillows were shredded, the quilt torn. Her clothing was thrown about as if by a cyclone. The dresser drawers were empty and thrown on the rug.

Only her old flannel nightgown had been treated with care. It was draped over the brass footboard, an intentional reminder of Ruth's humiliation at O'Malley's hands.

She opened the closet. The hangers were bare. Her dresses had been chopped into a pile of scraps.

Jagged ribbons of charcoal velvet and embroidered godet pleats delivered the final blow. Ruth sank to her knees and reached for the detritus of her armor.

"My dress." She could barely speak. O'Malley's rage leached out of the torn fabric. "My beautiful dress."

"Ruth." Henry knelt next to her. "You're safe. That's the only thing that matters."

"It's ruined, Henry. The most beautiful thing I ever had and he ruined it."

"I'll get you another."

"No." Ruth's chest hurt so much it was hard to speak. How could she explain what that dress meant to her? It had transformed her that night, given her the courage to triumph over O'Malley's cruelty and open her heart to new possibilities.

Henry gently lifted Ruth to her feet. "Gather up what you want, and we'll go home."

Very little had escaped O'Malley's destruction. A pair of shoes. A folder of papers for the Tapping Toes School of Dance. A few books. A new pair of silk stockings.

Everything fit in a single pillowcase.

Ruth left her key in the Galliano Club's mailbox.

CHAPTER 46

Trixie's place

Luca got out of the truck and followed Toby through a patch of woods that separated the freight yards from the whorehouse. Their search would concentrate on closets, attic and basement.

In dark coats both he and Toby were nearly invisible at this time of the night. Toby had sold a consignment of French wine to Trixie, the woman who ran the place, and was sure he could get them inside the house undetected.

No trains came through to mask the sound of their feet crunching on frozen leaves or the snap of icy branches against their coats. They came out of the woods on the east side of a big two-story house with a deep wraparound porch. It was perched well back from the road, with tire tracks through the snow all around. Several cars were parked in random fashion behind the place. Lights were on in almost all the windows. Tinny music spilled out, along with drunken laughter. Luca could hardly think of a less likely place to hide a child.

"Full house tonight," Toby observed. "Front or back

door?"

Luca considered. Anyone stumbling out the back to a car would catch them. "Front."

They trotted around to the front, staying in the cold shadows of the trees. Luca saw a blonde woman in an Oriental robe pass by the front windows, a glass in her hand. A man pawed at her and she foisted him off on a second woman, then hovered over a Victrola.

A pause of silence, then music blared and a man's voice began warbling. *Tonight you belong to me.*

"Trixie," Toby muttered. "A real tough cookie."

A car turned off the road, bumped along in the ruts left by previous drivers, but swerved to a stop in front of the house.

Luca grabbed Toby's sleeve. "That's Rotolo's Cadillac."

"The night keeps getting better." Toby produced a flask, tipped some whiskey into his hand and wiped it on his coat before taking a mouthful. "We'll go in the back. Pretend you're drunk."

Luca did the same.

The back door opened directly into a warm kitchen. A blonde girl with glassy eyes sat at a wooden table. She gave them a wide smile. "You're not supposed to be here."

"And where are we meant to be, sweetheart?" Toby

slurred with a silly grin.

She licked her finger, dipped the wet into a tiny mound of white grains, and sucked on it. "You better go upstairs," she said with her finger still in her mouth, shaking with suppressed laughter. The girl cocked her head toward a doorway.

There was something wrong with her but Toby gave Luca no time to find out. The Irishman half pushed, half pulled Luca through the doorway, which led to a narrow set of stairs. "Servant's stairs," Toby mouthed.

Luca mounted them cautiously, expecting to see Rotolo any minute. At the top, he cautiously pushed open a skinny door. A hall stretched ahead; half a dozen closed doors on one side and a banister on the other overlooking a wide and handsome staircase. They could see the foyer directly below. A wide opening framed with dark wood led to the parlor, source of the Victrola music.

Despite the warbling tenor, they heard the squeak of bedsprings and a chorus of grunts and panting from behind closed doors. Had Matilda been exposed to this sort of debauchery. Or made a part of it? A fresh surge of fury propelled Luca down the hall, Toby trotting behind.

The first bedroom he peeked into was large, the bed three times wider than his single at the boarding house.

A white painted dresser spanned the opposite wall, placed at an angle to a satin-skirted vanity heaped with bottles and jars. The closet was full of women's clothing, including a mink jacket and a thick black wool man's overcoat. A black fedora was tossed on a heap of frilly underthings. Matilda was not there.

A door slammed; footsteps pounded past. Bedsprings jangled. A new tune blared from the first floor. Footsteps thumped down the hall toward them. A woman sang tunelessly along with the Victrola music. The footsteps halted. A man and a woman spoke in low tones.

The doorknob turned.

Toby gestured frantically to another door, which opened to a tiny water closet. They crowded in, Luca just managing to shut the door behind. As soon as he did, a door on the other side popped open. The toilet could be accessed from two different rooms.

The girl from the kitchen stood in the doorway wearing the same glassy-eyed grin and not much else. A billowy robe canted off one bare shoulder. "Two at once," she said. "That's extra."

Toby winked, back to being a drunken lout. "Paid Trixie downstairs, so we did."

"Gotta pay me, bucko. Three dollars." The girl held out a hand and blew a kiss to Luca. "You're a looker, ain't you?"

Toby rolled his eyes and handed over the cash.

"All right, go ahead." The girl nodded toward the bedroom behind her, hair falling out of loose pins. "Nobody pays to watch a girl pee."

Luca and Toby edged past her and into the other room. She went into the water closet and slammed the door.

A rumpled bed, a dressing table and chair. A washstand with a basin and pitcher was tucked into a corner. A row of hooks waited for clients to hang their clothes. No closet.

"Look." Luc pointed up. There was a hatch in the ceiling above the washstand.

"Jesus wept," Toby marveled in a whisper. "The luck of the Irish is with us tonight."

A clanking chain and a rushing gurgle of water said that the girl was finished in the water closet. Luca saw the key in the lock and turned it. "We're not ready yet," he called as Toby dragged the chair to the corner.

The girl responded with a slurred string of vulgarities.

"Think you can reach it?" Toby held the chair steady.

Stretching as high as he could, his toes nearly coming off the seat of the chair, Luca managed to twist a small cabinet knob securing the hatch. As soon as he did, one edge of the wooden panel popped up a few inches, just enough for Luca to grab the lip by his fingertips. He dipped his head, pushed his shoulder against the hatch to bump it open, and hauled himself through the hole and into the attic.

The girl shouted from behind the water closet door. Toby hopped onto the chair. Luca reached through the hatch and hauled his friend up. As Toby's feet rose, his heel caught the ladder back and the chair toppled over with a resounding crash.

Luca closed the hatch, which gave a quiet click. Hopefully the girl would assume they were a couple of harmless drunks who staggered away, too drunk to do what they'd paid for.

Two dormers projected over the front of the house, letting in a dribble of moonlight, enough for Luca to see that the space was mostly empty. The attic was long and wide but not tall enough for a man to stand in. The floor wasn't solid but a lattice of rafters and newspaper insulation. If either of them stepped between the rafters, he'd fall through to the room below.

A few boxes and sacks by the hatch contained old magazines, glass Christmas ornaments, and shoes in need of new soles. No little girl named Matilda. Luca shook his head at Toby, sick with disappointment.

Thumps and bangs filtered up to the attic as someone moved clumsily around the bedroom below. The noise was accompanied by high-pitched giggling and an indistinct male voice. Bedsprings began a rhythmic groaning.

"*Oddio*," Luca swore under his breath as he squatted on a rafter. "Fisher lied. They wouldn't keep Matilda here. Too many people in and out."

"Or they moved her and didn't tell him."

A couple of shouts signaled the end of good times in the bedroom below. The girl's voice took on a rushed, petulant tone. Finally a door opened. Heavy footsteps stomped away. Bedsprings creaked, then the patter of a woman's steps. Water splashed. The door opened and closed.

After ten minutes of perching on the rafters, the room below the hatch was silent.

"Let's get out of here," Luca said.

Toby was closest to the hatch. "There's no latch," he whispered.

"What do you mean?" Luca maneuvered around Toby and saw what his friend meant. There was no knob or latch on the attic side. Too late, he realized that the magazines were there to keep the door propped open when anyone came up to the attic.

Even with two of them trying to pry it up, the hatch

cover remained stubbornly in place. Luca squinted around the cramped, low-ceilinged space. "How are you at climbing out windows?"

"Jesus wept, not even a sparrow could fit through those windows."

"You have another idea?"

Toby considered. "No, not really. All right then, off you go, you crazy dago."

Like a tightrope dancer, Luca picked his way across the rafters to the closest dormer, wadded his coat around his arm and smashed the window with his elbow. Glass clattered onto the roof shingles. Sleet and freezing air blew into his face. Empty, the window frame looked even smaller. Luca reluctantly gave his coat to Toby, knowing he'd never fit through the opening with the extra bulk, took a deep breath, and launched himself through.

For a horrible, heart-stopping moment, his arms and torso were suspended in mid-air with nothing to grab. Two stories below, the snow-covered roof of the porch promised broken bones and splinters the size of Roman Legion spears. Then his hands found the edge of the eaves. Luca twisted and slithered and pulled at the same time, ending up in a heap in the crevasse formed by the dormer meeting the pitch of the roof. He was freezing but alive.

Toby handed out first Luca's coat, then his own. Another few death-defying moments and then they were both on the ridgeline of the roof, out of danger, but stuck like two crows without a nest as fresh sleet blurred the dark landscape below them.

"Now what?" Toby shivered. "If we stay here we'll freeze."

"The chimney." Luca nudged his friend with his shoulder. "It's brick. We can climb down."

They slithered over to the chimney on all fours. Luca's hands were numb and he wondered if he'd be able to feel chinks in the brick much less to hold on long enough to climb down. His heart sank when he realized that the bricks were almost completely covered by ivy. The vines were slick with moisture and plastered to the brick.

"Jack and the beanstalk," Toby whispered.

Lying flat on his stomach, Luca eased his legs over the edge of the roof, dug his hands into the tangle of vines, and plastered himself against the wet ivy. The vine in his right hand pulled away from the brick, and he slid down the length of his left arm, only to be halted, still flat against the ivy-covered chimney, when his foot finally found a chink to hold onto. His right hand found a brick to grasp, only to have it pull loose.

Luca half fell, half slid to the ground. The impact

was worse than his encounter with the speeding car on Senate Street. Hands scored and bleeding, he lurched out of the way a moment before Toby landed in a heap at the base of the chimney.

"Jesus wept," Toby gasped. "Let's never do that again."

"Look," Luca breathed. "There's a barn."

They were on the west side of the house now. Luca could see a sagging roof and a wall with a definite list. It was an old structure. Yet a faint light seeped from the crack between the two large sliding doors.

Toby leaned close to Luca. "Remember, you're drunk and lost."

The Irishman hauled open the big sliding door. Luca slipped inside. A lantern on a wall peg cast a warm yellow glow over a dirt floor, bales of straw and rough wooden walls. A man sat up sleepily, his movements hampered by rough wool blankets, and barked out something incomprehensible.

Luca grabbed a wooden bucket and swung hard. The man fell back on the straw, arms flung out in unconscious surrender.

"So much for drunk and lost," Toby said in admiration.

"Saved time," Luca said shortly.

The guard, if that's what he was, had made himself

comfortable. Besides the blankets and lantern, he had a tin plate of chicken bones and an apple core, plus a Thermos bottle redolent of coffee.

Toby unhooked the lantern and held it up. Beyond the open space, they saw four sagging half-doors. "Horse stalls," he said.

"Matilda?" Luca's rush to the first stall left a trail of disturbed straw. A black void loomed beyond the half-door. "Matilda. It's Zio." He fumbled with the latch and finally swung the door out of the way, Toby on his heels with the lantern held high. The stall smelled like dry wood and old manure but it was empty.

The second and third stalls were empty as well.

The fourth stall was latched, the same as the others. "Matilda. It's Zio."

A muffled thump answered him.

There she was, under a pile of ancient horse blankets, trussed like a turkey ready for the oven. Her eyes were enormous in the beam of the lantern.

"Zio," she said as soon as Luca pulled away the gag keeping her quiet. "I'm ready to go home now."

CHAPTER 47

A simple solution

"Owen Forbes Fisher, you are a successful man." Owen whispered the words to his reflection in the bathroom mirror. "You are clever. You are capable. You are in the inner circle."

"Owen! Cynthia's voice floated up the stairs and shattered his fragile calm. "Your breakfast is ready!"

"Yes, darling," he called back, hearing the crack in his voice.

Owen murmured the mantra three more times. He was wearing one of his suits from Van Dyke's and his favorite silk bow tie, but still felt sick. Not even the whispered word *torpedo* made a difference. He washed the comb and put it in the cup.

In the dining room, Cynthia was dressed too nicely to stay home. "Are you going out?" Owen asked as she poured his coffee.

The breakfast table was set with the new Gorham sterling in the Etruscan pattern. The embroidered tablecloth and napkin were recent additions to the linen closet. His soft-boiled egg perched in a Wedgewood egg cup and toast fingers waited on a matching plate that probably cost as much as an Electrolux refrigerator. On the buffet, the new sterling champagne bucket promised a celebration.

Cynthia sat at her place and tapped the crown of her egg with the edge of her knife blade. "It's the Ladies Institute charity drive planning meeting this morning. After that I have a fitting at Van Dyke's for my new mink jacket."

"Mink jacket!" Owen nearly came out of his chair.

"You promised me a new mink after the cleaner ruined the other." She frowned, a storm warning in case he was foolish enough to protest. "I picked it out and they tailored it just for me. It's a little bit more than the other one but that doesn't matter, does it?"

"No, no, of course not," someone said using a squeaky version of Owen's voice. "I want you to be happy."

"Of course you do." Cynthia blew him a kiss across the table, sliced the top off her egg and dunked a sliver of toast into the soft boiled yolk.

Owen managed to decapitate his own egg but had no stomach for food.

Thanks to Dombrowski and his ruthless friends, there was no money for the new mink jacket or anything else.

But as Cynthia prattled on about the upcoming charity drive, to which Owen realized with a sinking heart they'd be expected to contribute a sizable sum, he said nothing. Telling his wife that his raise was fiction and that they had to go back to living on the pittance he made at Lido Premium was out of the question.

"You're not eating your egg," Cynthia pointed out, pearls swinging across her bosom.

"No, no, just thinking about something at the office," Owen hastened to say. He snatched a toast finger and jammed it into the egg.

This is what happened when immigrants like Dombrowski were given an inch. They took a mile. Owen had a good mind to write a strongly worded letter to the *Lido Daily Clipper* protesting Lido's lax immigration standards.

None of the three buffoons who'd cornered him even spoke proper English. It was inconceivable that such men could extort money from a Syracuse University graduate, a Deke from Delta Kappa Epsilon and a member of the Bison Club. The Membership Committee, no less.

Owen chewed a bite of eggy toast, washed it down with coffee and enlightenment dawned. He'd been so shocked when the three men confronted him that he didn't spot the flaw in their presentation, but he did now.

Lombardo had no idea how much beer the Lido Outfit was selling each week. He'd claimed to know of course, but that was simply a ruse. No one else had their finger on the accounts, not even Benny.

The simple solution was to cheat his blackmailers. After all, how much did it really take to satisfy a trio of immigrants who probably thought that five hundred dollars was the fortune of a lifetime?

He'd give them a portion. Forty percent of his quarter share should be more than enough for Dombrowski and friends to keep their mouths shut and the pocket ledger hidden away from Benny.

Leaving enough in Owen's pocket for mink jackets and charity events and Cynthia to keep calling him *darling*.

CHAPTER 48

Coffee with Finch

Luca looked up to see Inspector Finch enter the saloon, dusting snow off the shoulders of his coat.

"Mr. Lombardo," Finch said and took off his hat.

"Hello." Luca wondered what the inspector planned to accuse him of this time.

"Is this a good time?"

It was a surprising question. "Sure," Luca said. "The club isn't open yet."

Finch gave the barest breath of a smile. "I remembered from the last time."

They stared at each other in an uncertain contest of wills. The electric percolator on the work counter gave the dry gurgle that indicated it was done.

"Would you like a cup of coffee?" Luca asked. "On the house."

"I would indeed." Finch left his coat and hat on a chair and climbed onto a stool at the bar.

Luca wasn't sure what this display of settling in was supposed to tell him, but he duly poured the postal inspector a cup of hot coffee and set it in front of the man.

"Will you join me?" Finch asked.

Still wary, Luca filled a cup for himself.

"I thought you'd be interested to know that a detective from the Lido police department came to see me this morning," Finch said. "A Detective Dooley. Do you know him?"

"That's an Irish name," Luca hedged. He knew Dooley, who had investigated Jimmy Zambrano's disappearance. More importantly, the detective was a close associate of Toby Gleason.

"He's in possession of a number of letters from Vincent Salerno and is willing to represent the recipients who wish to remain anonymous."

"Does that mean you can arrest Salerno?"

"He's already in custody and out of business as a blackmailer."

"What about his local accomplice?"

"A farmer named Alphonse Genovese. Apparently, Dooley had been watching him for some time, suspecting him of cheating on some farm deals. Dooley will come to Gary to testify. None of the people who got the letters can identify Salerno. They never met him. All the evidence hinges on the letters themselves and the marked stamps. A nice, tight case."

Luca drank some coffee. Toby had come up with the

scheme, which covered Dooley with glory and gave him a break from Chief Doyle for a few days. The detective had all the letters sent to Vito, Enzo, and even Maria Teresa Procopio.

Finch put down his cup. "Genovese's wife said he'd been hanging around with some unsavory characters but didn't know names. He drove away from the family farm a few days ago and never came home. We figure he left with a sizable sum of money. Alerts are out. He won't get far."

No further than the river. "Did you meet his wife?" Luca asked.

"I would run away, too," Finch said.

For a moment, Luca wasn't sure he'd heard correctly. Then Finch actually grinned. They both gave a bark of genuine laughter.

"Are you leaving Lido, then?" Luca asked.

"In a few days."

Luca topped up Finch's cup.

"It seems that Italian crime is resolved inside Italian communities." Finch nodded his thanks and took a sip. "That's what allowed the Black Hand to become so powerful. What I don't understand is how Detective Dooley managed to win the confidence of the Italian community in Lido."

"He investigated when Jimmy Zambrano went

missing," Luca admitted. "Seemed a decent man."

Another grin stretched across Finch's face as he raised the cup of hot coffee. "I have a healthy respect for the way you orchestrated quite a number of things. I'm sure I'll never know the details. Unless, of course, you'd like to fill me in."

Luca realized his mistake and tried to cover. "I just make sandwiches and coffee."

"And try to stay out of the newspaper?"

"When I can."

"I think we both want the same thing, Mr. Lombardo. To help people who are scared and can't help themselves." Finch slid off the stool and retrieved his coat and hat. "Thank you for an excellent cup of coffee. If you're ever in Gary, please look me up."

He extended his hand across the bar. Luca hesitated, then grasped it for a firm handshake.

Finch took a last look around, doffed his hat to Luca and left.

Luca sagged against the work counter.

Vito had not admitted to receiving blackmail threats but he didn't ask what happened to the letters in the safe, either. He knew that Luca knew and Luca knew that Vito knew that he did. That was good enough. Neither mentioned the new safe combination or the loss of a dozen cases of whiskey, which no doubt were sold to pay *La Mano Nera's* first demands.

Both Luca and Vito knew that the other understood what had happened.

The relationship had changed, Vito silently ceding ground and Luca responsible for more than ever.

Rotolo was still circling around. Luca wanted to pay him back in kind for his role in Matilda's kidnapping. The shed fire and the damage to Vito's Packard, too. Eventually, he'd think of something.

In the meantime, the immediate threat was over. Fisher's money would pay off the bank loan. Another consignment of whiskey from Toby would help the balance sheet as well. New Year's Eve was always a big moneymaker.

He and Sonny had cleaned up Ruth's apartment and shoveled out all the glass in the dance studio. He didn't know if Ruth would reopen Tapping Toes but the apartment was habitable, if a little bare.

Best of all, Matilda was home and boasting about how brave she'd been. Rosaria hadn't killed Enzo yet.

Luca had everything he needed.

Except Tess. *Tessa.*

CHAPTER 49

The fireplace suggests itself

"The Pinkerton Agency has completed its investigation," Henry said. He folded a sheaf of documents he'd been reading at the breakfast table. "Ruth, you'll want to read this."

Ruth put down her fork. They were with Osa and Jack in the light-filled breakfast room overlooking the back garden, the same as every morning since Ruth came to stay. Henry and Jack discussed world events over eggs and coffee before heading to their respective offices. Osa jotted notes regarding her innumerable social commitments and occasionally took the men to task for eating too swiftly or thinking that Governor Smith was too radical.

Ruth loved starting the day this way; happy, companionable, safe.

She'd grieved for her pretty clothes, snug apartment, and the dance studio, but the Blick-Rutherford household welcomed her without reservation. Henry helped her create an inventory of what was lost and submit a police report. Osa brought her to Van Dyke's and Nelson's Department Store for new clothes. Jack devoted an entire column in his annual Chamber of Commerce report to the subject of vandalism.

More than that, they seamlessly folded her into their community of friends and family. Ruth attended dinner parties, charity events, family discussions. Quiet moments with Henry in the library.

All of her dance classes were canceled until further notice, except for the Christmas recital rehearsals which would be held at the Strand Theater.

Henry kissed her every night in front of the door to the guest room with the ivy wallpaper. He never stepped a foot inside. Her unfulfilled longing for him was as painful as the notion of his possible rejection.

"Pinkerton?" Osa said, a forkful of eggs in midair. "Don't make Ruth read your dry business papers, Henry."

"I don't mind," Ruth managed.

Jack tossed aside a magazine to slather marmalade on a slice of toast. "Byrd is in the news again," he announced. "Congress is going to pass a special act, promoting him to the rank of Commander. Going to get the Medal of Honor."

Henry set the Pinkerton documents by Ruth's plate as if they were only of mild interest and addressed Jack. "What about Bennett, the pilot?"

Richard E. Byrd, a Navy officer, together with pilot Floyd Bennett, flew over the North Pole last April. He beat out Norwegian polar explorer Roald Amundsen who shortly afterward made the journey over the Pole in an Italian airship.

"He'll get it too, I expect, but Byrd is a hog for publicity," Jack said. "Next thing you know he'll win the Orteig Prize. Twenty-five thousand dollars for being first to cross the Atlantic in an airplane."

"A silly contest," Osa said, rattling her cup in the saucer. "A steamship is perfectly good enough for crossing the Atlantic."

"Byrd will do it," Henry said. "If fame doesn't go to his head."

Osa and Jack finished eating and excused themselves. Henry went to the sideboard and poured himself another cup of coffee from the silver urn.

Ruth picked up the Pinkerton report, which was a thick assemblage of letters and documents. She browsed the documents, only skimming the typed pages until she came to two reports, each consisting of several sheets pinned together in the upper left-hand corner. One bore a dark blue letterhead proclaiming *City of Poughkeepsie* with the silhouette of a building with a steeple. The other was simpler, with *Poughkeepsie General Hospital* engraved across the top. The name

Ruthie June Crosswater was on both.

Her hospital and police records. Ruth blinked away tears.

Her arrest was duly noted, as was her transport to the hospital, jail term, and subsequent banishment from Poughkeepsie.

She had been pregnant and suffering from malnutrition when she lost the baby on a park bench. The record of her hospital stay was dispassionate. The doctor's notes were laden with medical terms Ruth didn't want to think about. *Cervical failure. Hysterectomy. Extreme blood loss. Anemia.*

In the police report, her miscarriage was characterized as *lewd and unhealthful behavior, indecent exposure, vagrancy,* and *public endangerment.* The prison record was attached, stating that she'd been a model of good behavior. The date and time of her release and subsequent departure from Poughkeepsie via train were carefully recorded.

"Did you read all of this?" Ruth asked.

"Yes."

Ruth felt ill. "Oh."

"Pinkerton is very efficient," Henry said. "Those are the original documents. There are no copies. Police and prison records have been expunged. The doctor who treated you signed a binding nondisclosure agreement."

Lewd and unhealthful behavior, indecent exposure. Cervical failure. Hysterectomy. Ruth wanted to die of shame.

"Would you like another cup of coffee?" Henry asked.

"Henry, these things . . . in the hospital report." Ruth closed her eyes. "These are terrible things for a man to know about a woman."

"Battlefield wounds," Henry said dismissively. He drank some coffee, the blue eye blandly meeting her embarrassment over the rim of the cup.

"What happens now?"

Henry put down the cup. "The fireplace in the library suggests itself," he said.

Ruth clutched the documents. "You mean . . ."

"Exactly."

Henry pulled out her chair and they went into the library, where a fire chased the morning chill out of the air.

Ruth fed the documents into the flames. Ruthie June Crosswater disappeared, the papers turning into brown curls before disappearing in a shower of sparks. A log shifted to show a glowing red belly, like a fat cat after swallowing a mouse.

"This came for me today as well." Henry handed Ruth a piece of brown butcher paper covered in grease pencil printing. "I debated showing it to you, but as it appears to be the final chapter, you should be aware of the promise it holds."

BLICK YOUR WHORE HAS A DIRTY PAST. WE NEED 5000 CASH MONEY TO KEEP MUM OR THE HOLE CITY WILL KNOW. PARK YOUR CAR ON HILL STREET AT MIDNIGHT ON SATURDAY. LEVE THE MONEY ON THE FRONT SEAT.

"O'Malley," Ruth gasped.

"Don't destroy it. The timing is quite fortuitous."

"Henry, this is awful. Just awful. He means to blackmail you."

"An excellent but not unforeseen turn of events," Henry said. He repositioned the glowing log with the poker. "Using the postal system to commit blackmail is a federal crime. Officer O'Malley has just earned himself a two-year stay in the federal penitentiary with absolutely no way to prove the validity of his claim."

"Federal crime," Ruth echoed.

"Exactly," Henry said. He sat at the desk, picked up the candlestick telephone and jiggled the wire to summon the operator.

Ruth sank into a chair as Henry asked to be put

through to the courthouse.

"Inspector Finch, Henry Blick here. We met at the Bison Club banquet." Henry nodded at Ruth as he spoke. "I need to speak with you as soon as possible. Yes, a matter of some urgency. I expect that Mayor Peabody will join us. I'll be in your office within the hour with the evidence."

Next, he asked the operator to connect him to City Hall. His conversation with Peabody was as brief and to the point.

"Oh my goodness, Henry," Ruth said when he finished. "When you said you knew how to organize a fight, you were right."

Henry left the desk and sat next to her. "In light of this morning's developments, may I have reason to hope that your concern regarding my intentions have been eliminated?"

Ruth took a shaky breath. "You're asking now?"

Henry slowly sank to one knee, his back ramrod straight as always, and took her hand. "Ruth Cross, I love you quite unconditionally. Will you do me the honor of consenting to become my wife?"

"Yes," Ruth whispered. "One hundred times, yes."

CHAPTER 50

Running away

"I'll be gone tonight." Tess opened her dresser drawer and took out her best camisole and matching tap pants, plus a clean pair of silk stockings and garters. "Tell Aunt Evelyn that I'm staying with a friend."

She folded each item and put it in the suitcase open on her bed.

"The doctor gave Miss Evelyn her laudanum," Annie said tartly from the doorway of Tess's bedroom. "She'll not wake up before the morning."

"Then you don't have to tell her anything at all." Tess rummaged in her closet for the plaid dress she'd worn to the bank the day she met Luca. And a slip, she'd need a slip. The white taffeta. She whirled back to the dresser.

"What do I tell Mr. James if he calls?"

"James Howland is not going to call." Tess found the slip and folded it on top of the silk stockings.

"Miss Muriel might."

"Goodness, Annie." Tess stopped vibrating with determination and excitement for one moment and turned to face the tiny housekeeper. "Fine. If Miss Muriel calls, tell her what I told James. The engagement is off. I don't love him and he doesn't love me."

Annie took a step back, almost tottering under the weight of the news. "Oh, no, Miss Tess. You surely did not break it off with Mr. James!"

"I surely did." The look of horror on Annie's face could win the housekeeper a role in the next Buster Keaton comedy. "His mother can find another girl stupid enough to marry him. I'll return all the gifts, write letters of apology and refund whatever it cost for the engagement notice in the newspaper. But it's over."

"It's those old letters," Annie gasped. "They've turned your head."

"They opened my eyes," Tess informed the housekeeper. "I'm not going to do what Aunt Evelyn did. Stay with a man she didn't love. Be a bird in a gilded cage that wasn't even hers."

"I never should have given you that box."

"Those letters made me realize how alone she was, even when Uncle Benedict was alive. You can say that she did the right thing in not going after Max, but she was sad and lonely and miserable for years. Her last regret was that she didn't go to him."

"What nonsense!"

"It's not. She's full of regret because she never had

the courage to be with the man she loved. The one who let her fly out of that cage. Now she's dying alone."

"Miss Evelyn was never alone," Annie snapped. "I was always there for her, just as I am now."

"It's not the same." Tess knew the housekeeper would never understand. Annie was blinded by loyalty. "I won't be stuck in a loveless marriage when I could have so much more."

"You're going to that Eye-talian, aren't you?"

Tess pulled the plaid dress off the hanger. She'd wear it tomorrow. The plum dress and matching cardigan she had on now would do for tonight.

The dress went into the suitcase, along with her favorite dusty violet nightgown. She chewed her lip for a moment, then tossed in trousers, an extra sweater, and suede shoes.

"Don't do it, Miss Tess," Annie begged. "Mr. James will take you back."

"I don't want him back."

"Think about Miss Evelyn!"

"I'll talk to her tomorrow." Shaking off her guilt, Tess closed the suitcase, flipped down the latch and fastened the leather straps.

"Those people live in the gutter," Annie said. "He'll have you taking in washing to feed a litter of half-breed brats."

Tess picked up her purse, hauled the suitcase off the bed and lugged it down the stairs. She'd probably packed too much but there was so much emotion fizzing through her veins that it was hard to think about sensible things.

Annie followed her into the front hall. Tess took her brown velvet coat out of the closet and found her matching cloche hat. She left her galoshes in the closet. No one got married wearing rubber galoshes.

"Don't go, Miss Tess," Annie said, practically wringing her hands.

Tess settled the cloche over her curls. She felt very strange and heroic and excited all at the same time. "This is my decision, Annie. For once, it's all mine. Not Aunt Evelyn's. Not yours. If it's a mistake, that's mine to own, too."

She picked up the suitcase and went out the front door.

CHAPTER 51

The surprise outside

Dear Mr. Lucky Lombardo,
You seem to be a nice man who didn't deserve the bad luck that came to you where you live so you may want to move where you live and come to live in a new place near where I live which would be very nice for both of us because there aren't so many men where I live on account of the Great War took all the menfolk from where I live and many of them didn't come back so it would be nice if you came to live here and we could be a courting couple and go for walks and talk about the weather. I would sure like it if you came to live where I live and we was a courting couple as I would like to kiss a boy who looks like you who lives where I live and you could be him but not if you is a dago like they say.
Mary Sue Pickley
Thurmont, Maryland

Seated on the bar, Luca put down the letter and received a chorus of ribald remarks and beery air kisses from his audience. The saloon was full. Every chair was angled toward the bar, the better to hear every word of the nightly entertainment.

He slid the letter across the polished bar top to Sonny. "The usual reply, please."

"You could always tell her you're not a dago." With a mischievous wink, Sonny palmed the letter.

Guido stuck his head around the pony wall, his moon face puckered with concern. "Luca, come outside."

"What's the matter?" Luca called, but the doorman had already rushed out.

Entertainment over, chairs scraped as men turned back to their beers and games. Luca trotted outside. "Guido, what's going on?"

The doorman pointed.

Tess stood on the sidewalk, clutching a small purse. Her green Ford coupe was parked by the curb. "Hello, Luca."

"Tessa." She was the last person Luca expected to see. "What are you doing here?"

"I'm running away," she said, face flushed pink in the glow of the streetlight.

"From what?"

"I've broken it off with James. It was wrong from the start. Somebody else's idea of what a good marriage should be."

Luca blinked. "You're not going to marry Mr. Howland?"

"No. I would rather marry the man I love."

He stared at her, unsure of what was happening.

Tess gave a tiny smile. "Would you like to elope with me?"

"Elope?" Another new word.

"It means to run away and get married without telling anybody."

"I don't understand."

Tess took a deep breath. "Will you please marry me, Gianluca Lombardo?"

"Marry," Luca repeated slowly. "You want to get married."

"Yes. To you."

Luca wiped his hands on his apron. Part of his brain was shouting in triumph. The other part was groping for an explanation. "What about James Howland?"

"It's done. Gave him back the ring and everything."

"What about your aunt? Her permission?"

"This is my decision. My permission. I'm giving it. What do you say?"

A wide grin spread over Luca's face. "I say that Tessa Lombardo is a good name."

"It's a perfect name." Tess flung herself into his

arms and Luca kissed her, right on the sidewalk in front of the club. She fit in his arms the way she always had, as though she was made for him.

"There's a justice of the peace on Jay Street," Tess said breathlessly when they came up for air. "He can marry us right now."

"All right." Luca kissed her again and again. "I'll get my coat."

Before he could move, a big car roared up, nearly smashing into the coupe's back bumper. James Howland leaped out of the vehicle, along with another man who was a younger and slimmer version of the banker. "Get your hands off her, you filthy dago," Howland shouted.

"James!" Tess pulled away from Luca, clearly shocked at the newcomers. "What are you doing here?"

Howland was red-faced and thick-waisted in a heavy overcoat unbuttoned over a pinstriped three-piece suit. "I can't believe you'd break it off with me and then run to some dago."

"The name is Lombardo," Luca announced. "If Tess told you it's over, then it's over. Go home."

"With pleasure," Howland huffed. The threadbare mustache stretched over his upper lip. "Come along, Tess."

"No," Tess exclaimed. "I could not have made

myself any plainer, James. I have no wish to be your wife. We are not getting married."

"Of course, we're getting married," Howland insisted. "It's all arranged."

"What don't you understand?" Tess shouted. "I dislike you intensely. Go away!"

Without warning, Howland slapped Tess across the face. She clutched at her spectacles and stumbled into Guido.

Luca's fist exploded into Howland's jaw. The plump banker spun across the icy sidewalk and fell onto the hood of his car with a sickening thud. "Richard," he moaned.

Howland's sidekick shrugged out of his overcoat and tossed his hat aside. "Come on, dago," he taunted. "This is going to be *swell*. I was Golden Gloves at Yale."

Luca put up his fists. Golden Gloves tracked him, teeth bared.

"We don't need to do this," Luca said as they circled each other. "Go home and take Howland with you."

"He's my brother."

"I don't care who he is."

Swinging hard, Golden Gloves rushed at him. Luca took one to the chin, landed the same on his opponent, and then it was an all-out brawl. As the punches flew,

Luca had a flashback to bare-knuckle fights in the Bowery. No ring, no neutral corners, no rules. Twenty dollars to survive five minutes. Seventy-five if he knocked out his opponent, the only way to win.

Blocking blows and weaving on his toes, Luca maneuvered his opponent toward icy spots on the sidewalk. When the moment was right, Golden Gloves skidding in his leather-soled shoes, Luca threw his weight behind a right cross to the jaw. The younger man's head tilted toward an indigo sky. His arms flew out to steady himself.

Luca jammed a knee into his groin.

Golden Gloves screamed and collapsed to the sidewalk.

"That's not fair!" Howland lurched off the hood of his car and rushed at Luca, overcoat flapping behind him.

A short jab spun the heavy banker off balance, giving Luca the opportunity to clamp one arm around his neck and lock a wrist with the other. Howland screeched in protest as Luca rammed his head into the brick wall of the Galliano Club building until the crunch of broken bones was audible above the man's inarticulate cries.

Luca let go and sucked in air. "Don't you ever touch her again."

Howland staggered away, gasping and mewling. His nose was surely broken.

"You fucker." Golden Gloves was on his feet again, fists up but wobbling badly. Snot and tears tracked down his face.

"Get out," Luca ordered. "Get out of here, both of you. Go home. Tess stays with me."

There was a noise behind him. Luca realized that the entire saloon had come outside. At least forty men in dungarees with work-hardened hands shifted restlessly on the sidewalk behind him. Gio Tulipano held Guido's steel-bladed snow shovel. Someone else had the broom. Sonny rested the baseball bat from behind the counter on one shoulder like Lou Gehrig waiting for his turn at the plate.

"Go home," Luca repeated. "It's over."

Golden Gloves had the good sense to lower his fists, retrieve his coat, and bundle his gasping brother into the sleek automobile. The crowd erupted in cheers as they drove away.

"Thank you," Tess breathed.

Guido stood guard in the vestibule over Tess and her suitcase while Sonny fetched wet bar towels and Luca ran down the hall to Vito's office to get the key to Ruth's apartment. The saloon was lively as everyone who witnessed the fight rehashed it, along with hoots and jokes about college boys and broken noses.

Luca unlocked the street door and made sure to relock it before he and Tess climbed the stairs to Ruth's apartment. There wasn't much in Ruth's apartment now, but it was better than standing on the sidewalk and bleeding. He opened the door and switched on the electric light.

"Are you all right?" Tess asked. She carried the bowl of wet bar towels. "God, I'm glad you hit James. And his smug little brother."

"I'm okay." Luca sat her down in the torn armchair and turned her jaw so he could see the welt blooming across her cheekbone. "Does it hurt?"

"Not very much," she said, clearly trying not to flinch. "How are you?"

Luca wiped his hands with a damp towel. The skin across his knuckles was split and bleeding. His face stung but nothing was broken and he still had the same number of teeth. "I've been in worse fights. Nothing's broken."

Tess pressed another cloth to the corner of his mouth. "It was like watching Jack Dempsey. You're amazing."

"He hit you," Luca said, tasting blood from a split lip. "He had it coming."

"No justice of the peace is going to marry us looking

like this."

"We'll find a justice of the peace in the morning," Luca vowed.

"What do we do about tonight?" Tess asked slowly. "I'm not going home."

"Neither am I," Luca said.

CHAPTER 52

Wedding day

"Wedding day," Tess said to her reflection in the tiny bathroom mirror. The giant purple bruise on her cheek matched the embroidery on her nightgown.

Luca's arms slid around her from behind. Complete with a swollen cheekbone and a split lip, his reflection smiled at hers. "Yes, wedding day, Tessa."

Tess leaned against his bare chest and crossed her arms over his. This was *intimate love.* She was so happy it hurt.

What Tess and Luca had shared last night was so much more than she expected and certainly more amazing, more *holy* than what friends at college had implied with whispered giggles and inarticulate descriptions. There had been a little awkward fumbling, a little laughter, and then a depth of emotion like a wave bursting through a dam.

It was impossible to sleep afterward. Tess didn't want to miss a moment of touching him, watching him watch her, of the sheer thrill of being together. Eventually they both fell asleep, still in each other's arms under a motley collection of blankets found in the back of the bedroom closet. When they woke up, Tess fell in love all over again.

Her cheek twinged as she smiled back at Luca. "I hope the justice of the peace doesn't ask any questions. At least by the time we have a church wedding, we'll both look better. We can have our photograph made then."

Luca's arms loosened a fraction. "Church wedding?" he asked slowly.

"Of course," Tess said. "We have to get married in the church."

To her surprise, Luca let go of her. His arms dropped to his sides. "I can't be married in the church, Tessa."

Tess spun to face him. "Not married in the church? What are you talking about?"

"Do you remember I said there was something I didn't tell you?"

"You said it didn't matter because I was going to marry James." Tess's hand flew to her throat. "Oh, God. You're still married. Your wife didn't die."

"No, it's not that." Luca paused. "A long time ago, I killed a man."

Tess gasped and backed away, but there was nowhere to go in the tiny bathroom.

"I told you about my parents," he said. "My father

was an army officer from the north. Sent to Eritrea. He deserted and came to Serra San Bruno, our village in Calabria. Married my mother. When the army caught up with him again, they executed him. A firing squad. They killed my mother, too. I was five or so and I saw everything."

His voice cracked. Tess waited.

Luca took a deep breath, the muscles in his torso flexing. "The officer in charge of the firing squad was named Humberto Orsini. When I was older, he came to our village. He was in charge of the army garrison in the area."

Tess found her words. "How did you know it was the same person?"

"He had a scar. It was more than twelve years later but some things are never forgotten." Luca's voice was very quiet. "I confronted him. I had my father's gun. I wanted him to beg for my forgiveness. He stabbed me and I shot him."

Tess's eyes dropped to the scar across his ribs.

"For a long time I told myself that it was an accident," Luca went on. "That I didn't mean to kill him. But I did. I wanted revenge for my parents."

"Were you arrested?"

Luca shook his head. "His death was ruled a suicide. I sold the gun and bought passage to America."

Tess blundered out of the bathroom, shrugged on her sweater over the nightgown and went into the kitchen. She'd make a cup of tea. Yes, tea and they'd talk about this calmly and rationally and then Luca would tell her it was a joke. He wasn't a killer.

But she knew in her heart that he was telling her the truth.

Outside on Hamilton Street, an engine rumbled into silence. Quieter vehicles hummed past. Somewhere, someone knocked. A male voice called out.

"Tessa." Luca stood in the doorway between the kitchen and the dining area. "I'm not sorry. I won't confess and repent. I live in a state of mortal sin for taking the life of another. But it means I cannot accept the sacrament of marriage in the church. I did that when I married Rafaella and she died. I won't let that happen to you. The justice of the peace will have to be enough."

Tess made a production out of looking through the empty icebox and single cabinet. There wasn't a single cup or plate in the kitchen. They'd have to drink tea out of a saucepan. Had Ruth Cross really lived like this? There was hardly any furniture and no dishes and the quilt on the bed was torn and . . . and . . .

"Tess?" Luca asked softly. "Say something."

She finally found a tin of loose tea even as their courtship unspooled in her mind's eye. Luca had shared the story about losing his parents. His father had been executed for being a deserter and his mother was shot when she protested. But that was all. Nothing about a military officer named Humberto Orsini.

Luca hadn't trusted her enough then.

There had always been a raw toughness about Luca that attracted her; he was so different from college boys and bankers with feeble mustaches. She remembered his stories of fighting for money when he first came to America. So novel, so exciting, so fierce and courageous.

Tess put down the tin and stared at the scar that sliced across his ribs, souvenir of being shot on his wild rumrunning trip. Bruises on his face and shoulders. The raw red of his knuckles.

Each mark represented something he did for her.

"Have you killed anybody else?" she asked.

Luca's eyebrows shot up. "No, of course not."

"Anything else you need to tell me?"

"Well, maybe one thing." He leaned against the wall. "Do you remember Mr. Fisher, the accountant who made that ledger? He helped blackmail my boss. That's why Vito took out that loan against the club."

Tess gasped.

"He and that bootlegger Rotolo and a farmer who lives near my cousin on Bell Road were blackmailing people. They had an argument and Fisher shot the farmer in front of Rotolo's brewery. I saw. Me and Karol and Toby, the rumrunner I told you about before. We saw him kill that man so we told Mr. Fisher that unless he pays Vito back, we'll go to the police."

Someone banged on the street door below the apartment. Tess was so tense that she nearly jumped out of her skin.

"It's probably the ice man," Luca said. "No one told him to stop coming."

"Wait a minute!" Tess pressed her hands to her head. "You tell me that you're blackmailing a crook and a killer and then go answer the door like it's not important?"

"I'll be right back."

He grabbed his boots and shirt off the settee, put them on and crossed to the apartment door. Tess followed him to the landing and watched as Luca made his way down the stairs. What he had just told her was impossible to believe, yet she knew it was all true. No matter what loomed ahead with this man, she knew she'd never be bored.

Luca opened the door. Over his shoulder, Tess saw two policemen on the sidewalk. A police wagon idled at the curb behind her green coupe, a big square vehicle with a yellow shield painted on the side. A third policeman was behind the wheel.

"Gianluca Lombardo?" the taller one barked.

"I'm Lombardo," Luca said.

"You're under arrest." The cop grabbed Luca by the arm.

"Arrest?" Luca exclaimed, trying to pull away. "What for?"

Tess flew down the stairs. "What is going on?"

"He's under arrest." The policemen swiftly fastened Luca's arms behind his back with big iron handcuffs. "Kidnapping and attempted murder."

"But that happened years ago," Tess said in confusion.

The policeman raised his eyebrows at the bruise on her face. "Looks more recent than that."

"No, wait." Tess realized her mistake and tried to get the policeman to stop moving. "Wait. This is wrong."

"Outta the way, lady."

"Tess, tell Karol," Luca shouted as the cops dragged him across the sidewalk to the police wagon. "Karol Dombrowski! He's the foreman at the mill. Tell him I've been arrested."

Early morning traffic stopped along Hamilton Street as the wagon swung away from the curb and accelerated toward the intersection with Union Street.

"Stop!" Tess pelted barefoot after it, screaming. "Stop!"

The wagon sped up, turned and disappeared.

A horn blared. Spinning around, Tess saw a line of cars. She was blocking traffic in the middle of Hamilton Street, wearing only a sweater and the nightgown meant for her wedding night.

CHAPTER 53

Plus and minus

Benny hitched up his trousers and thought about a slice of pie. He sure did like pie and nothing worked up an appetite like letting off steam with Annunziata.

He padded down the hall, the slap of his bare feet lost in the huffing, grunting, and groaning coming from behind the closed doors. Trixie had a full house tonight.

The light was on but the kitchen was empty. Trixie was upstairs with a fella, earning ten bucks and warming up for the main event with Benny later on. A couple of empty Mason jars were on the table. Benny sniffed. Gin.

He opened the icebox and found a bottle of buttermilk. There was apple pie under a cloth. Benny carved out a wedge, grabbed a fork and sat at the kitchen table. Toted up the pluses and minuses of the rackets business as he jabbed his fork through the crust.

On the plus side, the beer racket was doing fine. Brewing, distributing, and collecting dough as good as any outfit in Chicago. Customers knew not to complain.

On the minus side, Broz Siwak was doing lotsa

heavy lifting and Benny wasn't so sure he could trust Broz any more.

Who else knew that Matilda Russo was in Trixie's old stable? Benny, Al, Broz and a couple of Broz's boys who were supposed to stand guard and keep the kid fed. Then suddenly the kid is gone. Benny worried that the Polacks decided to run their own ransom scam right under his nose, something nobody in Chicago would have tolerated.

The Polacks must have traded the girl for a direct payment from Russo. Maybe they thought they deserved something extra for keeping their mouths shut about Genovese.

It had probably been a mistake to hire so much Polack muscle. In a showdown, they'd be loyal to Broz first, with Benny a distant second.

He stuffed his mouth with more pie. On the plus side, he was rid of Al Genovese and Owen owed him for cleaning up. Benny had a nice chunk of cash to buy off old man Spinelli. He'd do it, too, if Lombardo didn't get in the way again.

Thinking about money took Benny to the minus side again. Neither Russo nor Maria Teresa Procopio had paid up, which wasn't good for the rackets in general. If a fella was being blackmailed and didn't pay and the blackmailer didn't do anything, that was no racket but a lousy begging business.

It didn't really matter. The information racket was done. Yesterday, Benny got a telegram from the wholesale grocer saying they were out of bananas. What were the odds of that?

One of Trixie's customers had left the evening edition of the *Lido Daily Clipper*. Benny spread it out, looking for a distraction from his mental betting card. The headline took up the space above the fold.

MAGAZINE EDITOR IDENTIFIES RIVER WOMAN AS MODEL'S SISTER

A half-chewed bite of apple fell out of Benny's mouth.

Lido, New York: The woman pulled from the Mohawk River weeks ago was tentatively identified this morning as Marta Gorski, age 21, a Harvey Girl waitress at the Harvey House restaurant in Chicago's Union Station. She had been missing for more than 10 weeks. Originally from Warsaw, Poland, Miss Gorski emigrated to America as an infant.

The late Miss Gorski was identified thanks to Karl Edwin Harriman, editor of The Red Book

magazine, who contacted Mayor John Peabody in the belief that the unidentified woman, discovered during the search for the body of missing Lido Premium foreman Giacomo "Jimmy" Zambrano, bore a close resemblance to Mrs. Samuel (née Gorski) Vitello, the model on the cover of a recent edition of his magazine and the late Miss Gorski's sister.

A store model for Gossard's in Chicago, Mrs. Vitello stated that she will travel to Lido to officially identify the body and lay her sister to rest.

Miss Gorski's parents are deceased. She is survived by the aforementioned sister, Mrs. Samuel Vitello, and an uncle, Waldemar Gorski of Cleveland, Ohio.

The name jangled a bell in the recesses of Benny's mind. Not Gorski, but Vitello. *Samuel Vitello. Sam, Sammy Vitello.*

"Benny!" Trixie charged into the room, wearing a silk kimono and that prune-faced expression he hated.

"What?"

Trixie stabbed a finger at him, narrowly missing the bottle of buttermilk. "You did this and you're going to clean it up."

Benny's eyes fell to the headline.

"Are you listening to me?" Trixie swept the newspaper onto the floor with real fury. "I swear, Benny, you gotta take care of this."

"Okay." Whatever the problem was, if Trixie wasn't talking about the story in the newspaper, Benny could fix it. He summoned up his usual bad-boy grin. "Look, doll, calm down. One of the johns upstairs getting out of hand? I'll settle him down."

"You already settled things down." Trixie's eyes snapped with righteous anger. "You promised not to but you did it anyway."

Benny was flummoxed. "What are you talking about?"

"Annunziata is dead," Trixie said.

To be continued . . .

Find out what happens next in

REVENGE AT THE GALLIANO CLUB

ABOUT THE AUTHOR

Carmen Amato turns her 30 years with the Central Intelligence Agency into fiction loaded with danger and deception.

She is the award-winning author of the Detective Emilia Cruz police series set in Acapulco, the Galliano Club historical thriller series, two standalone thrillers and the Mystery Ahead book journal for mystery lovers.

Find out more at carmenamato.net.

www.ingramcontent.com/pod-product-compliance
Lightning Source LLC
Chambersburg PA
CBHW072020020726
47501CB00006B/1886